The Mandy Project

Mac Strack

DISCLAIMER:

This novel's story and characters are fictitious. Certain long-standing institutions, agencies and public offices are mentioned but the characters involved are wholly imaginary.

Dedication

This book is dedicated to all youth at-risk, challenged to survive in a world chock full of betrayal, mistrust and significant peril, as they negotiate their pathway through to an uncertain future.

Some do not make it.

Opportunities for a better tomorrow seem far out of reach, as their main focus is fixed firmly upon ensuring safety – day to day – minute to minute; physical, emotional and mental. Optimism does not shine within their complex web of survival strategies – skillfully constructed from necessity; and most often, trust is deemed a risk not worth taking.

These young people roam our community streets – some homeless, others in abusive living situations – group, foster or familial. Too many have left their mark on the wrong side of the law, resulting in further estrangement from a society that is often judgmental, fearful, ignorant and downright cruel; providing no value to the ones who are most in need.

These young souls are vulnerable – but also possess hard-earned incredible strength and tenacity - absolutely deserving of equal value in our society!

Consider this book a testament to hope for positive outcomes. While the characters are fictional, they are based on real-life people and their journeys mirror actual struggles.

I dedicate this message of hope to all of you, with heartfelt intention and encouragement to reach out for the hand that seeks to help you; in fervent hope that you can find it within, to embrace your worthiness.

Acknowledgment

While my loved ones – family and friends, will have my everlasting gratitude for their support and encouragement, there are others who deeply inspired the telling of this story.

To all the young people with whom I've been provided the opportunity to work with, love, help and grieve; in whatever capacity possible – you hold a unique place of value and love in my heart. I have gained such a wealth of education and experience; have been inspired to reach for greater heights, in witnessing your incredible strength and resilience. You have all demonstrated a depth of caring and compassion; even when it is not revealed – I both witness and feel it! I am profoundly touched by the level of trust that you have risked in me - thank you!

To those young souls who, through no fault or failings of their own, did not manage to surface from the horrible mire that marked their journey on this earth – my compassion and love follow you for eternity.

To the compassionate and caring individuals who strive every day to assist and walk beside vulnerable youth – partners in health and wellness; social workers, educators, medical professionals, community members, parents and family - the list goes on – you know who you are, and have my utmost gratitude and respect.

For those of you who find it within your heart to open this book and travel the raw pathway that Mandy has endured on the road to eventual liberation – I bestow my utmost gratitude. This message deserves illumination – into the dark and silent spaces where despair and hopelessness are assumed! It is here where sparks of hope necessarily arise – and with a leap of faith, flicker and grow.

Each one of you provide a critical spark – thank you!

Contents

Preface

This book contains graphic descriptions of violence, sexual abuse, physical abuse, emotional abuse, youth at risk, prostitution, vulnerability, peril and homelessness.

The content may stir PTSD triggers for those who have experienced any of the above.

The author was profoundly touched during her experience within the public and private education system. The opportunity to work with at-risk youth, in supporting them through their education; assisting them to scale the insurmountable maze of hurdles that seemingly deem impending failure, has birthed a deep compassionate drive to make a difference.

While working alongside children, she dedicated deliberate attention to the root sources – the inner struggles and insecurities; lack of faith in positive future outcomes, and strategically structured her intervention to incorporate a focus on these core roadblocks; setting kids up for success!

Her passion continues to flourish; Mae is deeply inspired to continue sharing the message of hope – illuminating the dark spaces and encouraging those leaps of faith that she knows – firsthand, *do* result in success!

Humanity's magic, idealism and hope for the future resides in our youth – they are hands-down; our wisest investment in educators!

Chapter One

Ten… nine… eight… *hold steady*… six… five… *that's it*… three… *you got this*… one… Bingo! It worked every time – had since I was six years old.

The woman fidgeted before me now.

Every nerve in my body slowly released, and the familiar, soothing calm washed over me. Yep - *I* was in control now! This lent an intoxicating sense of power, and I glared at her with all the animosity I could muster. Stupid woman! It wasn't personal, not really…they were all the same, and if I cared enough, I'd probably feel sorry for these lame people – they had absolutely *no* idea! This one cleared her throat now, obviously a tad uncomfortable.

"OK…Amanda."

I allowed a little smile – her nervous demeanor was increasing by the minute, and I couldn't help but wallow in her evident discomfort. She aimlessly shuffled the papers in the worn manila folder, my story resting neatly before her - on the cold, impersonal, black metal desk.

I sighed loudly and peered around – *so* losing interest in this charade. The aged furniture was scratched and cheap – seemed out of place for the woman – she was better than that. Surely, they could afford to give her a fucking, decent desk after all the crap she put up with from the likes of losers like me!

I allowed my eyes to wander over the room – old metal shelves housed well-used books, the kind that supposedly held all the answers; the deep, dark mysteries of troubled teens. Yep – diagnose and fix us all. What a load of bull!

"Amanda."

My eyes slid back to hers. She seemed a little more determined now - I couldn't afford to let my guard down. I shifted slowly, assuming a casual "I don't give a rip" slouch in the tattered, threadbare…and, yes, *smelly* old chair. The entire cramped space reeked of something I couldn't quite define, yet sickeningly familiar.

Depression…that was the best I could come up with – yeah…the smell of hopelessness! My nose wrinkled in disgust. I shook it off and focused on the woman's face.

Her eyes were actually quite pretty for her age – I guessed to be around forty-two. This was a game I had serious skills for, rarely off base. Yep – the tell-tale tiny bags underneath, a hint of sagging beginning around her lips, and creases etched into her forehead, right between the eyes – I was willing to bet, derived from frowning more than smiling. Her hair was the ultimate betrayal; tired and a little neglected, overdue for a root touch-up, at the very least. I studied the ragged split ends and deduced that she could use a visit to the beauty parlor - the sooner, the better!

"I know this is hard, but I need you to help me here."

The woman's keen gaze was really quite striking – in surprising contrast to the rest of her features. I felt a sudden admiration for this old gal – the smoky grey depths held a spark of resolve and revealed a calculated intelligent purpose.

I would need to keep on my toes around her. A rush of exhilaration flowed through me at the prospect of the fight! It was in the bag; I was certain of a win, and it would be an intoxicating challenge, for sure.

"You're going back, you know that!"

I felt the resentment flash in my dark eyes – my *father's* eyes – I loathed them! But I knew how to manipulate those orbs to my advantage. I stared her down once again. She met me eye-to-eye.

"Young lady, I'm giving you the opportunity to spill the beans here and perhaps alter your fate for the better…"

Ha! She wasn't as smart as I'd thought!

"What do you know of my fate?" I spat the words at her, "Are you coming *home* with me tonight? Will you *tuck me in*?" I nearly caved at the authentic concern on her expression, but that was a load of nothing, too. "Will you stay with me until I'm eighteen – keep me safe and warm?" I spewed out the words with as much venom as I could muster!

She didn't flinch.

My breathing labored with the boiling rage, and I knew that I needed to get a grip; control the emotions. Snapping my head away abruptly, I closed my eyes, refusing to meet her compassionate gaze.

"Just leave me alone – send me back – it doesn't matter anyhow."

I was done – there was no getting through to me now. As if there ever was a chance. Nothing would ever change, no matter how hard they tried! I was imprisoned in this fateful, dismal existence, and I knew with a clanging certainty that it would extend far beyond my teen years.

The silence was deafening – my ally now.

"All right, have it your way," she heaved a sigh of resignation, slowly picked up the phone, and spoke resolutely into the receiver, "She's ready to go…"

Daring a glance, I couldn't help but notice that even her phone was old – just like her. But as I waited for the lady cop to come and collect me, an aching yearning emerged from somewhere in the depths of my buried soul, and I wished for a fleeting moment that she would – could – take me home with her. There was something authentic about this one. The moment passed, and I quickly and efficiently, stuffed it safely into that dark, ugly abyss, where it belonged.

Chapter Two

The last thing – the absolute *last* resort, was to send her back! Del Greenwood ran a frustrated hand through the tousled and tired – yet still rich and luxurious auburn locks upon her thundering, aching head - for the umpteenth time. She slowly laid her forehead on the soothing, cold metal desk as she bleakly considered the options. Were there any?

With a frustrated sigh, Del eased gingerly out of the chair and onto her feet. God, she was weary – drained of all energy, all hope…damn it! How on earth was she going to get through to that girl? She'd come up against tough kids countless times – her life's work. But this one…she startled at the sting of tears starting.

No – she couldn't afford to go there! Her investment here needed to be detached and practical – it was critical for the sake of the child. Yet, the dull, persistent ache in her gut betrayed the unavoidable truth – who was she kidding? It was virtually impossible to keep the emotions out; her heart always took a thorough thrashing.

It was a bone of contention between her and Jack. From a coincidental common bond, they'd invested what seemed like a lifetime into each other over the past several years. Both of their spouses had ducked out, unable to deal with the passion and intensity – and yes, the substantial number of hours that she and Jack

- friends and trusted co-workers then, had doggedly devoted to their work.

Del gazed intently at her mirror image above the file cabinet in the corner. The pain and uncertainty there in the dark grey depths glared back at her accusingly - a haunting reminder that some hurts never die. She broke eye contact swiftly and gave her head a firm, clearing shake.

He, of all people, should be compelled to understand. She'd trusted that he'd be the one person in her world that she could count on! But he'd bailed on her. She had backed him all the way in his decision to change gears with his career! Hell, it was a nightmare on a good day, and she'd truly been happy to see him get out from the trenches – still with the same dysfunctional bureaucracy, but safe, behind the confines of a critical solutions brainstorming group. It was a good gig, and she was proud of him!

In retrospect, if she dug down into the druthers of her painful confusion, she was aware - even then, of a burning feeling of abandonment that his decision had evoked deep within her soul.

And she knew…oh yes, she got it, but hated the fact that one of the driving, motivating factors in their devotion to one another – the sole reason they had risked moving beyond the friendship, was, in large part, a huge co-dependent ball of enablement; in which they were both hopelessly entangled within. They validated each other's overwhelming dedication to excessive hours on the job – hell, there was nothing else! They'd both lived and breathed it until now.

A deep surge of resentment threatened to reduce her to tears for the second time within the span of fifteen minutes. What the hell was the matter with her? She had to admit that it *was* her – not him. He'd made a great decision for himself, and here she was, almost hating him for it. It wasn't equitable, she knew.

Yet, there he stood, on the opposite side of an insurmountable barrier – of course, with all the right words of assurance. He knew how hard it was for her - after all, he'd *been there too*; and now, he *needed* her to embrace the same transformation because her stagnancy was sucking the health out of their relationship – his words.

It amounted to nothing more than ridiculously impossible ultimatums, and she'd never felt so utterly, desperately alone.

Chapter Three

Oh God, Oh God, Oh God…stay still! I couldn't prevent the violent shaking, convinced they could hear my teeth chattering wildly – *he* would hear me. I shoved back the hysteria and forced myself to breathe calmly – the panic was welling up like an erupting volcano, and I knew I couldn't let it get hold of me; my fateful undoing.

It was critical that he not find me, in his present state. My survival was ultimately at stake! Come on, calmer breaths now – slowly. Oh God – fuck you, tears! I hated that weakness in myself!

"Where the fuck do you think you're going, you piece of trash?"

I tried in vain, to ignore his threatening bellows, filtering in from the floor above me. I knew he was relentlessly stalking Gen in the kitchen – could hear her shuffling around the island, knocking things to the floor, in her panic.

"Please, Paulie, calm down!"

The pleading whine in Gen's tone sickened me – why didn't the pathetic woman grab a knife and defend herself? Defend them all! But Gen had started this one – stupid scrag!

Crash! The first blow had firmly landed, and I shoved down the rising well of panic. I well knew what that felt like - I had risked it just once. Couldn't go to school for a week. There was no good outcome in defying Paul Miller!

"Get up, you rotten filth!" He was exceptionally pissed.

I tried to quell a sudden fear that he just may kill her this time. Gen loved to goad him – I could not fathom that level of stupidity! This time, she had accused him of diddling the office secretary, and though that was entirely believable, it was ironic that I could likely testify on his behalf. Oh no, it wasn't *her* he was diddling. But I knew who it was. Disgustingly so…the vomit threatened to erupt once again, and I needed to breathe it away.

"Paulie, get a grip, I have to go to work!" Yes, it was her lucky night…for now! "You know that I just love you so much, it drives me crazy, jealous!"

Oh God, I *hated* that sickly, sweet voice – I *was* sure to puke now!

"You are one damn lucky woman, Genevieve! It so happens that I need your money, you cheating bitch! Oh yeah, I know all about that young buck who loves giving you rides home! Well, I fuckin' know exactly what you are *riding* on the way! Get outta here – you make me sick!"

The door slammed, and I knew Gen was scurrying down the sidewalk with her powder puff makeup kit in one hand, dabbing expertly at the spot where an ugly bruise was rapidly coming to the surface.

I held my breath - Gen's fate forgotten in my immediate concern for survival. I had inadvertently, mercifully found this clever little hiding spot out of necessity shortly after that first time.

No, don't go there! My skin screamed at the biting friction from the cold concrete basement wall, scraping my back. I was scrunched in there so tightly - I knew it would be a challenge to walk for a bit afterward. But that didn't matter. Nothing mattered except that he *not* find me.

I listened intently, hardly daring to breath…where was he?

Slam! Yep – the whiskey! It was easy to predict the clink of glass - one, two, three – four shots, and another refill. His footsteps were slow and steady above - stalking…stay calm, calm…

"Girl! Get down here!"

My body involuntarily spasmed in the tiny space. Not on your life, you bastard! Good, though; he thinks I'm upstairs. Hopefully, he'll have another couple of shots before he resumes his search up that steep staircase – with any luck, he'll trip and tumble on his way back down!

"Hey! Right now!" His footfall was even and calculated – with deadly purpose - it was utterly terrifying!

I gulped back my panic in calming breaths, so grateful that Gen had given me that tool – at least one thing, I suppose!

"Girlee," He was changing tactics now, drawing out the name in honey-glazed disgust, and I wondered hysterically if he really believed that this strategy would make a whit of difference!

"Come on out!"

His tread on the stairs was deafening – he'd soon realize that I was not there and become further enraged. I never managed to come up with a good escape route, and I was well aware that nothing would save me in the end, but I couldn't surrender; I would never stop fighting! I knew, without a doubt, that my very life depended upon it.

My ongoing, fervent hope was that he would drink himself to a stupor before he ruthlessly tracked me down. There had been other nights that I'd been spared.

Creak! The basement door!

Oh my God – I felt utter humiliation as my bladder suddenly gave way. I held back the whimpers; he wouldn't like that at all, and I would be certain to pay for my weakness! I didn't dare breathe as he made his way down the stairs, but every nerve in my body was screaming. I heard him shuffling around, ruthlessly kicking things out of his way, as he navigated the junk-cluttered cellar.

"C'mon now!"

His voice was so close that I nearly shot right out of the little nook – oh please…in my head only, in my head only! The shuffling stopped right in front of me, and the sirens went off in my mind – stay still, so still…

Suddenly, he turned and made his way back up the steep cellar stairs. The relief was palpable, and I thought my pounding heart would never slow – was I to die here from sheer terror? Damn, I should be welcoming such a demise!

Creak! My heart flew into my throat. Was this a trick?

I couldn't take the chance and accepted my fate, tortuously crammed inside that small crate-like space behind the hot water tank against the cold, clammy concrete wall. I would rather die here than face the alternative.

As my heart finally slowed, I mused over my good fortune to have stumbled across the recess in the cellar wall. I supposed that it was designed with the intention of storing freshly harvested vegetables, as it was flush with the drywall; the space replacing what should have housed insulation - without such, it was bone-chilling cold. The opening was just a loose piece of drywall, really, and I'd come across it quite by accident when I'd tripped into the wall in sheer panic.

That time, I had been hiding from the fighting – little had I known that soon, I'd have a far more horrifying reason for seeking that refuge.

The space was barely two feet deep, three long, and three high – it was a brutal squish, and my body was screaming for relief now. But I waited…once I heard the stumbling, I knew it wouldn't be long. Yep, disgusting snores – passed out grotesquely on the sofa.

I slowly unfolded my aching limbs from my haven, carefully replaced the drywall, and slunk quietly up the stairs to my room.

It was only a matter of time, I knew. For sure, I had been unable to get to my safe spot too many times and was ever grateful whenever I managed it. It was a fine line to balance because if I squirreled myself away too many times, the violence increased when he finally caught up to me – the piper always demanded payment.

Crying myself to sleep, I couldn't erase the vision of the smoky-eyed Child Protection Services lady and the compassion glowing enticingly from her intelligent, knowing gaze. Fuck you, lady! Just fuck you!

Chapter Four

On this night, Del Greenwood reflected on one fateful blessing; she and Jack had never quite deepened their commitment to the merging of households.

Grateful for the peaceful solitude, she engaged in a deep soul search, complete with three glasses of Merlot. It was a deviation from her steadfast policy. Wine - and she *did* adore a fine one, was reserved for weekend relaxation. Seldom did she imbibe through the work week. However, tonight was a time for introspection.

True, she worked too damn hard, cared too damn much, and devoted more of herself to her career, than was remotely healthy – she'd have to ponder on that some.

After the second goblet of soothing red spirits – nowhere near inebriated, Del determined that it was not her responsibility alone to *fix* her and Jack's stressed relationship.

There was a simple truth here – he was in the fast lane, aimed in a direction where she was not headed, one she was unquestionably not ready for. Just as with a drug addict, it was futile to tackle change for the sake of anyone other than herself – she well knew this; she had engaged in criminally expensive training to claim ownership of this wisdom. After the third hit of magic juice, she was struck with an epiphany!

She cared deeply for the guy – she truly did! But she loved her work too – especially the kids; loved to hate the dysfunction, and was simply and unequivocally unwilling to sacrifice her passion for making a difference – even if it was a mere shot in the dark. Del knew, at a soul level, that it was worth it and, yes, the beauty in this bombshell? She believed in it still – in her heart of hearts, she knew without doubt that she could make an impact. Not all flowers and happy endings, but when she did get through to a kid or even a caregiver, it was the epitome of success, however small.

Oh, Jack, she mused fondly. You really just stopped believing, and it's time for us to face our new reality.

Finally, Del Greenwood crawled between the sheets - though a little sad, feeling a calming sense of peace flow through her that had nothing at all to do with the wine – a renewed purpose. As her breathing slowed and she began to drift off, she couldn't keep her thoughts from swaying toward the young and feisty Amanda Goodchild.

She fell asleep with a smile and a striking vision of the fifteen-year-old girl in her dark, fiery, determined defiance – and yes, the fear; she'd get to the crux of that, Del vowed.

Chapter Five

A thundering bang on the bedroom door crashed through my exhausted yet ever-guarded slumber. Geez – my heart slammed painfully in my throat as I gulped in breaths, waiting.

Gen's muffled scream punched through my growing awareness as she was ruthlessly hurled upon their bed. The tell-tale, rhythmic creaks that followed always gave it away and more. Abandoning all hope for further sleep, I pulled the covers over my head and tried to block out the disgusting noises – oh yeah, Gen was going to get it good tonight!

I was safe in a cozy log cabin - a Snow-White hideaway in the middle of a thick, wooded forest, secure in the knowledge that there wasn't a soul on earth who could find me here! I had neatly arranged it so that poison apples and deception belonged in other worlds. Venturing out into my perfect woodland sanctuary, I breathed in the aromatic wildflowers that bordered the edge of the forest in abundance and basked in my haven, knowing that I was thoroughly protected. Here, I didn't need to remain on high alert - there were creatures who devotedly had my back. I rested in a feather-soft hammock, floating in my serene existence amidst a heavenly serenade of fluttering birds and buzzing bees. The perfect breeze caressed my skin, and I soared...

Smack! Gen's wretched cries tore me rudely from my

Nirvana as the assault carried on. Though violence was a regular occurrence, during these bouts, it sounded particularly intense – God, I hated this!

"Teach you for takin' it from that sad excuse of a man – that fuckin' schoolboy – now you had yourself a *real* man, and you'll never forget it!" The shatter of his whiskey bottle sent a thousand shards of pain through my skull – pins and needles of anxiety! I heard him stumble awkwardly and land heavily on the mattress. I was flooded with a welcoming comfort; at least for tonight, I would be left in peace.

Turned out I was dead wrong!

Jolted rudely from slumber, I couldn't breathe as his filthy, calloused hand clamped tightly over my mouth and nose; I panicked as my airway blocked completely. Thrashing in my desperate need for oxygen, I whimpered as he chuckled softly in my ear. There was no need for him to threaten me into silence – I knew the drill; he let a little air through my nostrils.

The faint light of dawn revealed the wild excitement in his eyes as I voraciously – greedily snuffed in air, tears of terror escaping my eyes. He sought my helplessness, thrived on it, lusted after it, and I seethed with internalized hatred at my self-betrayal. The stench of his sour whiskey breath and nicotine-stained fingers had me fighting staunchly against a wicked gag reflex. I was terrified that I would vomit, either causing myself to choke to death or suffer at his hand – it would enrage him completely!

I managed to calm myself enough that he removed his hand from my mouth, and I gulped in oxygen, willing myself not to scream in my terror – I had to stay quiet. This wasn't my first rodeo with the bastard, but the horror never abated.

Then, his hands were everywhere, and revulsion was a living poison – he pinched and bit as he bestowed a myriad of abuse upon my body. Silent screeches echoed inside of my brain, reverberating down into my soul.

Through the horrific pain, I began to fall into a state of numbness – my blissful escape – no longer caring as the brutal violation continued – it was beyond bearing, and I fell gratefully into the enveloping darkness.

Slam! His fist plowed into the side of my head, and little points of light threatened to drag me under. It infuriated him when I stopped fighting - when the smell of my fear no longer permeated his senses.

And then, mercifully, it was over. Every nerve in my body sang with pain, and I wondered just *who* had gotten it good tonight. As he stumbled from my room, I gingerly touched my head and knew for certain that there would be no school for me in the morning.

I lay there until the sun streamed into my bedroom, teeth chattering violently, trembling uncontrollably – thoroughly abused and helpless. I dared now to release my hiccupping sobs, which, ironically, could not come close to drowning out his chainsaw snores in the next room. Hideous at best, it was the safest sound in my world at that moment.

Chapter Six

Del was thoroughly sparked by the clarity of mind that was hers this morning after. The realization that she had been losing her edge, compromising focus, in a pitiful quest to control the mess - that was currently her and Jack lent a fair measure of determination. Now that she'd accepted that it wasn't her responsibility – can't control or change it – her brain was in full gear, currently honed in on the plight of one Amanda Goodchild.

The girl was in serious trouble – of that, she was certain. A sudden vision of the teen swam into her mind's eye; slight and slender, but even the baggy clothing she'd worn did nothing to conceal her fully developed figure. Her deep brown eyes were stunningly gorgeous; long lashes enhanced their magnetic power. Though the girl's coiffure was clearly self-attended to, the dark, spiky style expertly framed her heart-shaped face, which only served to enhance her femininity. Del smiled at the irony – quite certain that this produced the exact opposite effect that Amanda had sought to achieve.

With Amanda's file not currently on her case load, Del wasn't privy to the background details. But her gut never lied, and the twisted knots warned of a real threat here.

To complicate matters, Amanda Goodchild was actually on Jack's plate, and with him leaving, the department was scrambling to reallocate his cases. Jack had shared with her only that the history was unbelievably sad, and so Del was strongly compelled to take her on; was now awaiting the bureaucratic bullshit that always assured a frustrating delay. She made a swift decision to employ a surface dig into this one on her own - to wisely leave Jack's perceptions be.

A quick skim of the internal database brought up the current foster address and information, which Del swiftly added to her digital contacts. Paul and Gen Miller – why on earth did that name ring bells? She made a mental note and filed it away for further consideration at a later time, adding details of the secondary school that Amanda attended to the list.

Del decided to swing by the home address before carrying on to the school, where Amanda would likely be, at this mid-morning hour. Cruising slowly along Springfield Boulevard, Del couldn't ignore the tingling sense of alarm trickling up her spine. The neighborhood was old and run-down, with most homes in sad need of upgrades.

There it was – number thirty-five! She cruised the car out front, pulling over to the curb for a better view. Window shutters that were once likely rather striking - against what was now flaking, sun-bleached, hunter-green wood siding dangled precariously on rusty, single hinges. Absent boards from a rotting wooden fence revealed a peek-a-boo glimpse into a truly junk-strewn, overgrown back yard. Overall, Del decided, the home appeared forlorn and neglected, which drove her feeling of unease upward another few notches.

As Del pulled away from the curb, she reflected on her decision to speak first with Amanda before diving headlong into the middle of a volatile home situation. Intuition guided her firmly – she knew she needed to earn the girl's trust in order to gain any leverage with her investigation into what she was certain to be an extremely unhealthy environment for Amanda.

Parking in a visitor stall, Del noted that Birchwood Secondary School was every bit as old as the homes in the Miller's neighborhood but stood in stark contrast with the obvious care and pride that was evident in the building and grounds. No doubt, there were likely structural issues. Del observed the aging sidewalk that led to a community garden space, spanning one entire field alongside the school. She mentally reviewed the neighborhood demographics, comprised of low to mid-income families – more the former.

Following the directives on a sign that was posted on the office entrance wall, Del picked up a miniature school bell that rang to announce her presence, fighting the impish feeling that she'd just done something naughty. She smiled a little, realizing that the apparatus was firmly anchored to the counter, likely to prevent its untimely disappearance. A small, post-middle-aged woman immediately popped out of a side room to greet her, smiling warmly.

"Lou Harris, how can I help you today – are you here to pick up a student? I don't recognize you…"

Though this slight little gal seemed meek and altogether too sweet to deal with hormone-infested teenagers on a regular basis, Del wasn't fooled. She was instinctively aware that this grandmotherly woman ruled the school with an iron determination – nothing and nobody got past her.

"Good morning! Del Greenwood, from Child Protection Services," she extended her hand in greeting, which was returned in kind. "I am here to arrange a quick meeting with Amanda Goodchild, if I may – I am her assigned social worker."

Ok, that was a bit of a stretch, as the case load transfer was not yet officially complete. The sudden change in expression on Lou Harris's features sent another shiver up Del's spine – her spider senses on full tilt now.

"I'm sorry but Mandy…Amanda is absent today," Lou looked her firmly in the eye, assessing, "but perhaps you might wish to call on her at home?"

Del was fully aware that school secretaries were officially

bound by ethics to remain neutral, at least professionally, when dealing with sensitive issues. She harbored no doubt that Lou Harris had just delivered a silent – yet loud and clear critical message and Del received it in earnest.

Amanda needed help. She nodded firmly, and Lou Harris returned the gesture, lifting her hand slowly to cover her heart.

The determined look on Del Greenwood's face and her steady departing gait would not be lost on those who knew her well – she was on a mission and would not accept defeat!

26

Chapter Seven

The bedroom door flew open!

I instinctively cowered against the wall at the head of my bed, trembling beyond control – but it wasn't him! Intense relief instantly weakened my knees.

Instead, I gazed in horror at Gen, whose right eye was grossly swollen shut, with some kind of fluid leaking down her cheek. Blood crusted down her legs, and her arm hung grotesquely from her shoulder at an odd angle. In shock, my eyes took in this hideous sight – there was dried blood in her matted, bleach-blonde hair, and full clumps were missing, leaving gaping bald spots. The appalling apparition before me was akin to a grisly zombie! Her already too-thin frame accentuated her appearance as eerily skeletal.

For God's sake – what had he done to her? I found my voice as the pathetic woman teetered precariously in the doorway.

"Gen, you need to get to the hospital," I started, not even aware of my own bruises and bleeding from the horrific abuse that I had endured, as well.

"You little bitch!"

Gen launched herself off the door frame with surprising agility and lunged for me, but I was quicker! She careened into the dresser.

"You constantly flaunt yourself at him, playing your little cat and mouse game – catch me if you can – hot and cold." Gen sneered hatefully; her voice muffled by what I suspected was a broken jaw.

That was so ridiculously far from the truth, and I suppressed a hysterical giggle.

"Oh yeah, you think I didn't hear your little moans and groans last night? You little filthy floozy! What man wouldn't come lusting after that kind of offer?"

I could not believe my ears – was she fucking kidding me right now? She continued stalking me around the room.

"Gen, look at me! Do I look like I enjoyed that disgusting abuse?" She faltered a little as her eyes glanced over my body, "please, Gen, you need to believe me – we need to get away from Paul before it's too late!"

"Don't give me that shit!" She was screaming hysterically at me now, "it was your dirty little plan all along – get rid of Gen – convince her to leave, so you can saunter your sultry little ass back here to make him squirm for you!"

I was taken off guard as her uninjured hand connected firmly with my cheek – throwing my head violently sideways. I pondered with alarm if my neck was injured as I stumbled into the bed frame.

"Gen, please, you have this all wrong! He's going to kill you

– kill us both!"

"Shut up, you rotten trollop! Filthy whore!" Her eyes took on a maniacal glaze, and I was cognizant of the fact that she was in shock – she had most likely been unconscious until a few minutes ago.

"You get out of this house *now*!" She began tearing clothing from the dresser and hurling it wildly in my direction, "I will tell them all that you ran away - that is what you always do anyway. Why the hell haven't you?" Gen's pitch rose in a strange, calm tone, and without question, I was hell-bent on doing exactly what she demanded! Grabbing my bag from the closet, I hastily stuffed my meager possessions inside before running out into the hall and down the stairs.

Feeling strangely surreal, I burst out onto the street, toting the same worn-out green garbage bag that I'd come to that house with - not even three months ago. Yet, it was an eternity. I began shivering violently.

Where the hell *was* I going to go?

Chapter Eight

Del guided the car flush to the curb in front of Amanda Goodchild's foster home and gazed thoughtfully at the door, weighing out her approach. If Amanda was home, there'd be no guarantee that she would agree to see her. She decided to bank on the likelihood that both Gen and Paul Miller were away at work, catch the girl off-guard, perhaps.

A fresh wave of uneasiness assaulted her senses as she caught a fleeting glimpse of what appeared to be someone moving away from the window as she approached the crumbling sidewalk to the front door.

Del knocked firmly, doubling her efforts by squeezing a button that was hanging precariously by a wire from the door frame. The responding ring from inside took her by surprise. She waited a minute or so and tried again – accepting with a sinking feeling that no one was going to open that door.

Well, she'd just have to keep trying. Amanda would return to school sooner or later – if she had to doggedly stake out the house, so be it! She pulled away from the curb and headed back to the office, intent on tackling more investigate digging, before heading home in time to get ready for her dinner with Jack. Against her better judgement, she'd allowed herself to be talked into dining at their favorite haunt. She gave herself a mental kick.

At precisely 6:00, Del entered the restaurant and smiled warmly at Mike, the head Host, who expertly plucked two menus from the stand and led her to *their* table. Del thanked him cordially after he pushed in her chair. She glanced casually around the room, wondering if anyone else in the room felt a similar trepidation as they contemplated their dining experience this evening.

Truth be told - for once, she was grateful that Jack was late. It afforded her a moment to collect her thoughts and muster up the necessary courage to broach the conversation that she conceded was long overdue. She felt no regret, really – not for her part, but wondered how Jack was going to react. No matter what transpired, she did not wish to cause him pain – she did love and care about the man!

Spotting the object of her thoughts now, a little flutter tickled her stomach at the familiar ease of his stride as Jack ambled toward her. Del returned the perfunctory meeting of lips before he sat down and grabbed his napkin from the glass. She acknowledged, watching him smooth it neatly onto his lap, that her reaction had no connection to romance. It was about caring and friendship. OK, if she admitted it, the flutter part was sheer anxiety in the anticipated wake of this uncomfortable evening. She took a deep, calming breath.

For a time, they chatted amicably about their last couple of days and some upcoming work commitments. Del decided to get into the source of her professional frustration first.

"Jack, you remember Amanda Goodchild?"

"Yeah, sure - tough cookie, that one."

"I've taken her case." There - the first hurdle and his expected reaction didn't disappoint.

"Del, what the hell? Why?"

His look of exasperation underscored her firm resolve to take control of her own career without Jack's opinion or judgment influencing her direction.

"Because she needs help sooner than later, and I'm the most familiar with her background."

"Give it to Grady, Del! You don't need this nightmare – and trust me, she *is* a nightmare; you will get too wrapped up in it - you know I'm right!" He picked up the menu in dismissal.

"Jack, it's a done deal – they've agreed to transfer her file over to me, and I'm not asking for your blessing on this – I want a little more insight."

"Let me get this straight. You want *me* to help *you* dig deeper into this hopeless pit of a career by taking a case that will rip your heart out because you won't be able to do a damn thing about it!"

Ok, it was time.

"Jack, it's not about saving everyone – not about the foreseeable outcome. For me, it involves putting my best effort forth and believing in possibilities. Perhaps not this moment, week, or even decade - but some day down the road, Amanda may draw upon those memories and experiences and decide that she is worth the effort of self-care. It's about hope!"

The look of incredulity on his features spurred her on – he would never get it – not anymore.

"We don't always lose, you know that. I'm truly happy that you've moved on, Jack, but the truth is – you've outgrown me, and I'm simply not ready to pack it in yet."

"C'mon, Del, that's a copout – you can do exactly what I'm doing! All you need to do is take the leap – you won't regret it!"

His matter-of-fact, condescending assumption that he was entitled to determine what was right for her was the clinch.

"Jack, I really have no intention nor desire to walk your pathway – frankly, I need to follow my own!" Her tone was clear and assertive, and his silence signified his realization that she was serious; this wasn't going away easily. He slowly placed the menu that he'd been casually skimming onto his plate.

"Even at the expense of our relationship? The long hours and sudden plan cancellations? I'm so over that, Del – I thought you were too!"

"It's the price of passion, Jack – I'm not ready to abandon that yet. I haven't hit that fork in my own road," she softened her tone at his wounded expression, "if I gave this up for you, I would be miserable."

She reached for his hand across the table, "It's no different than if you came back to this career for me." Now *he* looked miserable, and it broke her heart a little. "Jack, I have to move on."

Despite her resolve, a sudden sadness overtook her, and a tear trickled down her cheek, "I love you enough to be totally honest."

"So, you've put your career above me, then," he was angry now.

Interesting choice of words - *me* and not *us*.

"Perhaps we are at an impasse, where that is concerned – let's take our pathways, and if someday, we meet on common ground again, it will be the right time for us."

"Don't count on it, Del, you just blew the best thing you'll ever know! Have a nice life!"

With that, he abruptly rose. Watching him storm out the door, she wondered if the anger was masking hurt or pride. Maybe a bit of both, she decided with a sigh of resignation. Relief did not always bring resolution, but it sure was a welcome reprieve tonight.

Chapter Nine

"Fuck you, Asshole!" I was shaking with rage – how dare that disgusting jerk presume that I was standing there, hooking?

I didn't care to admit that this was a glaring possibility for my survival if I did not figure out what to do – like, *right now*! It was a total irony that the very person I was here to find was currently imprisoned within that profession.

My heart softened at the thought of Jessi. We had been sisters once – mingling each others' blood on our wrists, sealing the oath that we'd never break that bond.

But fate made damn sure that I was brutally ripped from our shared foster home; when Simon had dropped from a sudden heart attack, and Millie was aging and unable to care for us both. Guess who was last on board? A long time had passed since I'd shed a tear over that loss – Millie and Simon were the closest to family I'd ever known; everything before and since had been nothing short of pure hell!

Roaming these familiar hoods now, the smell of hard luck and poverty permeated my senses, and I wondered if, perhaps, that had all been some elusive dream…but I had found Millie – couldn't believe my luck, that she still lived in the same little bungalow on Tenth Ave, a few steps up from this area.

Hard times had hit after I left, and Jessi had apparently been adopted out from under her. Millie had managed to keep tabs on Jessi over the years and found out that the adoptive parents had been abusive – surprise, surprise! Jessi had left at fifteen and had ended up on the streets – a year ago now.

More than a tad anxious in this neck of the woods, closer to the waterfront, teeming with addiction and homelessness, I glanced at the address Millie had scribbled on the paper – Ninth and Forty-second Street. It was a large, run-down, brownstone multi-complex in Downtown East Vancouver beside the Corner Stop convenience store. Gawd, this area was a slum – trash everywhere, and I almost stumbled on the quaking leg of a druggie shooting up. I quickened my pace across the street and gingerly entered the foyer.

The bars on the inner glass did nothing to calm my jitters, and there were remnants of some kind of mush that had dried in rivulets down the filthy wall. A shiver of revulsion ran down my spine. The background noise of the bustling city, surreally out of my realm, grew fainter.

Jessi's code name was "Destiny," Millie had informed me – look on the buzzer box. Sure enough, there she was. I hit the buzzer and waited. A voice crackled over the rusty intercom speaker.

"You know the word," the tone was soft and low.

Did I have the wrong place? I hesitated.

"Jessi?"

"Who the hell *is* this?"

"It's Mandy!" No response – oh crap!

"Mandy, from the Jenkins?"

"Mandy?" the voice was now very much Jessi, and I almost melted to the floor with relief.

"Yes, it's me! Can I come in and see you?" Eyeing the used condom, smooshed into the corner of the filthy window frame – eww, I averted my eyes and stared down the buzzer on the door, fervently willing it to chime my admittance.

"I'm a little busy right now – how did you find me? No, let me guess – Millie, right?"

"Yeah, look…Jessi, I need to see you. It's really urgent!"

Another hesitation. Maybe she's decided to blow me off – I couldn't blame her! I came with a shitload of baggage and bad memories, which I was certain she'd likely rather leave firmly buried.

"OK, go back down Forty-second 'til you see a little café – Daisy's Diner, on the corner of Fourth. I'll meet you there in half an hour." My knees went weak with relief! "Oh, and just tell 'em you're with Desi – you'll be taken care of." She broke the connection before I could thank her.

"Get outta here!" A tattered and toothless woman growled fiercely as my trek past interrupted her intense forage through a stenchy trash bin. I picked up speed and glanced back; she was eyeing me dubiously, hugging some treasured finds protectively to her chest.

Damn…what kind of life was this ragged old lady forced to endure? Realizing I was just a step or two away from that reality was sobering, to say the least. The thought of growing old on the streets blasted some common sense into my brain. I needed to find a place to stay – pronto!

It was surely the longest five blocks that I'd ever traveled on foot, at least in my current state, homeless and vulnerable. Hell, who was I kidding? I was one of them now…

Holy crap! I stopped short at the startling image reflected in the glass window of the little diner; dried blood grotesquely smeared on a blackened, swollen eye and through a nest of matted hair. A tattered and torn hoodie barely covered the blood-stained, oversized nightshirt, hanging askew, on the girl's inadequately clothed – clearly beaten and bruised body. The untouched eye was wide and reflected terror and fear – she appeared shell-shocked and dreadfully familiar!

Damn – it was probably the most horrifying, vulnerable image that I'd ever gazed upon, and I could not believe she was me!

This girl looked so fragile – I'm tougher than that…still, I could not control the single tear trickling down, casting a trail to the aching, tangled ball of pain in my chest that was threatening to choke the life out of me!

What the hell? I couldn't afford weakness or sentiment – not now. With an inner shake, I tried to muster up at least the appearance that I was in control.

Hanging outside the door seemed to make the most sense, given the spectacle that my appearance created. I practiced calming breaths as I surveyed the activity around me. I'd always been a people-watcher – felt safer somehow, on the outside of it all.

"Oh my God, Mandy! What happened to you?"

Jessi materialized from nowhere, it seemed, and gathered me up in a firm embrace – only *she* wouldn't flinch at the grisly possibility of contamination from the blood and grime smeared all over me, and I melted into her, in a heap of gulping sobs.

She was the lifeline I needed, and my heart ached with pent-up misery, built-up during all the time I'd been missing her. I couldn't speak through hiccupping whimpers. She pulled back now, with tears streaming down her own face, and herded me inside, to the washroom, down a dingy, back hallway.

After her gentle administrations, I pondered upon my

considerably-improved reflection – so much of a person's pain and trauma was only visible on the inside. We emerged and took a table away from the window. Jessi grabbed my hands, and the shaking began to subside.

"It's so good to see you – I totally lost track of you!"

The caring and compassion in her eyes melted my well-preserved guard. I knew I could trust her – that had always been a given.

"I am in trouble." My lips quivered, and I shook my head for much-needed clarity. "The bastard from my current home is out of control – I think he will kill me if I return or if he finds me."

"Did he…?"

Jessi's eyes were traveling my profile, and she nodded knowingly before I responded. I knew that the truth reflected in my gaze mirrored both of our stories.

"God, Jess, he's not the first – I should be used to this by now," I inhaled deeply, "but the violence is epic – more serious than I've ever encountered. The creep is so unpredictable – I think he messed up his wife - significantly, last night." I paused as a thin, older waitress plopped two glasses of cola in front of us.

"What can I get you, two beauties?" Bestowing an affectionate wink upon Jessi, she insisted, "it's on the house today!"

Jessie ordered grilled cheese sandwiches for us both.

"Thanks, Daisy," Jessi smiled gratefully, "I'll get you back!" Daisy, whom I now assumed owned the joint, waved her off dismissively, smiled compassionately at me, and glided off to the kitchen.

"I truly have no idea where to go right now, Jess," I looked at her beseechingly, "some annoying social services do-gooder is trying to pry into all my shit, but you and I both know it's a dead-end road - got me here in the first place! It's useless to go there."

"We'll think of something!"

Jessi eyed me with determination, but behind the sparkle was a haunted look, reflecting desolation and hard times. No matter – she was still the stunning beauty that turned heads everywhere – dark exotic features from her Cree ancestry. I wondered why she didn't just seek out an easier life – her physical attributes alone would buy her way off the street. Even exotic dancing would be safer.

But she was like me, and it just wasn't that easy; the deeper in the mire, the harder it was to extract yourself – acceptance was a survival skill, a strategic comfort zone – of nightmarish proportions. Jessi simply had no other home to go to.

But now I needed a solution, and a city shelter would just

land me back into government care before I could even make it past the front desk.

"If I can stay on your couch – even for a day or two until I find a job…"

"God, Mandy, it's complicated. Russell is a bit of a stickler – a real control freak and would not tolerate you there." She eyed me with genuine fear. "In fact, you'd be in big-time danger if he found you – I can't let that happen to you."

This girl before me, the only true friend I've ever known, was more worried about me than herself – profoundly moving! My heart melted. She didn't need to tell me – the jerk was her pimp, and I'd move mountains to ensure that I did nothing to endanger her.

"Jess, look at me," I paused in earnest. "I can't be at greater risk than I already am – I'll take my chances. I just need a place to crash for a few hours a day and will make myself scarce whenever you say! I've become the boss at disappearing when I need to."

I needed her now and knew that desperation was written all over my face. She regarded me with a troubled expression.

"Mandy, there are things you don't know," Jessi sighed, "Russell controls everything about me – even what, where, and how much I eat. As long as I follow his rules, I'm safe and well-cared for." She leaned forward. "I don't know how we could swing it to keep you safe as well – for sure, food will be an issue."

"I'll manage that. How often does he come around?"

"It's sporadic – part of his control over me, but he does usually give me a bit of a warning to ensure he doesn't interrupt the income stream."

I smirked at Jessi's raised brow.

"OK, only for a couple of nights, right?" Jessi smiled softly.

"Anything you say – I'll completely follow your lead." I nodded enthusiastically.

"Where will you try to find work?"

"Hell, Jess, I'll do anything it takes to survive," I knew she was worried, and I needed to reassure her. I paused at her pained expression.

"I promise not to fall under Russell's spell!" I grinned at her with feigned optimistic confidence.

"OK, let's get back - you can tell me all about your foster home, and we can plan the bastard's demise together!" We both giggled and finished our meal. I felt a surge of confidence – I was back on my game.

Chapter Ten

The tiny apartment was surprisingly tidy and clean, in stark contrast to the general shitty condition of the building. Jessi imparted that Russell was adamant with his expectations in this regard. Looking around, I noticed the sparse furnishings; only a well-worn love seat, coffee table, and floor lamp adorned the living space. That's cool. I could squish myself into it quite nicely – apparently, I'd mastered a useful skill. There was an aged, 60s variety, a metal dining table with 2 chairs, a small galley kitchen, and a bath. The bedroom, in comparison, was a decent size with ample space for clothes and storage – not that your average hooker had many possessions, I reasoned.

"Just throw your bag under the bed." Jessi looked like she was ready for work at a moment's notice. Hell, it didn't matter – she'd be drop-dead gorgeous in a burlap potato sack! I headed to the shower – figuring I should be grateful that Gen had, at least, allowed me some extra clothing, as she had thrown me to the curb.

God, this felt like heaven! As the water streamed liberally over my body, I relaxed a little, pondering my situation. I was determined to scout out every possible opportunity to earn some cash – maybe enough to rent a room in a hostel, until I figured things out. For the next few days, I planned to clean and keep up laundry, etc., for Jessi. I jumped as my reverie was broken by the sharp rap at the door.

"You need to get out, quick!" Jessi sounded really stressed, and I quickly complied, opening the door to her frantic pacing. "Russell is on his way – he's bringing a trick, and you need to leave *now*."

"I'm on it!" Drying myself on the way, I quickly gathered up my soiled clothing and stuffed it - towel and all, into the worn plastic bag. After throwing on clean duds, I gave Jessi a hug of gratitude on my way out the door and sauntered across the street into the park. Predictably, the green space in this run-down area of the city was clearly uncared for; needles strewn on the ground, and trash everywhere. No shock to me.

I picked a bench with a convenient view of the building entrance and waited. A few minutes later, a scrawny but tough-looking dude walked up to the doors, followed by a well-dressed society type – likely the john. I watched them disappear into the building and figured I had a bit of time to scout out some food alternatives. I'd already decided to ask Daisy for a job – any job! I could eat, at least.

The diner was quiet, and Daisy greeted me with a friendly smile and a steaming cup of hot coffee that promised warming comfort. I was about to protest – no way that I could pay for that, but she quickly assured me it was a freebie.

"I'm aware that you have no means – you have the look of someone on the run." she studied me now, and I decided to get right to the point.

"I need a job." I watched closely for her reaction.

"Honey, we aren't hiring right now, and besides, despite the name, I'm not the only owner."

My heart dropped – this had been the most promising prospect. But what the hell had I expected? She regarded me thoughtfully.

"Tell you what, I'll talk to Joe and see if we can use a dishwasher – it just so happens that we lost our most recent one to another restaurant; he upgraded to a waiter." She rolled her eyes. "We were planning on making do, but I happen to have some influence." She winked. "Come back tomorrow."

"Hey, thanks, I really appreciate it!" My spirits took a hopeful leap!

I needed to be on my best behavior – I knew how to play it.

"Don't thank me until tomorrow – this has to get past the big guy," she gave me a no-nonsense stare, "and don't mess this up! Desi is very dear to me." With that, she grabbed some menus and glided over to a couple who'd just come in, the little bell signaling their entrance.

She must think I have shit for brains!

I made my way back to the park bench – my outlook considerably brighter. Sweet! If this worked out, I could end up in the best shape ever – with a future I hadn't even dreamed possible. Earning enough income to make my own way, no matter how meager, was a gigantic leap – one that opened doors. The first one was to get Jessi out of this hell-hole, out from under that asshole's control.

Suddenly, I spotted a light flickering in the second-floor window of her unit – that had been the all-clear signal we'd agreed upon. I made my way across the street.

"Sorry for the short notice." Jessi was in a particularly perky mood as she opened the door to let me in.

"No worries – I just appreciate what you're doing for me," I smiled – her high spirits were infectious. "Hey, Daisy may have a job for me – washing dishes! Why are *you* so chipper?"

"Awesome! She is a good head!" Jessi laughed. "I just landed an upscale john – if I keep him happy, he will be paying four times my regular rate. He's a friend of a friend of Russell's," she sighed contentedly, "apparently has a thing for aboriginal chicks." She shrugged. "Russell promised me the same percentage split, which means I'll have extra cash that belongs only to me!"

"Sweet!" Jessi looked absolutely radiant! "I'm really happy for you."

But it struck me –

A bit pathetic, isn't it? Celebrating success as a hooker? Oh, there was a good living in it if you got the right gig – the right pimp. I had my doubts about Russell though, but chose wisely to keep them to myself for now. It was necessary that I wandered the neighborhood twice more that evening before we both reconvened for a catch-up chat.

"It was so hard leaving Millie," Jessi related wistfully as we munched on some leftover nachos, "and the last asshole who actually adopted me started dicking me almost right away. My so-called new "mother" sat in a chair in the bedroom, while she watched him rape my ass." Jessi smiled sadly. "Running was my only option, and it was fucking hard, but it led me directly here, and believe me, for the most part, the sex is infinitely more bearable. There are quirky tricks, but mostly safe. And, as long as Russell is happy, he protects me."

I got it! I understood the reasoning. Hell, for as much as I vowed that no asshole would ever force me to prostitute, I had to concede that it was a far better option than the rapes and abuse that I had endured in foster care!

I shared those tough details with Jessi before we called it a night. She agreed that I could stay, until I saved enough to secure a place to live. My pessimistic realism kept me from getting my hopes up about the future, but tomorrow just might be a rare good day!

Chapter Eleven

Del fidgeted in her seat, stiff and drained from her lengthy vigil in the car, feeling like the classic private eye or undercover cop. Ha! Her skills were totally inept for that job! Clearly, it was time to come up with *Plan B*, as she'd yet to spot Amanda or either of her foster parents, though she'd sat here in focused diligence the entire day, barely noticing the vehicle and foot traffic around her. Luckily, her usual work load was conveniently accessible on her laptop, and she could easily touch base on her cell with clients and colleagues alike.

OK, here we go - showtime! She peered closely across the street as a car pulled up to the curb in front of the home, and a brawny man got out and headed to the house, letting himself in. A mass of butterflies, born from anticipation, messed with her stomach as she waited, in contemplation of the wisdom in approaching the home. Before she could make that decision, the door flew open, and the man, whom she now recognized from a file photo as Paul Miller, awkwardly shepherded a woman, who she assumed to be Gen Miller, down the porch steps.

The poor lady appeared to be in appallingly rough shape, with a massively bruised face, a significant limp, and one arm hanging uselessly by her side. Del knew instantly – from the gnawing pangs in her gut that Gen Miller had very recently been subjected to a significant beating. She set a mental alarm to move quickly on her commitment to investigate the reason that Paul Miller's name was ringing warning bells in her head.

As he edged away from the curb, Del followed at a safe distance. In line with her expectations, the car pulled into the UBC Hospital's Emergency drop-off; the closest ER to their home. Del carried on to the exit and traveled toward the office. She would connect with her head hospital administrator contact to find out the scoop with one Gen Miller.

Back at her desk, Del took a large gulp from her Café Mocha, heaved a deep sigh, and opened the file for Amanda Goodchild. Ignoring the increasing clutter of paperwork that had been building during her absence, she began to pour through the documents in more detail. Jack had not been exaggerating with his dire assessment of her case.

OK, she mused - need to start at the beginning, to determine any connections at all with which to establish possible communications. She unconsciously tuned out a series of emergency sirens just outside her window; it was apt background noise.

Now that Del had witnessed the dire, physical state of Gen Miller, she was completely certain that Amanda had fled the home for her own safety. In that vein of thought, niggling worry seeped in. The girl may think she's tough, but danger lurked for a fifteen-year-old wandering the streets by herself. She was a smart young lady, and Del knew instinctively that Amanda had been forced to make a choice based on her determination of which was her best chance for survival.

"Oh, good Lord," Del muttered expletives as she combed through it further. From the start, Amanda's fate with the system was certain.

Her mother, Selma, had been born to a prostitute. Amanda's grandmother, Candice, was murdered when Selma was a little girl, but by that time, Selma had already been in foster care, with the identity of her father unknown.

Selma had hooked up with Amanda's father, Rick, at a very young age, and both were hopelessly addicted to Crystal Meth. Hence, Amanda had been born a *crack baby*. It was during one particular drug-induced rage, that her father had beaten Selma senseless, causing permanent brain damage.

Amanda had been just four years old at the time and entered the Child Protection system malnourished, severely neglected, with significant developmental delays, and several previously ill-healed bone fractures. One nurse's testimony indicated evidence of possible sexual abuse – she had to have been a toddler, for God's sake!

Del fought back an intense wave of nausea, took a deep breath, and walked off some steam, trying to deal with the emotional turmoil from the ugly story unfolding before her eyes.

She completely understood the anger and outrage that average, well-balanced citizens denounced when these types of stories came into public light. How, indeed, could a newborn baby, addicted to Crystal Meth through her birth mother, be allowed to stay in that home?

The sad truth? Legal snags, missed information, and documents not submitted by deadlines often resulted in vulnerable children falling through the cracks. Suffice it to say that Amanda had dropped through a mammoth crevice.

The Crown Prosecutor, at that time, had been unsuccessful in convicting Amanda's father in the attack on her mother due to a lack of viable evidence in the form of a witness. Therefore, by the time Amanda was six, Social Services released her back into the care of her father, whom they deemed was fit to raise her. Amanda's alleged abuse seemed to be attributed to her mother, and it was ruled that there was no clear evidence to support the nurse's observation of prior sexual molestation.

Rick had, by this time, conveniently left Amanda's mother to her terrible fate - withering away in long-term care, and was living with a common-law partner whose brother, it was later discovered, was a convicted pedophile. Not shocking, Del surmised, disgust flooding her senses. How could this get any worse?

But the horror continued, as Amanda's father and his partner had turned a blind eye to the sexual abuse that Amanda suffered at the hands of her so-called "uncle" and his like-minded friends.

When Amanda was eight years old, the school administration called Social Services, relaying that a teacher had noticed a spot of blood on Amanda's pants. Upon questioning, Amanda admitted that her uncle's friend had *played down there* before she left for school. Subsequent investigations and arrests put an end to that one source of evil in her world – complete with a ten-year sentence.

From here, the foster care journey resumed – Amanda's fate sealed, as Selma had passed away a year earlier, eliminating any other possibilities for familial care. Amanda had never heard of nor seen her father again. Thank God!

Amanda presented as an angry, mistrusting little girl - understandably so, and it was extremely difficult to secure a foster home that could handle her emotional needs and outbursts. Del swore heavily under her breath, as she calculated that Amanda had been placed in twenty-two different foster homes throughout the next seven years – Paul and Gen Miller bringing up the rear. Although not proven, it was documented that she suffered alleged sexual abuse at three of them. Now, Del surmised with a sick feeling in her gut, that number may rise to four - officially. The actual tally was possibly higher.

OK, this explained the extreme hostility and mistrust that Del had slammed up against with this young teenager. All of these kids had their issues – necessarily significant, to end up in care, but Amanda's case was, by far, the most horrific child protection failure that Del had ever come across.

She stood up and self-massaged the back of her neck. God, she was tired. Well, no flipping wonder, she deduced, picking up her cell as it chimed – 7:00 p.m. The sound permeated the silence like an ominous warning.

"Del," Janet Freeman, her hospital contact, was brisk.

"Hi, thanks for calling – what have you got for me?" Del braced herself for what she suspected was coming.

"It's brutal. I won't candy-coat it. Gen Miller was severely beaten, raped, and sodomized. The rape kit confirmed penetration – likely both human and foreign objects; the latter confirmed. She is messed up from that and has a broken jaw, six cracked ribs, a ruptured spleen, a dislocated hip, and her arm was almost ripped clear from the shoulder. She will require surgery for most of it, including an eye socket, that may or may not be successful. She will most likely lose vision in that eye."

"Oh my God – the poor woman!" Del took a deep, shaky breath. "Janet, I can't find their foster daughter, Amanda Goodchild – she's fifteen!" Del was completely horrified. "You will let me know if she's brought there? She may have been victimized, as well! If not, she most likely witnessed this or, at least, had been at the home when it happened, and she hasn't shown up to school today."

"I will for sure, and I'll also scope out the other city hospitals – ask them to advise me if she shows up there. Sorry for such a grim report, but there's more."

Del held her breath and slumped back into her chair.

"The perpetrator was either unable to or must have finished his business elsewhere, as there is no trace of semen – so, no definitive DNA evidence. What do you think the chances are that she will testify against her asshole husband?"

Del groaned her frustration and felt bile rise – had Amanda been subject to his abuse afterward, then?

"The woman's pretty much looped right now and unable to talk yet." Janet paused, and Del knew there was more.

"Paul Miller insists that the perpetrator attacked Gen in the morning after he'd left for work, and that Gen was able to tell him that the *boy* was an acquaintance of Amanda. He alleges that Amanda had let him in the house instead of going to school.

According to Paul Miller, she likely fled with the kid afterward to escape getting caught."

"Thank you so much for letting me know – you are an angel." Del rang off with a heavy heart, more anxious than ever and not buying a bit of the low-life's fabricated story, determined to dredge any possible dirt on Paul Miller first thing in the morning.

Chapter Twelve

What the hell? I was startled rudely awoken by screaming and violent pounding from some unknown source in the unit above. What a dive! I quickly showered and headed to the diner.

Daisy greeted me warmly – that alone pricked my suspicion – why so friendly? But I well knew, when I had no choice but to play the game. I smiled.

"Hey, Miss Early Bird – looks like you've earned a worm," she plopped a cup of coffee in front of a stool and motioned for me to sit. "I'll be right back, and we can chat."

I peered around at the breakfast crowd absent-mindedly, picking at a rip in the faux leather that covered the perch which my butt was currently parked upon. It was a fairly obvious lot; construction workers, business people, and a couple of old farts. A younger waitress dashed around, quite efficiently managing a half-dozen tables. No way that I could deal with a crowd like this – no tolerance for putting up with people's bullshit!

Suddenly, a plate heaping with breakfast fare was slid under my nose. Oh God, that smelled delicious! My stomach audibly growled in response.

"Time to chow down, and then we'll talk about your work commitments here." Daisy winked cheerfully and took off with a steaming coffee pot for refills.

Hell, I'd work off this meal, I assured myself as I caved into my extreme need for sustenance. I would owe no one!

I kept a wary eye on her as she stopped to chit-chat with all the customers. By the time she returned, I'd wolfed down the entire feast – my stomach gurgled loudly as it worked overtime to digest the first real meal that I'd had in days!

"Mandy, is it? That the name you prefer?"

"It's the only one I have!" Maybe she thought I was set on working the street like Jessi and used a pseudonym. In any case, it was mandatory that I keep a pleasant approach with her – I was under no illusion my survival depended on it.

"Hey, thanks for helping me out." I forced a pleasant smile.

"We can keep you busy all day – breakfast and lunch are the prime times here, so it will be eight-to-ten-hour shifts, depending on the crowd, with a half-hour break included, to be taken between rushes, but it's minimum wage." A gentle smile softened her tough demeanor. "The first week will be sink or swim, and Jeff and the girls will show you the routine."

"That's great!" I couldn't believe my luck, "I really appreciate this – I won't let you down!" Hell, I'd never made any wage – this was beyond awesome!

"OK, sure, we can use your help. Are you ready?"

"Right now?"

"Unless you have other pressing things to attend to…" Daisy's assessing gaze broke through my shocked stupor.

"No, no – I'm good to start!" Truth be told, I was terrified – what the hell had I gotten myself into? I had no idea what I was doing! I guessed I was about to figure it out…

I followed her through the squeaky swinging kitchen doors to a surprisingly tiny space with very little room to move. The first word that came to mind was *chaos.* The guy flipping food, in steaming pans and a griddle, was everywhere at once, singlehandedly filling plates and yelling the order numbers, as he slid them on the counter for the waitresses to pick up. By now, there were two servers, not including Daisy, and I noticed the place was full!

"Hey, can you peel those for me?" He shoved a mountain of potatoes to what seemed to be the only working space left on the counter, grabbed a peeler, and, without looking up, held it out to me. Wait – I thought I was the dishwasher! I looked imploringly to Daisy for direction.

"Jeff, this is Mandy." Daisy took the peeler and placed it into my hand. "She's a bit green, so go easy." She shot him a warning look as he finally looked up with a grin.

"Whenever you have time, you'll also be helping Jeff in the kitchen." She must have seen the look of terror in my eyes. "Don't stress, Bree comes in at noon – she's the kitchen help, and stays over for the dinner rush. She'll be very glad to see you! Don't sweat it, Kid, you'll be fine." With that likely inadequate prediction, Daisy disappeared into the hustle and bustle of the breakfast crowd.

Well, at least I was painfully familiar with the task at hand and grabbed a potato to start. Jeff slid a large stainless-steel bin my way to put them in. It was fascinating, watching the speed and skill unfold, as Jeff managed the endless breakfast orders that were constantly pinned on the spinner. Not a chance in hell, that I could ever hope to keep track of it all!

I studied him from the corner of my eye. Had to be about twenty-five or so, blessed with dark, good looks. The one grin that he'd afforded me was easy and friendly, not to mention refreshing - transforming his features. I had to admit, he was a bit of a hottie – not that I was in the market.

I quickly made short work of the potatoes.

"Thanks. Would you mind rinsing them? Slice half for frying, and the rest, put into a pot – we'll boil them later for lunch."

I looked around and grabbed a pot, covering the rinsed

potatoes with water, and placed it on a back burner that seemed free. The remainder, I sliced them in accordance with my observation of the cooked version on the plates that were going out to the customers.

"You are not that green," he awarded me another winning grin, which I returned with a genuine smile. Jeff immediately threw the potatoes into a large frying skillet with a generous dose of butter.

I really liked him – there was something warm and honest that I could discern in his expression. Too, I held a fair measure of respect for people who worked their asses off – without expecting the world to gift them a living. I aspired to be someone like Jeff one day – sooner than later, I hoped.

"I can chop onions and mushrooms for the omelets if you want." Keep busy, girl – your day will fly by. My first day on the job and every second counted – income for my survival. I would *not* screw this up.

"Sweet! I'd really appreciate that." Motioning to the knife block, he passed the vegetables to the cutting board. An hour went by in relative silence, and the dishes were piling up. Damn, I'd better get to them!

"Are you good now for me to handle this?" I motioned to the piles of trays.

"Oh, sure. Soak them in bleach water first, though."

My anxiety levels were rising – what if I messed up?

"Bleach is on the shelf above you – two capfuls are all that you need, and fill the sink about halfway with hot water."

I took a deep breath – hadn't realized I'd been holding it! I had enough sense to rinse the food off first and began the soak, bleaching the second sink to transfer them. Suddenly, a young girl burst through the door.

"Hey," she threw me a smile and playfully punched Jeff in the arm. "How's the run today?"

"Would be much worse without Mandy," he smiled, motioning to me with a spatula.

"Yeah, Mandy, you know your way around dirty dishes, it seems. Do you know the drill?"

"I'm pretty sure they have to be sterilized yet - the ones in this sink are ready to go," I replied, eyeing the large stainless-steel contraption with some trepidation. Yeah, I could properly wreck this job!

"Awesome, that's the easy part. I'm Bree, by the way."

She was right – the process was quick, and I soon had an efficient routine going. Lunch rush hit me by surprise. Wow, the time was flying by! We stopped for a quick bite to eat after the onslaught. Food was included in this deal – sweet!

At precisely 4:00, Daisy came in and motioned quickly for me to follow her. My dish duty was in good order, and I had just been helping Jeff and Bree with supper prep. I'd met the other waitresses, Carrie and Lucy, and was feeling like I won the lottery – everyone seemed so nice and easy-going.

This was the honeymoon phase though – I knew all about those. I trailed after Daisy with a sense of apprehension. Had I screwed up? She led the way into a small office down a hallway, next to the washrooms, and motioned for me to sit, in a near threadbare chair across from her. I was afraid to say anything and waited anxiously.

"How do you feel after your first shift?" Her smile was genuine, and I heaved an inner sigh of relief.

"Great – everyone here is very helpful and cool." Daisy eyed me astutely.

"There are many of us still in this world who care about each other. The tricky part is caring about yourself."

Her assessing glance made me squirm. No way that I was ready for this level of intimate conversation – I didn't need another savior to take me on.

"You are going to have to trust yourself with this."

She was dead wrong, but I nodded for the sake of compliance. What I *needed* was to keep this income gig – do my job well; no attitude; show up on time, and refrain from screwing up! They'd have to drag me, kicking and screaming, back to that hell-hole that I'd been living in! Just the thought brought a wash of nausea through my guts.

At the first inkling of trouble, I'd run – I had this!

"We just need to handle some necessary red tape, and you'll be on board officially." Daisy slid a formal-looking document in front of me. "Just fill in the blanks in the first section – I can do the rest."

I scanned the paper. Lucky - I already had a Social Insurance number from being in the system, and I was now officially old enough to hire. My guts tensed when I got to the residential address portion. I looked up to find Daisy studying me. Her keen gaze astutely followed my finger, and she advised that she'd handle that one for me. How much had Jessi told her, and when? Well, I wasn't about to offer anything further and quickly nodded my agreement.

"For now, you'll work five shifts per week – Monday to Friday days, eight – four. If you are open for overtime opportunities, we could sure use weekend help, same shift Saturdays, and a four or five-hour one on Sundays – not required, but comes with OT pay. We will first see how the next couple of weeks play out. Sound fair?"

Hell, that was more than fair – I'd gobble up those extra shifts and be out of Jessi's hair – perfect! I nodded.

Daisy's gentle smile unnerved me. I couldn't afford any emotional investment – to get attached. I'd seen a thousand of them, just like it, turn to devasting betrayal.

"I'll pay you for the full eight hours today – you're free to go."

"Thank you."

"You bet, Sweetie! Oh, I forgot to mention – meals are included for every shift, payday is every Friday, and I'll have diner-logo aprons for you tomorrow." She paused. "I don't suppose you have a bank account yet, do you?"

Panic seized me – I had to remain incognito. That was critical!

"It's OK, I can pay you in cash for now. And Mandy?"

The relief weakened my knees. But what the hell else did she want? I needed her to shut up and let me escape for tonight.

"Heed Desi's advice – stay away from her business. She must care very much for you – she'd get a fair bonus for bringing you on."

Humiliation invaded me as sudden tears of emotion flooded my eyes and threatened to spill. I held them back – every drop would release all the courage and fortitude I possessed. I couldn't afford weakness now. I turned abruptly and stumbled blindly out the door.

Chapter Thirteen

Del woke, plagued with a deep, throbbing headache, and hit the shower in hope of some semblance of relief.

It had been a rough night.

Sleep had eluded her, with haunting visions of Amanda Goodchild swirling around in her head – brutally raped and beaten, like Gen Miller; wandering the streets with no possessions or money; hiding somewhere unsafe - or worst of all, lying dead in a cold, deserted ditch.

Stepping from the shower, she popped a couple of extra-strength Advil and prepared for work.

In Timmy's drive-through line-up, she firmly pushed the images from her brain and focused on this morning's task.

Paul Miller…she ran that name around in her mind – searching for a connection that she sensed was just out of reach. It was so damn frustrating! Jack!

Del abandoned *that* avenue of strategy immediately – no way, under the circumstances, would he likely be willing to help, and she really didn't need that awkward complication anyhow. She'd figure this out – whatever it took.

"Good morning!" Del plopped the Café Mocha, complete with a still- warm cream cheese Danish, on Sherri's desk with a grateful smile. The girl was the epitome of a perfect executive assistant, and Del would frankly be buried ten feet under without her. Sherri expertly handled the mess of four social workers in total – no easy feat!

"Right back at you!" Sherri groaned her pleasure as she took a long pull from her cup. "Oh, Janet Freeman called to let you know that there were no admissions for Amanda Goodchild in the city or surrounding area hospitals."

"Thanks Sherri. Hey, can I ask you a favor? Please see if you can find anything on Paul Miller – the name tweaks, and I don't know why." At Sherri's smiling nod, Del headed into her office and closed the door.

Well, it was a good thing she supposed, that Amanda hadn't showed up at Emergency. However, her identity may be simply unknown, she mused. Thankfully, Janet was thorough and would have picked up on a young, unidentified teenager as being a possible Amanda. It was time for some serious digging.

Unfortunately, *his* was a common name, and Google immediately highlighted at least fifty *Paul Miller*s. Scanning the Facebook, Instagram, and LinkedIn profiles brought no matches to light. A nudge from her struggling memory bank strongly suggested that she was on a dead end and that the name was likely a pseudonym. She opened the file once more to study his picture as if staring at it hard enough would shed the necessary light.

Back in the search bar, she decided to pair his name with "pedophile." This narrowed it down to two – neither of which was a match. Damn! She knew that Sherri was already scouring the government database but had the sinking suspicion that it would be fruitless.

Del repeated the same steps for Genevieve Miller, with mirroring results. She tried the maiden name "MacPherson" that was on file, with still no hits, even paired with Paul Miller. What the hell was she missing? Well, she needed to figure it out – not for love nor money, would she enlist any input from Jack at this point.

After one more scour through the files, Del released a weary sigh and tackled a few pressing tasks from her other caseload files. An hour later, the sunlight sneaking through the blinds had her feeling sleepy and she grabbed her purse and headed to the front lobby; her focus now shifted to finding Amanda.

"Hey, Del," Sherri halted her exit through the double doors. "When was the last time you took a break?"

Yeah, when was the last time? Exhaustion screamed that it was far overdue, but swimming in that murky pool was familiar to Del; rest would come only once she made some measure of headway. The situation was far too volatile, and Amanda's very life may be at stake – assuming she was still alive! A chill of premonition traveled down the length of her spine.

"I'll be OK, thank you." She leveled her irreplaceable assistant with a genuine smile of gratitude, thinking that she was the luckiest person alive to have Sherri on her team.

"I'll be watching you all the same."

"You are an angel," she blew a kiss before heading out to her car.

Del had to tamp down her growing impatience at the lack of results from their investigation thus far. She knew, in her gut, that Paul Miller was a dangerous man, and the sooner that she could dig up the evidence to support her intuition, the better the outcome for Amanda's predicament. She quickly scanned her cell notifications and put the car in gear.

Right now she was grateful for her choice, in the little Honda Accord. She'd opted for practical yet comfortable, in direct opposition to Jack's urging. He had tried to persuade her toward a more luxurious, larger American-made vehicle, insisting that her money would go further in terms of options and space. But Del had held firm. There were enough perks in her little ride, and the fuel cost was minimal in comparison. It didn't hurt that she remained inconspicuous in this little gem.

At this moment, she decided to cruise the neighborhood

where Gen and Paul Miller lived, hoping to find a glimpse of Amanda or either of her foster parents. Earlier at the office, she had confirmed that Paul had been showing up for his usual day shift routine. Still, she resisted the urge to go to the house. Her anxiety had escalated upon learning that Amanda had not yet returned to school. Janet had sent a text as well, informing her that they'd released Gen from the hospital that morning, pending further surgery appointments. Poor woman – her safe haven was defunct. With no luck here, Del considered her next move.

Having burned through the list of prior foster homes that Amanda had had the misfortune to land in, Del moved on to other areas of the city, deducing that it was likely safe to rule out the ones where she'd suffered the greatest abuse. Still, she mused, Amanda would have made connections, even through her various schools. Del decided to focus first on the one home where she'd spent the longest time – Millie and Simon Jenkins.

Their home had been in a relatively decent area of the city, though just a few blocks shy of the poverty-stricken waterfront neighborhood where young girls, laden with similar circumstances as Amanda's, ended up turning tricks for their survival.

Truly, Del deduced, it had likely been a fortunate move for Amanda, with Simon's steady income and Millie's preference to stay home with her foster kids. According to the records, her reputation as a devoted caregiver to these needy kids was stellar. It was Amanda's misfortune to be once again uprooted without warning and transferred to a new home after Simon had died suddenly from a heart attack. How sad…

Millie had stayed in the home with only one other girl, who had been adopted shortly afterward, and her health and finances had deteriorated to the point where she was forced to stop fostering.

Having no luck in cruising the neighborhood streets, Del made a quick decision to try Millie's place – she might still be alive, and if Del had learned anything in this hellish career, it had been to leave no stone unturned.

Chapter Fourteen

Pulling up to the curb, across from the little green and white wood/stucco home, Del immediately noted that it seemed well-cared for. It was one of the originals on this street, where urban renewal was rejuvenating the neighborhood. Many homes were either under renovation or torn down completely, making way for upscale multi-unit rentals.

Del made her way up the walk, noticing the spring tulip bulbs peeking out merrily from the flowerbeds bordering both sides of the cobblestone path. They would soon be in full bloom, and the thought of spring brought relief from knowing that, at least, Amanda would not have to battle the cold nights for much longer. Del pushed the door bell buzzer and heard its faint hum within.

The ensuing silence was deafening.

"Yes, who is it?" The voice seemed muffled.

"Hello, is this Millie Jenkins?" Another pregnant pause.

"Who is asking?"

"Del Greenwood, from Child Protection Services. If you are Millie, please consider chatting with me. It's about one of your former foster children, who may be in grave danger."

Millie opened the door immediately, dubiously eyeing the ID card that Del held out before motioning her inside. Del noticed the same care, evident in the clean and tidy space, and offered Millie a gentle smile.

"I'm sorry to barge in on you unannounced, but I believe that time is of the essence."

"If it's about Mandy, I've seen her already."

This was indeed a shock and rendered Del momentarily speechless. A lucky break for sure – it would be easier to find the girl now. Millie must have read the hope within her expression.

"Don't go thinking I'll tell you where she is, even if I do know!" Mistrust was oozing from her expression. "No personal disrespect intended, but not one iota of good has come from any part of your department's involvement in Mandy's life." A single tear trickled down her cheek.

Del's heart lurched. She could not deny any of it! For sure, government intervention had contributed significantly to the young girl's strife in her life thus far. Damn! Had there been any alternatives? A little niggling inner voice taunted her – *background checks*.

How did this so often get missed? Oh, she was under no illusion regarding the less-than-honorable motives sometimes in play for foster parenting; and acknowledged ruefully the importance of thorough investigation.

It made her sick every time they found a great home for a child, only to have them ripped out because some long-lost relative had learned that there was financial compensation inclusive with the package.

Her last case was heart-wrenching, as the child was born meth addicted – the third sibling, all with different fathers, and was taken into custody. The mother had immediately signed over all parental rights to government care, just as with her first two – good on her. This little boy was taken in by a wonderful family, just a few days old – their own kids were old enough to engage completely in the fostering experience and considered little Timmy, their brother.

Life was good for Timmy, and the family had undergone the rigorous and lengthy adoption process, as all known relatives had declined to take him.

Del's blood boiled every time she thought about it! In the midst of finalizing the adoption procedure, the Department had written one of the grandmothers who lived clear across the country; assuring her that she would receive the same financial compensation that is awarded to foster parents for the rest of his minor years. The woman promptly altered her decision and requested to have Timmy.

His birth mother immediately wrote a letter to all government authorities, begging them not to allow it because this grandmother had lost custody of her own children due to physical and mental abuse as well as severe neglect. So much for background checks! One chilly fall day, nine-year-old Timmy was ripped from the only parents he'd ever known.

Del whipped her attention back to Millie.

"I have no excuses to offer – you are right," she needed this woman's alliance in order to find Amanda. "It is a flawed system, overwrought with ineffective processes and ridiculous red tape." She took a deep breath and met Millie's gaze head-on. "Please, may we sit?"

Millie led her to a worn but clean and comfortable loveseat in the living room and took her place in the matching chair facing her. Del leaned purposefully toward this woman, who quite obviously still bore immense love for Amanda Goodchild.

"There is no question – Amanda…Mandy has lived a horrendous life under government care, and yes - it's frankly unacceptable!" Del was grateful that Millie was allowing her to continue.

"Millie, I can't change that reality. I can only assure you of my solid commitment to making this right for her, moving forward." She reached out to gently touch Millie's arm and took a deep breath. "Most of us in this system throw our hearts into it, even knowing the pitfalls that are often in place. You are no stranger to this - it is often a case of the *lesser evil*." The hurt, evident in the older woman's shaky demeanor, would haunt Del – she knew it.

"I will give you my word that Amanda will not be shuffled through the same pathway. She is of an age that I am planning to work out a support outreach residence for her. Mandy would be with other kids like herself – under house supervision, of course. She will have options for her education and future – possibly blending in career-focused employment opportunities."

"Oh, I don't blame *you*, Ms. Greenwood…" Millie's face softened.

"Call me Del, please."

"Del," Millie bestowed a hint of a smile. "I know that your heart is in the right place and you seem to care a lot, but I've been fostering in the system for so many years, I find it hard to believe things have changed." Mille shot a calculated glance at Del. "Did you know that she was sexually abused at the hands of foster parents?"

"I have just taken on her case and have reviewed the file – it's unthinkable what she has been through!" Del nodded with a troubled sigh. "It sickens me, to be frank, and I have lost much sleep over the years, but for me to move on equates to abandonment within my moral ethic, so I stay to do what I can within a flawed system."

Millie reached out and patted her hand. "I believe you – I

appreciate those of you who put your heart and soul into these kids, I really do!"

Millie shifted her body in the chair in an obvious effort to ease some physical discomfort. Her long white pleated braids still shone like silk, and the years of hard-earned survival were gently etched onto her face; creases around her eyes and mouth marked untold stories. Del decided she really liked this woman.

"I understand Millie, your reluctance to trust the power of my influence with the system, and I share that concern." Del took the woman's weathered hand. "I will do absolutely everything within my power – it's all that I can give you." She pinned her now with a determined gleam in her eyes. "Come hell or high water, I *am* going to find her, but it would be significantly easier with your help." Del sat back, anxiously awaiting Millie's reaction.

"Before I lost her, Mandy was coming around – leaps and bounds!" Millie's misty gaze focused on another era. "Oh, she still had her fiery moments – after what she'd been through, it was a necessary defense. But she and her foster sister, Jessi, bonded like superglue. Jessi may well have been the sole human being alive with whom Mandy risked trust." Millie turned her eyes to Del, her expression softened with nostalgic reverie.

Del sat riveted, transfixed on this quiet, gentle woman. She knew that underneath the surface, Millie possessed fearless strength and commitment – the qualities necessary to walk beside these at-risk youths – through their pain, suffering, and hopelessness. One thing was certain, Millie Jenkins had forever impacted many a young life in a profound, positive way.

"I began to see a ray of hope sneak through every now and again. Simon and I were planning to adopt the two of them – not take on any new ones. Simon was tired, and we were getting older." A single tear trickled down her cheek.

"Then we lost *him* – just like that, it all changed. Even with the government payments, I was unable to keep both girls on, with unpaid medical bills from his brief illness and my own health faltering. He was my true soulmate – my partner through all of it." Millie sat up straight and gave herself a shake. "First Amanda, then Jessi was gone, and I could no longer keep up – broke my heart."

"Suffice it to say that Mandy went back into the jungle with absolutely no choices available to her. I didn't hear from her again until just a week ago or so – they wouldn't tell us where the kids were sent." Millie threw Del a measured glance. "You are one determined lady, Del Greenwood, and I will give you what little help I can."

Del let out a huge sigh of relief, figuring that she must have been holding that breath through almost all of Millie's words!

"Thank you, this means so much! I'm assuming that Mandy

is on the run and did not have a lot of time to fill you in." At Millie's curt nod, Del continued.

"After she left your home, the picture turns grim." Del drew in a deep, steadying breath. "At more than one of the placements, she suffered mental, physical, and sexual abuse." Millie closed her eyes, and Del knew instinctively that the imparted news – some of which Mandy must have already shared - was causing the woman deep pain. She reached to take her hand and was encouraged when Millie did not refuse.

"Amanda is tough – we can give her that! She ran when she got the chance and, thank God, her social workers at those times intuitively knew that things were not right. Unfortunately, even though there was obvious physical evidence, Mandy would never talk, so the best they could do was put the homes under strict surveillance."

"I am not sure yet about the home she just ran from, but my gut tells me that Mandy's experience there may even have put her life in danger." Del went on to explain Gen Miller's brutal beating within twenty-four hours of Amanda's disappearance and watched Millie's reaction closely. She was bang on in her assumption that the woman was made of sturdy stuff – there was only a fierce anger evident now.

"I appreciate all that you've shared – I know it's

confidential, and I will honor that." She studied Del for a moment before continuing. "I have little to go on except my certainty that Mandy had nowhere to run except to Jessi. That alone is trouble, as Jessi is turning tricks, but I know, at least, where she lives, as does Mandy. I am aware that Jessi has not managed to get out from under that son-of-a-bitch's stranglehold, so it is a good lead." She nodded with the conviction of some inner decision.

"I will take you to her," her sudden grip on Del's arm was surprisingly strong, "but…it will have to be on my terms – it's dangerous for Jessi and now Mandy too, I assume." She stood up slowly. "Let's have some tea."

Del nodded her agreement, troubled by the knowledge that she was about to operate *far* outside of protocol for her position. But once again, everything within warned her that Amanda Goodchild's very life was at stake.

Chapter Fifteen

"Geesh, Jess! What the hell is *in* this stuff?" I couldn't believe how quickly I was totally baked! I was normally pretty cautious about substance intake. I couldn't afford addiction woes – no way would I turn out like my loser parents! Not to mention the fact that I had to be on my toes at all times. Besides, I never had the cash for it. Until now…

Jessi had been over the moon when her slimy pimp allowed her to keep a percentage of the take from Slick Dick – *SD*, we'd dubbed the business man. She'd pocketed over a hundred dollars in just the last two days. Apparently, he's a horny bastard!

There's something about Russell, though – I couldn't quite put my finger on it, but the man gave me the creeps. Of course, I hadn't met him or even seen him up close, but I had a pretty fair vantage point from my little spot across the street, and with the small advance that Daisy had insisted I take, I had picked up a small pair of binoculars from the pawn shop, next to the diner – sweet!

Jessi never says much about him – in fact, she's suspiciously vague. However, who could knock having some cash in your pocket? Maybe soon she could run, and they'd find a place together. I'd have to find the right time to bring forth that suggestion to her.

"Mandy, Mandy…you are totally wasted!" Jessi folded over

in giggles, and I figured that she was in about the same shape! It was infectious, and I almost peed myself laughing so hard.

"Crap, I need to open a window, quick!" Jessi shot up - there were only two of them. "Can't have this funky odor – *wouldn't want to offend the customers*," Jessi mimicked Russell, and we both fell to the floor in howling laughter.

"Relax, Jess," I tried to interject and get a grip on my AWOL self-control, "you have the night off, right?" Jessi nodded and flopped heavily onto the couch, still giggling.

"I'm done anyway – need to sober up!" As much as the chilling fest was like a gift from the gods, I knew I couldn't afford to let my guard down. I grabbed a piece of pizza from the table. Jess had been so excited to be able to order in, without Russell's permission. I settled in beside her, determined to eat my way to sobriety.

Click! A key in the door.

"Shit!" I flew off the sofa and into the bedroom, diving underneath the bed, pizza and all! There was no time to worry about what else I might have left behind. I heard his voice and tried to still my tremors.

"Well, well, what have we here? A little party?" I recognized the silky threat in his tone.

"Not really, just chilling on my night off."

I could almost smell the fear in her voice. God, please let there be no trace of my presence here! Where is my jacket? Shit – on the couch, I think! Thankfully, my shoes were still on my feet. I held my breath.

"Surely, this is a lavish celebration for just *your* sweet little ass. Perhaps we'll have to rethink your percentage. I'm not so sure you are ready to manage this level of income independently just yet."

The click of a lighter. Cigar smoke wafted into the bedroom, making my nose twitch.

"OK, no matter – this works out quite conveniently actually – you will be more than pliable with the change in plans."

Silence from Jessi. Wise move, girl – be cool!

"It's fine, Russell, what's up?" She was playing it well.

"Your favorite customer has decided to visit tonight with a little surprise." A cell phone chimed.

"Hey there – I'll let you in."

I heard the faint buzz and knew her john would be soon about to make this one a threesome, unbeknownst to him, of course. I wracked my brain, but there was just no way out of this. At least cramped spaces were no stranger to me, and I'd be a silent partner.

I stifled a hysterical giggle.

I heard a commotion at the door as SD arrived. It sounded like an entire party out there.

"OK, I'll leave you to it then. I'm very sure you'll be in good hands with the ever-talented Destiny." I wanted to puke with Russell's departing suggestive leer.

Wait! Was he still here then? Definitely, two male voices were currently in play. Jessi was cool as a cucumber, drawing them in provocatively towards the bedroom.

Towards *me*!

I didn't dare move a muscle. I could tell that her audience was pleased by the sounds of anticipated pleasure in their wordless murmurs. What the hell? Russell too?

"C'mere baby, show us a little sweetness. I knew you'd be up for treating my buddy here, too. I've been talking you up, and he just couldn't resist this tantalizing opportunity."

"Not yet – first, we get you ready for a sweet time…"

Oh lord, I knew, but I hadn't actually heard Jessi in action. The rustle of clothing being removed was confirmed when it hit the floor randomly around the bed – around *me*!

"That's it, on the bed!" Jessi was rocking the control here! "Now it's showtime…" her voice was sultry, seductive, enticing. I knew the dickheads on the bed would be drooling already – Jessi had the body of a goddess and the best come-on look imaginable; she knew how to use her goods!

A subtle movement above bounced the bed springs – oh God, one of them was masturbating – the rhythm unmistakable. I heard one suck in his breath as Jessi's clothes slid slowly to the floor. Then, felt her weight add to the sag of the mattress.

I was definitely cold-stone sober now and felt a tell-tale itch. Fuck! I was going to sneeze – please, not now! It was a weird thing for me. Every time I came down from a good weed high, I had a round of sneezing, and I cursed that weakness now.

My body was pinned so tightly that I was unable to slide my hand up to squeeze the bridge of my nose to stop the onslaught. Sheer panic loomed as claustrophobia set in – I couldn't breathe! The increasing movement above, together with escalating moans of pleasure, added to my sense of helplessness. And to my growing nausea. I knew her fate – with two or more of the assholes. Soon, the leverage of power would switch, and she'd be at the mercy of their lusty appetites.

Achoo! Oh fuck! It reverberated through my brain like a pipe bomb explosion. Keep still…if I'm lucky, maybe they can only hear with their slimy dicks right now. The second sneeze hit without warning – I'm sure they felt my head smack against the bed frame.

"What the hell?" The new guy.

Still, I waited and prayed.

"Are you hiding something from us, sweet Desi?" SD.

"No, is something wrong?" She was scared; I could hear it. The pressure eased on my body as he got off the bed. Shush! I nearly peed myself when his face appeared before me on the floor.

Chaos ensued as I was suddenly and none-too-gently dragged from under the bed and hauled to my feet. My breath came out in gasps as the two men checked me out.

A glance at Jessi confirmed our perilous situation – fear was written all over her features as she stood shivering in all her naked glory.

"Well, now, it seems we have a visitor." SD inspected me thoroughly from head to toe, and I resisted the urge to spit in his face. I couldn't put Jessi in further danger. Crap! This would get back to Russell, for sure!

"Please, can we leave my friend out of this?"

Her pleading tone caught my heart. What have I done? The only real friend I've ever known, and I've put her in danger and messed up her world.

"I was supposed to have the night off. She had just dropped in for a visit, and things got going really quickly with you two!"

"Ah, but she laid there and listened, all the same – why didn't she just leave with Russell, I wonder?"

He was no fool, that's for sure.

"She was just scared, is all," Jessi was pulling herself together now, a little.

"I'm thinking this could all be salvaged if this little lady would be amenable to joining in the fun."

Revulsion flooded my senses as he trailed his fingers from my face down to my breasts. Don't move!

"She's not in this business, Tiger." Jessi reached out and began caressing his body. He didn't resist but kept his attention on me with a calculating gleam in his eye. His buddy began masturbating as he leaned against the wall, watching us. My heart dropped into my stomach.

"Well, consider this, Sugar," he remained focused on me, seemingly fascinated, "our little pleasure fest, which I paid dearly for, was rudely interrupted."

"Oh, I will make that up to you, and then some – no extra charge." Jessi was negotiating for both our sakes now, I knew. I really appreciated her efforts, but in the end, I'd lay my body down, if need be, to save her. I just wasn't sure if that would be enough now. Russell!

"I've no doubt you will, Sugar. However, I would still need to run this by your big daddy, as I prefer to arrange my compensation for this…mishap up front."

"No, please…" The game was up now.

"Unless…" his voice was silk, "your delightful little friend here will agree to join us, fully engaged and willing." His eyes bored into mine now. "Totally at our whim – both of you!" He slid a meaningful glance to Jessi, who now closed her eyes, trapped resignation evident in her body language.

"I'm in," I couldn't let Jessi take the fall for me, no matter how the prospect sickened me, "but if I do this, you agree to leave Russell out of this." I was bluffing – knowing full well that I had no leverage in the situation at hand.

"The little lady has guts - I'll give her that." Both hands now were squeezing and caressing my breasts. It was all I could do not to bite him!

"I'm sure we could work something out, right Buddy?" This from the masturbator, who had abandoned that activity, at least temporarily.

Hell, it's not like it was the first time that more than one disgusting prick had forced their lewd attention on me. I could survive this and considered the wisdom in Jessi's attitude regarding her reality; it was far better than the abusive rape the both of us had endured in foster care.

"OK, but she comes with the original deal – same compensation," SD shot a warning glare at Jessi, who merely nodded, sending me an apologetic stare.

"Well, let's get this ride on the go, then." I'd never prostituted before, but I knew the drill and was infinitely certain that it would be far more tolerable than forceful abuse.

"Back to the bed!" Both men did my bidding, the evidence of their excitement immediately escalating, likely at the prospect of having two of us at the mercy of their pleasure.

The session began, and through it all, my stomach railed in repulsion. Their aggression increased with lusty abandon as they insisted that Jessi and I perform various sexual acts upon each other as they watched – this, to me, seemed unthinkable.

But here we were – our eyes met, and we decided together, without words – at a soul level that we would put all of our caring and love for each other on the proverbial table. Our shared pleasure incited the dickheads to no end but also served to significantly lessen the impact – the importance we placed - on their thorough use of our bodies to satisfy their every whim, in ways they could never hope to experience at home with their own wives.

In this way, we robbed them – gained a measure of control. Our experience together was so much deeper than physical – it was our empowering gift to each other, and we knew that they couldn't touch it. No words needed to be said. Both of us accepted that it would be reserved for these moments only – our usual friendship would stay intact, albeit with a deeper bond and commitment.

After the two johns left, we draped ourselves on the sofa, thoroughly exhausted and sore – every muscle, bone, and every part of our bodies had been thoroughly worked over.

While I assumed that Jessi and I would not resume shared sexual activity outside of that situation, I was grateful for the opportunity to experience ultimate pleasure with an activity that normally delivered only pain and trauma.

Chapter Sixteen

The waiting was killing Del! It had been two days! Every moment that passed increased the odds of Amanda facing threats and trauma. However, Del was significantly calmer and grateful to learn of her whereabouts and that she was alive, at least!

She'd left Millie after securing the woman's promise that she would contact Del when the time was right. Millie agreed that she'd get in touch with Jessi when it was safe, and they'd take it from there. There could be no involvement with Child Protection Services – it was the caveat. Del had no choice but to trust.

Of course, this meant that not one iota of their meeting, nor the details, were on record. Del was well aware that if anything went sideways, her job was on the line. Hell – she'd be fired! The thought was sobering and she swept her hair back, determined to see this through, no matter what the outcome.

Del had been glued to her desk for the past two days, scouring internal records, court orders and decisions, and newspaper articles on file – all in an effort to nail that son-a-bitch, Paul Miller. The horrible reality was that he and Gen were free to operate their foster home until any charges were laid against him.

Spousal abuse, as long as his wife laid charges, would immediately suspend the foster licence, pending the outcome of the investigation. This was her ultimate goal. She needed to talk with Gen Miller.

Pulling up to the curb, Del reflected on how the events of the past few days had made no impact on the scene before her now. The house still sported the same sagging shutters, and as she walked up to the front porch, she noticed that the cigarette butt in the corner had not moved, almost mocking her ominously.

She rang the bell, knocked at the same time, and waited. Trying twice more, she was about to abandon the quest when she heard shuffling inside. Suddenly, the door creaked open, just enough for Gen Miller to peek at who was calling.

"Yes, who are you?"

"Gen Miller? Del Greenwood, with Child Protection Services. Can we talk, please?"

"We have nothing to talk about – there are no foster children here."

"But Amanda Goodchild was here until a week ago, correct?"

"She ran – damned girl always does. I knew she would – so ungrateful for all that we gave her."

"Mrs. Miller, do you know…"

"I have no idea where she went, nor do I care." She moved

to close the door.

"May I please come in just for a moment? There are things I need to speak with you about." At her hesitation, Del plunged in, "I know that you were physically abused, and I really would prefer to have this conversation with you here, outside of a formal investigation."

The door slowly swung open, and Gen Miller reluctantly motioned to follow. Del stepped in and looked around with a trained eye. While well-lived, the home was relatively neat. She took the seat that she was motioned toward.

"Mrs. Miller, our department is required to investigate any violence that may have occurred in one of our foster homes." She eyed the woman speculatively. "This is ultimately for the protection of the children under your care, but also for yourself."

"That no-good friend of Amanda's beat the shit out of me – that's all you need to know!" She glared accusingly at Del. "It's all in the police report from the hospital – surely you have access!"

"I have seen the report, yes," Del confirmed, "however, there are often discrepancies, and frankly, you did not give them much to go on." Del pinned her with an astute gaze, noticing her nervous shift in position on the sofa.

"Your description of the suspect is vague – not enough detail to know where to start. Not to mention the fact that you don't even know his name or what his connection is to Amanda – not even how they met."

"How am I supposed to know all that shit? She's a defiant little trickster – can't trust her as far as you can throw her." Gen Miller regarded Del warily.

"Don't get me wrong, I'm all for helping the kids that are at risk and underprivileged, but some are just beyond my help – I'm not God, and there's only so much I can do."

"Gen – may I call you Gen?" Not waiting for an answer, Del changed tactics. "How would you describe your marriage to Paul Miller?" Watching closely for a reaction, she waited.

"What kind of a question is that and how is that any of your damn business?"

"It is relevant to the well-being and safety of the children under your care." Del took a deep breath. "So, please answer my question."

"We have the same struggles as any married couple, but nothing out of the ordinary." Gen Miller swallowed nervously.

"Let's talk about specifics. Do you and your husband ever have disagreements that may involve significant outbursts of anger – physical or mental abuse?"

"What the hell are you getting at?" Gen spouted her indignation. "My recent injuries were caused by a beating from that no-good boy who hangs around Amanda – I wouldn't be a bit surprised to learn that the little bitch set it up."

"Why would you suggest that? Has there been past violence, then?"

"No, but Amanda is after Paul – always strutting herself in front of him suggestively - for her own agenda, I know." She sniffed loudly.

"So, has Paul ever taken advantage of Amanda's alleged seductive antics?"

"Hell, no – he's not stupid!"

Del thought it interesting that she hadn't responded with outrage at such an idea, one that might involve pedophilia. Instead, Del was left with the suspicion that he likely would work to avoid getting into trouble – smart enough not to get caught in it. Del leaned forward for direct eye contact, and Gen shifted once more.

"Has Paul ever hurt you – laid a hand on you in anger, roughed you up, controlled you, either physically or mentally?" Del had her now – the body language and fear in her eyes confirmed everything. The trick now was getting her to admit it.

"You need to leave now – you've gone way too far with your

questions and insinuations!" Gen stood up and moved shakily toward the door. Del followed.

"Gen, I know that you were significantly injured with this beating and that you have further corrective surgeries to endure. No one on this earth has the right to do this to you." Gen flinched but did not pull away from Del's gentle squeeze on her arm.

"It is important that the right person be prosecuted for your injuries." Del handed her a card. "Please call me if you have anything more to share or if you hear from Amanda. We will find her either way and put things right." Del was further alerted by the ensuing fear in the woman's eyes, signalling that the prospect of them finding Amanda troubled her deeply.

Heading home for the evening, a familiar exhaustion flooded her entire body. All she could manage tonight was a frozen dinner, bath, and sleep – in that order! The ring of her cell through the Blue Tooth startled her, and she instantly pressed to receive the call – eager to hear from Millie.

"Hey, how are things going?"

Jack? Crap!

"Same a usual, Jack," she needed to head him off at the pass if he was about to seek reconciliation.

"Jack, I meant what I said."

"I know, don't worry," he paused. "I do miss you like hell, Del, and am sorry about the way we ended things."

Oh Jack…

"But that's not why I'm calling. I was thinking about the Amanda Goodchild case that you so foolishly took on – sorry! Something occurred to me to pass on that was not included in the file," he heaved a deep sigh, "for the simple reason that there is no evidence to support it."

Del's heart thudded in her chest – was this the break she was looking for? Something that could nail that asshole to the wall? She could no longer contain her enthusiasm.

"Something to do with Paul Miller, I hope?"

"Perhaps, but it's more to do with his wife, Gen Miller – not her real name. Well, at least not originally – it's her legal name now. When they entered the foster program, another foster parent called me." Del was on full alert.

"She insinuated that Gen Miller had applied for fostering under another name prior – not her maiden name, though, and was denied. At the time, I could find no record anywhere of that application, but the person who brought this forth was a well-established and trusted care provider, in our system."

"Jack, this is huge!" Del couldn't still her heart. "Amanda is missing, Gen has been beaten to a pulp, and this information may just help me find her."

"Well, I no longer have access to the file and cannot remember who contacted me – it was vague, and I wrote it off in my busy mental queue. What I *can* tell you is that it was one of Amanda's prior foster placements, though the woman had no way of knowing then that Amanda would be placed with the Millers."

Oh my God! I had to check them all out, but a trusted one…Millie could fit that description for sure! My heart melted now, thinking of Jack and how I'd sorely misjudged him. He did care about Amanda enough to put his resentment aside and help where he could.

"Jack…thank you so much – this means everything." Del heard his sad sigh. "I'm sorry, too."

"Take care of yourself Del – I hope we can be friends, still."

"Absolutely!" Del ended the call, just as she pulled into her attached garage – she thought about how Jack had insisted that she opt for the home security, having safe access into the house. In their profession, one never knew. The thought hit her – these poignant emotions, in the complexity of relationships, were the catalysts for staying. She mustered her strength and let it go.

Her mind flew to the possibilities, now armed with this new

information. Every cell in her body cried to head back to the office, but the reality pointed to Millie as a first investigative resource, and Del knew that the woman would be calling her within a day or two.

For now, she was content in knowing that Amanda was safely away from the Miller household, so she surrendered to her original evening plans and considered Sherri's advice for rest. Yes, now she had enough progress in play to allow common sense – her body would rejuvenate at least a little tonight.

Chapter Seventeen

"Geezus, Jess, let it go!" I softened my gaze, searching her eyes. "Honestly, I'm fine! It is what it is!"

Jessi was wallowing in a well of guilt for involving me in this sex tryst between her two most affluent johns. Their accomplishments and position meant nothing – they were still just horny, cheating pricks, serving their own needs. The only distinction was that they wielded considerable power to get more bang for their buck. I sniggered inwardly at the pun.

"I mean it – we are in this together, and I'm good."

For now, my inner voice reminded me. When the time was right – I'd have a talk with her. Meanwhile, she was apologizing for it all – carrying the blame, including turning me to lesbianism.

"Do you really regret what's happened between us?" I stared her down. "Look me in the eye and tell me you'd rather that we'd fucked each other with fear, anger and hate!" Jess shook her head and let a tear escape.

"I am no more lesbian than you, and even if I was – there's not a damn thing wrong with it! We both learned a long time ago how fucking stupid it is to put our trust in men!" My heart broke at her troubled expression.

"Jess," I took her hand, "this literally changes nothing

between us – other than a testament that no matter how low it gets – we can lift each other above it." This brought a small smile to her beautiful face.

"Don't worry – I'm not going to jump you in your sleep," she blurted.

We both hooted with laughter over that one, catching the eye of a few diners in the sparse mid-afternoon crowd. I was on a break, and we'd agreed to have a late lunch together. Daisy, Jeff and Bree gave me full flex now for my hours. I'd worked hard to earn their trust and thanked my lucky stars every day for this gig.

"One positive thing, I suppose," Jess was more relaxed now, *SD* and *M* insist on evening tricks, and Russell has decided to restrict all my other clientele to day time in order to keep prime time open for them."

"Sweet!" I smiled at our clever acronym – *M* being short for *the masturbator*.

"Should be three to four evenings per week – I suppose that's all their wives would allow," Jessi snickered sarcastically.

She had insisted on giving me half the take, but she couldn't stop me from saving it for her – I'd find an opportunity to return it!

"Cool, I can stay at the apartment now for the evenings then."

"We just have to still be careful with Russell."

I nodded my agreement, but we'd already serviced the johns twice since, and Russell hadn't returned yet. We both agreed that I'd keep all of my belongings under the bed, including my coat and shoes, in the event that he should pop in unannounced. We were both relieved – apparently, they had kept it from Russell. Understandably so, as the price would be double to go through the pimp with a second girl in play.

It seemed to be going well – almost too good to be true. A little niggling jab in my gut, from time to time, warned me against complacency. Sometimes, too, the speculative gleam in SD's eye set the hair on the back of my neck to standing straight up. I shook it off now and headed back to the kitchen to help with supper prep.

Jeff stuck his tongue out playfully as I grabbed the cutting board and reviewed his menu for the night. I set out to retrieve the items I'd need from the fridge and pantry.

"At the risk of blowing your head up a notch or two, I have to say that my job has become much easier with you on board." He threw me a grateful smile. "I know Bree would echo that sentiment."

Jeff and Bree had both become solid friends – as close as I would let it develop, that is. They were genuine and downright good people and treated me like gold. When had that ever happened in my life, before? Still…good people didn't know about my reality and couldn't change it anyhow. Nothing good ever lasted forever in my world!

The shift blew by quickly, and Jeff sent me home with a meal for two – leftover from last night's dinner. Woohoo – time for chilling tonight. I assumed we'd have a night off, as the creeps had come by last night.

So much for assumptions, we'd just settled into a flaky, B-grade action movie when the buzzer rang. Damn! Jessi let them up, and we'd cleaned up the supper dishes just as they knocked.

My anxiety immediately flew into my throat when they entered with two other men. What the fuck was this? SD had that *cat who swallowed the canary* expression plastered onto his face.

"Two nights in a row – luck is with us." Jessi's smile was welcoming, but I knew that she must be concerned too.

"Well now, you girls are *so* skilled at your profession," SD sent me a satisfied leer, "it is hard to stay away. Our friends here are eager to sample your delights, and so – here we are."

"Let me get this straight," I had a lot less to lose than Jessi, "you are expecting that we will now entertain four of you at once?"

"Well, the more the merrier – quadruple the pleasure, so to speak."

Shit! My heart was pounding, and I noticed Jessi's

complexion turn pale. What the hell? It didn't matter how much money was on the table. This development took our vulnerability to a whole new level.

"Do you have an issue with this? If so, *do* speak." His eyes held a dangerous glint, daring me to try it.

"My concern, of course, is how best to maximize your pleasure." I could tell that I had disappointed him by not rising to his bait. "A better strategy may be to pleasure two of you at a time – the other two would be privy to a dynamite view – don't you agree?"

"Oh, I'm not the least bit worried about that," he was smiling now. "You see, Sweetheart, we will be in complete control of taking our pleasure, and so you need not worry on our behalf." My heart dropped. Fuck!

"And payment?" Jessi had found her voice,

"Our payment agreement is already in place, Sugar."

"So, you would expect that we take care of four for the same price?"

"It seems to me," SD moved over to Jessi and began squeezing her lewdly, "that you are in no position to bargain." He pinched her nipple hard, and she winced. I wanted to go bite his dick off!

"Unless you'd rather I run this through Russell – that can be arranged."

We were fucking hooped, and we both knew it! He shooed us into the bedroom and ordered us to strip – very slowly. With little choice, we did exactly as he asked. I prayed for mercy – hoping that their tastes did not involve any measure of pain. I watched, wanting to wretch with revulsion, as they rubbed their crotches, undressing as they went.

We clearly had a ring leader, as SD called all the shots, ordering us onto the bed side by side. My panic surfaced as they tied our hands to the bedpost in such a way that they could flip us face-down or up at their will. Down first – I felt their heavy breaths and groping hands on my neck, back, buttocks, and legs – everywhere.

Then the blindfolds rendered us sightless – perhaps that was a blessing, but it terrified me, nonetheless. Suddenly, they hauled my ass up in the air and began the assault; I had no idea who was first or last. All I knew was utter torment. I was whimpering with fear, more than pain – not knowing what was next to come, and I could hear that Jessi was suffering the same fate.

In a swift motion, I was flipped over. My nipples were on fire already, from brutal pinching, but now this included merciless bites and I cried out, hating myself because I knew it was increasing their excitement.

It went on, we figured out later, for three hours, with no reprieve to us, as they took their turns. One of them commented on the power of some fucking drug that must have kept them going. We gagged with the oral sex that was forced upon us. At one point, all four coordinated to molest us both simultaneously and without mercy; the pain was excruciating.

When it was over, they untied our hands and left us there on the bed, bleeding and weeping softly. I found enough fight left to send them a parting shot.

"What kind of desperate assholes get more pleasure from rape rather than a willing, passionate participant?" SD sidled back into the bedroom for one last fondle.

"I don't know – Sweetheart, you seem ready to go still – perhaps we'll come back, yet again tonight."

I felt the bile rise in my stomach as they left the apartment, and I quickly limped my way to the bathroom to empty my supper into the toilet. After cleaning myself as best I could, at that moment, I grabbed some fresh, warm cloths and brought them to the bedroom. Jessi was shaking now with her sobs, and I gently cleaned her body. I lay beside her, and we cuddled for a bit.

"Crap – we didn't get our orgasms!" I let out a shaky giggle at my ill attempt at humor, but that broke the horrific aftermath, and we both laughed and cried at the same time, deciding to get up and hit the shower together. Sore as we were, we slowly took that step to preserve our right to pleasure without their fucking evil male intervention. It felt right and good. Fuck their repugnant souls!

"The assholes didn't use condoms!"

Jessi had a point there – it had become glaringly apparent with the forced oral sex. Were they fucking crazy?

Then again, what was the risk for them, aside from STDs? That we might go squeal on them to Russell? Geezus – we were the only ones at risk here. If one of us were to get pregnant, we didn't even know their fucking names! Yes, this is exactly why I had avoided getting into this potentially lucrative trade in the first place! I was damn lucky that I hadn't already been knocked up by my disgusting abusers in the past, although some did take the time for protection – for their own asses, of course.

Jess and I both figured that we were not currently ovulating, so it would likely be OK. Russell insisted that his girls be tested for STDs on a regular basis, and I planned to do the same – it was not my first rodeo.

One thing was sure – I was not prepared to endure this nightmare again – I'd rather die. It was time for that talk. I prayed that Jessi would listen and come with me – where to? I had no idea just yet, but I had a bit of money saved. Not enough for a place of my own, but it would cover a cheap motel for a week or two, until we could figure it out.

"Jess, we need to talk…"

"Mandy, you need to leave – tonight!"

"Are you fucking nuts? No way I'm leaving you here alone, lady – the gig will be up with Russell. Those assholes won't like it a bit!" What had I done in this life to deserve the selfless friendship of this beautiful soul? Well, we were in this together, and I still had a voice in the matter.

"And what do you think Russell will do about it? He'll likely beat your ass and leave you lying in a gutter!" I took both her hands. "Jess, we need to leave together – tonight!"

"I can't do that – he'll hunt me down anyhow!"

"You can, and you will – you have me, and I have some cash! There are two of us now, and we'll figure it out. Get your shit – only what you need." I could tell she wanted to argue with me further, but she was also beaten and battered - beyond terrified now, and I was adamant!

I watched as she grabbed anything of importance, stashing her own clothing into my bag, and when she was ready, we snuck out into the park across the street to gather our wits and make plans. There was no turning back now, and at least neither one of us would have to go it alone anymore.

116

Chapter Eighteen

Del gave up on trying to sleep through to the alarm and was at her desk by 6:00 a.m., pouring through Amanda's file. She decided to start with eliminating those homes where Amanda had allegedly suffered abuse. By the time she'd plowed through the records, it was close to 10:00, and she'd polished off an entire pot of coffee.

Could it really be possible? Out of all her placements, only seven homes could likely be a candidate for the established stability, that Jack had referred to. But she'd start with Millie, and if the woman didn't call this morning, she fully intended to drop in for a chat.

Gen and Paul Miller had applied for their licence, only two years ago. Hardly long enough to establish a record of any kind. But Del needed to dig deep and leave nothing to assumption.

They'd had only two placements before Amanda. Neither had stayed long. The first one involved two siblings – brothers. After just one month, they were removed from the home on the grounds that the children were incompatible.

The second involved a young twelve-year-old girl, who reportedly ran away several times over the few months that she'd been placed there. The last time she'd fled, no one had ever heard from her again. Shit! Del wondered whatever had become of her and quickly searched the data base for the missing child.

Her picture pulled at Del's heart strings – the trauma in the eyes staring into the camera was haunting, the image of a trapped soul. The file was still open, but little progress was made in finding her. She had been pretty much alone in the world – father unknown, and mother had been hospitalized from a drug overdose, and hopelessly lost in the world of addiction, though sporadic, supervised visits had been arranged, with long years in between. No known relatives were on file. What were the odds? Unfortunately, this was not as unusual an occurrence as the public was aware of. Young girls almost always ended up on the streets. Damn it!

Amanda was their third and had been with them for two months before fleeing. There was very little on file. Jack had visited the home, only once before his transfer, to find things in seeming good order – Amanda was attending the local school and so far had not run, as per her usual behavior. He'd had no reason for immediate concern.

Del had entered the picture with Amanda's first attempt to run – at least, that *she* was aware of. Amanda had been apprehended by the police, as she'd been found wandering the streets, seemingly traumatized. But, of course, she had clammed up and offered no insight into her situation. Then things had escalated before Del even had a chance to speak to the Millers.

Judging by what had happened to Gen, this was undoubtedly a blessing.

Shit – she was getting nowhere fast! Grabbing her purse, she popped an Advil to stave off the beginning of a nagging headache and made a firm mental note to back off from the caffeine. Sherri waved as she exited the building.

Heading over to Millie's, she mulled the possibilities over in her head. It was almost certain that Amanda had suffered some sort of trauma at the Miller home, and it was sheer luck that Del had found her at all. Millie opened the door immediately and waved her in.

"I hope this is a good time – I know you said you'd call, but we need to talk."

"It's good timing, actually. I'm afraid there's been a disturbing development."

Oh God! Del's heart sank – she knew instinctively that they'd just hit a major snag. She sat down and waited.

"I have a young neighbor who cares for me now and again – taking my trash, going to the store for me, etc. He's a good kid." Millie smiled and continued.

"He also is a smart fellow and has been watching out for

Jessi – not contacting her by any means, but he knows where she lives and who her pimp is." Millie put a hand up. "We cannot involve him in any way."

"Of course not, but this is valuable information."

"It's gotten more complicated. My young man, who shall remain nameless, has just reported that he had seen a young girl go into the building of late. Once, he spotted the two of them enter together. It's very likely that Mandy is staying with her."

"This is great – but have you gotten the message to Jessi, then?"

"That's where it goes south. I had contacted him to do just that. As soon as he'd given me this update, he headed off to the task." Millie heaved a troubled sigh.

"But, just this morning, he came by and informed me that Jessi had left and moved on. Word on the street is that her pimp is apparently livid and has turned the apartment upside down – out there tearing the streets apart, looking for her now."

"Oh my God – they are both in serious danger! It may be time to call the police." Del bit her lip in agitation, contemplating the wisdom of that move, and Millie immediately echoed her fears.

"No, that will put the girls in even graver danger at this point. Besides, the complexities of this situation would slow down their search for the girls anyhow; and would expose both your outside of protocol actions and my young friend. I can't agree to that."

"Fair enough, and you're right," Del gave her a reassuring smile, "we will tackle this another way." But how? We had to find them!

"There is a diner that Jessi frequents – the owner, Daisy, has taken a shine to her and provides a safe place to come for a meal etc., now and again." Millie regarded Del thoughtfully. "Jessi goes under an assumed name – Desi. Short for the name on her apartment buzzer - Destiny."

OK, this was big.

"I'll head there and see what I can come up with. Can you please ask your young angel to keep his eyes and ears open, too?" Millie nodded.

"One more thing. Amanda's current foster placement is with Paul and Gen Miller – I hadn't given you the details when we spoke. Do their names ring any bells?" Millie's expression revealed instant concern.

"Yes, I called your office a couple of years ago, when I saw them on the roster – I recognized Gen Miller's picture. I had known her under another name, and at that time, her foster application had been declined. For what reason, I was not privy to."

"Do you remember the previous name?"

"Yes, I think the last name was Richards." Millie grabbed her arm. "If you find Amanda, there's no way in hell that we can let her go back to that Miller home – I had a bad feeling about it back then."

Del's mind raced on the short drive to the diner. She would set Sherri onto one Gen Richards when she got back to the office. Where the hell had the girls gone? What had happened? Del's instincts told her they were together. She pulled into the small parking lot and took a deep breath as she needed to take caution to avoid scaring them further away. If Daisy had Jessi under her wing, her guess was that she'd act as the proverbial mother bear. While this was somewhat of a good thing, Del knew that the woman would not be able to keep them safe for long.

Upon entering the diner, her training kicked in, and with quick efficiency, she sized it up - worn but comfortable eatery; capacity enough for a regular crowd, mid-to-low-income clientele; reliable food and menu, and care was evident in the orderly cleanliness. The diner was off the beaten track – far enough from the sketchy area to avoid riff-raff squatters and close enough to Millie's neighborhood to attract a loyal clientele.

There were two waitresses handling the incoming lunch crowd, and Del chose a small table by the window. Almost immediately, an attractive young girl placed a menu, a glass of iced water, and a cup on the table.

"Coffee?" Lucy, as the name tag indicated, provided an immediate warm welcome. Del nodded and thanked her.

Intuition guided her to sit back for a bit, order lunch and observe. She could not see into the kitchen, as there were swinging doors that automatically closed. A very small window, where the food was placed, on a waiting, stainless steel warming counter, provided no view either.

Lucy took her order and placed the Daily News on the table for her convenience.

"Lucy, have you worked here long? You seem very good at your job."

"Oh, about a year now – it's a great place to work." She beamed at the compliment. "The boss is one in a million! I haven't seen you here before – are you just passing through?"

"First time for sure, but I don't live too far away and may very well see you again another time!" The sentiment was genuine – there was something charming and enticing about the place, and…safe – yes, that was it. This provided a measure of peace to Del – at least the girls had somewhere to land, now and again.

Lunch was delicious – a cob salad with toasted pita strips,

complete with a raspberry balsamic vinegar drizzle. Everything was fresh, the vegetables crisp, and Lucy brought a complementary slice of lemon meringue pie to top it off. This could become a viable surveillance post, for sure!

It was time.

"That was delicious, Lucy, thank you!" The waitress was busy clearing dishes and chatted pleasantly.

"Is it possible for me to speak with Daisy?" Del wracked my brain for a plausible reason to give. "She's your boss, right?"

"Yes, I can check, but I think she's out running errands right now."

Damn!

"It's OK. Please just give her my number and ask her to call when she gets a chance." Del scribbled her personal cell number on a sticky note from her purse – unwilling to reveal her Social Services connection at this point. To be honest, it was useless anyhow, Del conceded; it was personal now. Hell, it had been from the get-go.

Chapter Nineteen

Crap! Shit!

What the hell was she doing here at the restaurant? I couldn't figure it out! Well…I knew that she'd likely been looking for me, but there was no way she'd know that I was working here – Daisy was paying me in cash for now.

OK, I need to get a grip! It was shit-ass luck that I had been forced to wait for Lucy as she'd come into the kitchen. I had caught only a glimpse of the lady sitting at a table – Del Greenwood? I'm not sure why her name stuck in my memory bank. I had been headed through the doors to go pee – now I'd have to hold it!

Calm down – just get your work done, I chided myself. Lunch was the usual busy parade, and Jeff and I worked our asses off – making the time fly by. I was still so impressed with his culinary wizardry – talented dude! I would venture to wonder why he was stuck cooking in this diner, but hey – it *was* a pretty good place to land. It was now clear to me that he and Lucy had the hots for each other – cool beans!

Lucy and Carrie were steadily stacking dishes in the bins now, Bree showed up, and it was perfect symmetry – like a well-oiled clock! I made fast work of the dishes and turned on the first round to sanitize before taking the opportunity to sneak a peek through the door glass.

She was gone! Holy hell, I needed to pee. On my way back from the washroom, I considered my predicament. Was it just a coincidence, then? What if she came back? Damn – my safe haven was a bust if the woman did start to frequent the diner.

My mind whirled, along with the activity surrounding me. I worked on automatic, reviewing my options. Jessi and I were the only ones, thus far, that were in the know. Would it be better if we chatted with Daisy? No…she was awesome and cared about us – that much was clear. But because of that very reality, she may decide that we needed help and protection from the system. I couldn't risk that. My skin crawled at the memory of Paul Miller's slimy hands and putrid breath all over me.

I needed to chat with Jessi – as soon as I got home. We'd discussed our situation in the park the previous couple of nights past. I had secured a little motel kitchenette room down the way. It was a bit of a dive really, but surprisingly clean and not overly unsafe. It was well-known for transient bikers, etc., who really had no permanent home, so they'd rent by the month sometimes. The rate was dirt cheap by the week, and I had enough cash saved already to cover the next four.

The unit provided a small cook top, a two-burner unit, with a built-in mini-fridge underneath – good enough for our needs. The shower was decent, and the queen bed was acceptable.

Jessi and I had easily accepted our newly formed sexual connection and gloried in the beauty of our passionate shared pleasure. I hadn't dreamed it possible, but it made sense, really. It wasn't born from any particular sexual orientation. Trust was a given – the love had been there almost from the day we had met as pre-teens. And it was a pleasant and natural development. Jessi was beautiful, soft and warm in all the right places – I felt safe, cherished and loved. I knew it was mutual. We held nothing back. No *man* had ever looked lovingly into my eyes while bringing me to the pinnacle of ecstasy.

They took their rutting pleasure selfishly.

The only exception had been a young man, another former foster child, who had stayed with the current family. The fucking bastard – our so-called *father*, hosted sex parties from time to time, where I was the main course. At one particular event, there were ten piggish guests, all excited to sample the goods. I'd been totally grossed out as they'd arrived – with the evidence of their anticipated delights already bulging in their pants.

It didn't matter how many times I'd been abused as a young girl – it was equally terrifying every time. These parties left me completely sore and bruised – I would bleed for days afterward - the men were so rough – pigs!

This time, the party got going very quickly – they'd ripped off my clothing and leered at my twelve-year-old, fully-developed female form, which served to fuel their lust.

My foster father ordered the young former foster kid, eighteen now, to strip as well – though I knew Jake didn't wish to be part of it; he had always done what he could to help me avoid these situations. In spite of that, he couldn't control his body's reaction as the others took their turns with me. When he came around, his apology glistened in the form of tears – offered to me, and as he looked directly into my eyes, he whispered for me to relax. He then reached down between us and fondled me slowly, with a gentle rhythmic stroking. My body reacted naturally, with a burning, moist heat from the friction. He'd expertly ensured that I received at least a little pleasure – along with the horrific pain, while shielding me from the others' view and muffling my confused gasps of pleasure.

It was the first, and only time since, with a man, but I was completely horrified at having received pleasure from what could only be termed as rape. The shame has never left me.

Fuck! Why do I allow myself to get lost in this mire! Time to buck up and get on with business here. My shift ended, and I headed to the motel.

"Hi there!" Jessi was looking proud of herself for having

conjured up a stir fry of some sort for supper.

"Hey, that smells delicious!"

We sat down at the small table for two and ate companionably, sharing tidbits of our day. I knew that Jessi was not comfortable with what she considered freeloading, and she discussed ideas for employment. I could hold it off no longer.

"Jess, that social worker I told you about was in the restaurant today," Her eyes reflected immediate fear. "I'm not sure if it was a coincidence or not – I can't see how she'd know where to find me."

"Shit – that's not good! You may have to just get away, Mandy! Maybe Daisy could help."

"No!" I was adamant. "The less people who know, the better." I could kick myself now for not using a false name – where was my common sense?

"Jess, we'll just have to be careful – there's no reason for them to connect you to all this, so let's concentrate on getting us to a safe place for you, out of that bastard's clutches." I squeezed her hand. "It will work for both of us if we do this right." Jessi nodded tentatively.

"Well, I think we'd better make a plan then – our time here might be limited, depending on if she returns." Jessi retrieved a note pad from the night table drawer by the bed, and we began a list – of options with pros and cons.

It really boiled down to three things: stay here long enough to save for our own place – contingent on Jessi finding employment, and perhaps a change in my own; enlisting the assistance, whatever that might entail, of Daisy – risky; or, parking our asses at Social Services – over both of our dead bodies, we decided.

"Hey, there is a fourth option," I regarded Jessi with feigned optimism.

"Do tell."

"We could set up our own escort service – you *do* know the business rather intimately." We both guffawed over that nasty suggestion.

It came down to this – Jessi needed to find work. To that end, she could chat with Daisy and let her know, at least, that she planned on changing her income source. Daisy would be very pleased to hear it, I knew and would do whatever she could.

We hung out for the evening, watching old cartoon re-runs – not much else to choose from without cable TV. It felt really good, having come to some form of consensus on a plan of action. At this moment, it seemed that life was looking up.

Chapter Twenty

Del licked the oozing Bavarian cream from her fingers, one by one, increasing the effects of a formidable frown, etched upon her face. She really had to quit eating this shit. True to that line of thought, she stuffed the remainder of the doughnut back in the bag and turfed it in the trash bin.

Sleep had eluded her throughout the night. She'd taken a long soak after a light meal in an effort to ease away the worry. Truth be known, she could not ignore the ugly premonition that for every step of progress, a dark force lurked. Del gave herself a shake now – no time to waste.

She was anxious for Daisy to call; so far, no luck. Kicking around the idea to head back to the diner, Del considered all angles. There was always a possibility that her presence and chat with Daisy could further complicate the outcome. But she had to do something. Both girls were in peril from Jessi's former pimp – if he wasn't already aware of her safe spot at the diner, that would soon be a bust.

Del took a measure of comfort in the fact that Jessi was street-smart and would likely avoid the place like the plague. Did her pimp know about Amanda, then? She had to operate under the assumption that he did. Based on this premise, talking with Daisy was, first and foremost – a necessary risk. She prayed that the woman wouldn't send her packing. Sherri appeared at her door just as she stood up to stretch.

"Got a hit!" Sherri held out a sheet, still warm from the printer.

Jesus! Del could not believe it! The news article was dated almost a year ago. A young girl's remains had been found, but thus far, they'd been unable to confirm the identity of the victim. It was speculated that she had been a homeless youth, likely living a high-risk lifestyle as a minor, an under-aged prostitute. Hell, she remembered this in the media – but not much else had been reported since.

It went on to further suggest the possibility that she may have been prey to a particular convicted serial rapist, who had been recently released from a five-year mandatory sentence. The name of the perpetrator chilled Del's blood – Everett Paul Richards. The picture they provided was unmistakable, albeit dated. This man's hair was long and dark, and he sported a full beard and mustache, while Paul Miller was silver-haired and clean-shaven. Same cruel eyes though.

It all came back now. The name Paul…Del remembered the court trial. His conviction involved fifteen known cases of child sexual abuse, and with his sentence came a label – he was registered now on the federal record as a child sex offender. How in the hell had this slipped through the system?

Her mind raced! Could this young girl's remains be that of the same girl that disappeared from the Miller's foster home less than one year into their operation? She voiced her thoughts to Sherri, who nodded solemnly.

"I will dig into this and the police records and get back to you as soon as I can." Sherri touched Del's arm. "You better sit for this." Del did as she was bid while her assistant perched upon the very same chair that Amanda Goodchild had habituated, seemingly a lifetime ago.

"The original application for foster parenting that Gen Miller applied for was under the name of Gen Richards." No surprise now, Del surmised. "Gen MacPherson had been a frequent visitor to Everett Richards throughout his incarceration," Sherri continued, "and married him before he was released. The media reports, at that time, suggested that she may have been with him at the time of the child abuse offenses, abetting him in his disgusting violation of children, but there had been no proof of this."

"Gen had applied for the foster application on her own. Even though she and Everett Richards were married, he was living in a halfway house by this time, under the terms and conditions of his parole. Seems Gen was not overly astute in wiping the traces of their past."

"If we can somehow connect this girl's remains as their

former foster child, the police will hit him hard as a suspect." Del figured there was a strong possibility.

"To ice the cake, the body was found in a ravine, a mere ten blocks from their first foster residence. They moved shortly after she'd allegedly disappeared," Sherri added.

"We are going to nail this scumbag!" She squeezed Del's arm.

"Let's pray that we do before he finds Amanda." Del rose to give her a hug.

"I've already forwarded this alert up the chain of command, so Paul and Gen Miller's licence will soon be suspended – they won't get Amanda back – at least, not legally."

Del heaved a sigh of relieved gratitude, blew a kiss, and headed out the door.

Millie invited her in immediately, and Del imparted the new information. Both women shared the concern that if Paul Miller found Amanda, he may feel he would have no choice but to eliminate her as a potential witness; to whatever evil he'd been up to. The only hope that offered any solace was that both Paul and Gen Miller did not seem overly bright in terms of covering their bases.

Del was incensed that the internal screening for Gen and Paul Miller's application had missed the connection between the application under Gen's former surname. Especially considering that Gen's marriage to Everett Richards was the reason it had been denied. Further, Sherri had easily accessed records to show that Gen Richards legally changed her name to Gen Miller shortly afterward. She was still searching the data base for Paul Miller.

"I missed Daisy the other day, so I'm going to head back to the diner. I'm sure Jessi will stay away from there." She gave Millie a brief hug.

"Daisy is very discreet, and Jessi is careful, so I doubt the asshole has any knowledge of their relationship." Millie scratched her chin. "Still, I think you are right. We have to assume that he knows Mandy has been there, though he controlled everything from clothing, shelter and food, so, he could have been lax, keeping tabs on Jessie. We can only hope."

Del considered the best approach as she made her way to the little diner. How would she earn the woman's trust, remotely assuming that Daisy would even grant an ear? Well, at the very least, it was lunch time, and she was starved for healthy fare.

Immediately upon entering, she noticed the astute appraisal from a middle-aged woman at the counter, serving coffee to a couple of customers perched on stools. She was still stunningly attractive, Del mused. Daisy, Del assumed, turned her attention back to her task as Lucy breezed by the table with a welcoming smile.

"I'll be right with you!" The young girl was truly an asset to the business. Once again, Del was impressed with the warm atmosphere.

"I knew you'd be back!" Lucy handed her a menu, "Same order? Or try something new?"

"I'll take a look, thanks." Del noticed Daisy's watchful eye upon them. Lucy moved off to grab another order and hurriedly pinned it to the wheel on the counter. She and Daisy exchanged a quick word, and the older woman touched her shoulder affectionately as Lucy grabbed the coffee pot and wandered out onto the floor again.

Immersed deeply in the tempting menu choices, Del jumped a little at Daisy's voice so close beside her.

"Hello there, I've been told you are looking to speak with me." It was a statement.

"I am," Del admitted, "I would really appreciate it if you have a moment to sit."

Daisy gave her a measuring glance and slid into the opposite side of the booth, maintaining her silent vigilance. Del accepted this an invitation to speak.

"Up front – all cards on the table," Del looked her square in the eye, "my name is Del Greenwood, and I am the Senior Child

Protection Worker with Child Protection Services," Del noted the expected wariness in her eyes.

"I am not here in that capacity, however." Del heaved a steadying sigh. "There are two young girls who are likely in significant danger, and I know of your association with one of them, for sure. I have information to share with you – please just grant me your ear before deciding on my trustworthiness and the value of our collaboration."

"I can see no reason why you would come to see me regarding these two girls," Daisy's tone was curt, but Del knew she had piqued her curiosity and concern.

"For the sake of the girls, you need to hear what I have to say," Del pinned her with a determined stare, "we need to talk privately."

"I will hear you out," Daisy narrowed her eyes," but please do not harbor any expectations for the outcome." She motioned to Lucy that they were moving to the back.

Del had no sooner settled into the office chair across from Daisy, when Lucy came to take their orders and hurried off. The woman facing her was truly a force to be reckoned with. Del had been intimidated by much less.

"Go on."

"I am aware that you provide a measure of comfort and friendship to a girl known as Desi. I am sure you know that her real name is Jessi." At a lack of any response from Daisy, she continued.

"I have recently been assigned a file for Amanda Goodchild, who has fled her foster home, and I have reason to believe that she has been staying with Jessi."

"Assuming this is all true, what do you want from me? You are the one with the legal leverage – I fail to see how I can be of any assistance to you."

"There are recent developments that you may not be aware of."

"Go on."

"A few days ago, Jessi fled from her pimp – abandoned the apartment, and he is now turning the neighborhood upside down, looking for her." Del knew by the flicker of concern in Daisy's eyes that this was, indeed, news.

"How do you know this?" Daisy was invested in gaining the information, at least.

"A former foster parent of Jessi's has been keeping an eye out for her over the past few years." Del sighed, "There is much to the back story that I can tell you, but right now, the girls need help." At Daisy's wary gaze, Del continued. "Believe me when I tell you that my professional cap is off the table – I am here on a personal level and would likely be fired if my boss discovered that I was here with you now."

Lucy knocked and brought lunch in for both of them and left without a word. Daisy looked intensely thoughtful – clearly in the throes of making a decision, as she unwrapped the cutlery from the napkin and slowly placed it on the desk.

"You seem genuine, Ms. Greenwood, and it's obvious that you do care for the girls' welfare," she pinned Del with a willful glance, "and that you are clearly a woman of high intelligence. So, I'm sure you understand the danger that I might place upon the girls should I so much as acknowledge to you any involvement with them." She paused for a moment. "Certainly, in my shoes, you would do everything you could to preserve their identities, whereabouts and safety."

"Absolutely," Del nodded firmly, "and I have formed the same assessment of you. Therefore, I am sure *you* know that I do not come to you lightly." Daisy afforded a single nod. "Please call me Del."

They both regarded each other as they took a breather to dig into their lunches.

"You may already know that the girls developed a strong bond in a previous foster home, where they lived. Further, that they were separated by unfortunate circumstances, for the past several years." Del continued.

Another solitary nod.

"Amanda has endured horrendous abuse and neglect over these years and has just fled from her current foster placement for reasons of peril, I am certain." Del drew in a deep breath.

"What I'm about to reveal to you is highly classified, and my sharing of it is against every oath that I've taken with my employer – I sincerely hope you will keep it in the strictest confidence."

"As long as there is no consequence for the girls in doing so, you have my word."

Daisy was clearly invested now – thank God!

"Amanda fled her foster home within hours of a brutal beating to the foster mother – I believe it was the foster father who did this, and I am suspicious that Amanda may have received similar treatment. Hence her flight."

"I tracked down her route by speaking with their shared foster parent from years back. As luck would have it, the woman knew where Jessi was living and agreed that Amanda was likely with her. She had come to Millie in search of Jessi." Del heaved a frustrated sigh. "But Amanda has been one step ahead of me for the past week. Not to mention the fact that I am the absolute last person she'd want to see. The system has not afforded her, nor Jessi, any favors."

"I need help!" she threw an impassioned plea to Daisy.

"Recent searching has unearthed a very dangerous situation," Del noted Daisy's keen attention. "The current foster father, under a different name, is a convicted pedophile who was released from prison two years ago after serving time for fifteen counts of child sexual abuse. His wife is suspected of being an accomplice for some, or all of it – at least by association."

"Jesus! How did the lowlife manage to qualify as a foster parent?" Daisy exploded. "This is disgusting!" She was thoroughly enraged.

"I know – believe me, I share all of your questions, thoughts, and disbelief! Our system is significantly flawed. And I hope you understand that this very reality is why I cannot run this on record – we have too little time for that."

They were two women in partnership now. Del knew that she had earned, at least, the woman's guarded trust. The haunted look in her eyes provided a glimpse of what Del's gut told her – Daisy carried a history of abuse. Perhaps as a child or a spouse – it was something along those lines, Del knew.

"I have, at least, arranged to have the information hotshotted up to the powers that be, and the Millers will lose their foster licence immediately," Del regarded her solemnly, "however, that will not ensure Amanda's, nor Jessi's safety, should Paul Miller find them.

"We have to ensure that does not happen," Daisy was adamant.

"Yes, and that Jessi stays away from the diner, away from the pimp."

"That scum-of-the-earth piece of shit will never set foot into my establishment," Daisy growled, "I can guarantee you that!" Not another word of explanation was offered, but Daisy studied Del for a long time before continuing.

"I know about your Amanda and can attest that she is currently safe. At least she was, until this latest development." She rubbed her forehead. "The girls are still together, I'll wager that." Daisy stood up, and Del followed suit.

"Let me chat with the girls, and I'll call you – I do have your number." Daisy smiled.

"Thank you so much!" Words could not express Del's level of gratitude. She knew, with dead certainty, that Daisy was a powerful resource moving forward.

Del decided to swing by the Miller household on her way

back to the office. Parking across the street, she settled in to watch from a distance and take a breather from the bombardment of information and speculation that was currently weighing upon her weary brain.

She would give anything to exercise a search warrant at this moment but knew that Sherri would be covering that step already.

Mulling over all the fine details, Del speculated that it was useless to approach Gen Miller at this point. If the woman managed to muster the courage to come forward, she would call. Truthfully, in her shoes, Del would likely not take the risk. If the man was as volatile as she suspected, the woman would not be safe – no one could protect her. Oh, they might arrest him, but too often, bail was readily made, and Gen Miller would find herself face-to-face with a violent man whom she had just betrayed - a lethal combination.

144

Chapter Twenty-One

"Hey, you are an eager beaver today," Daisy gave us both an appraising glance. Jessi and I had decided not to delay the conversation and hoped to catch her before my shift.

"C'mon into the office," Daisy had accurately assessed the situation.

We sat across from her, and my vulnerability was paramount. We had agreed to reveal as little as possible, but this was one smart lady that we were dealing with, and I had the uneasy suspicion that she just may be able to read my mind. Let Jessi do the talking!

"Daisy, I'm in a jam," Jessi jumped in, "one of my tricks has become unmanageable, and I'm not confident that my main man can offer protection." She heaved a shaky sigh.

"I know, I know…you've warned me," Jessi blurted.

Both of us had expected Daisy's retribution – the *what did you expect,* attitude. But she was distracted somehow – in seeming speculation.

"Daisy, I've taken your advice to heart and am leaving the business," Jessi was nervous as hell - I could feel her shaking beside me, "In fact, I fled the apartment a few nights ago. Well…we did." Jessi motioned toward me.

Something was off - not just a lack of surprise, that I detected from Daisy. It was more as if none of this needed to be said - no news to her. My mind whirled. Jessi had stopped speaking, and I knew that she sensed it, too. We waited.

"It pisses me off that you took three days to come and tell me." At what must have been stunned expressions from the two of us, she continued.

"Yes – word is on the street." Her gaze softened a little. "Don't ever leave me in the dark again – surely you know you can trust me?"

"It's not that," Jessi began.

"The hell it's not!" She growled fiercely. "It's a good thing for you that I already, just yesterday, learned of this latest development, or Mandy would be grilled like a well-done steak by now."

Daisy took a deep breath.

"Also, you need not worry about *my* protection – there's not a lot you can tell me that I am not already privy to, should I choose to call upon my sources."

Jessi flushed, and I knew she was feeling a little ashamed for choosing to hold back information from this true friend that she had found in this ugly existence. But it wasn't on her – I needed to jump in.

"Daisy, this wasn't Jessi's choice." I looked her square in the eye. "My showing up here has escalated the situation, and I carry my own share of crap along with me. I insisted on discretion."

"Fair enough, but no more secrets!" She leveled us both with a formidable glare. "Every detail you keep from me creates precarious situations for us all. If I am to help you, my condition is that you will come clean."

Shit! I was in a pickle now. My every instinct told me to run. There had been do-gooders before, along the way, and not one of them had been able to do a damn thing to help me.

This plan was fricking, blowing apart, like a time bomb! All we had intended was to secure some assistance for Jessi's independence. My shit was supposed to stay out of it – I have a good job! Running would sacrifice that, too. I needed time to think.

"Jessi can't go back there. She needs an income." It was time to take a bit of control back.

"Daisy, that is why we've come to you. If you know of anyone who'd be willing to take a chance on me, I'll work my ass off to stay away from turning tricks." Jessi looked at her imploringly. "We've got this. We'll get our own place and…"

"Where are you staying right now?"

Jessi and I looked at each other. We really did need her help, and there'd be no screwing around with her – she was too smart for that. I nodded.

"Mandy has paid for a full month at the Sleep Eazy, just off Granville, a couple of blocks."

"And you thought you'd be safer there?" Daisy's expression was unreadable.

I swallowed nervously. Hell, there was no safety in my life or Jessi's.

"Jessi is much safer there; trust us."

Daisy gave us both a speculative glance.

"Hang on, I'll be back in a minute – don't go anywhere!" When Daisy left the room, I let out an audible sigh.

"Mandy, something has to give – I don't think she'll help us if we don't let her in."

I chewed my lip in nervous contemplation. How far in was the question?

"OK, if we can keep this about you, I'm fine with it. I agree. She needs to know how dangerous that fucking slime ball Russell is."

"Mandy, you are under threat from him too now, too, I'm sure of it. There's no way SD is going to keep that to himself – at least the part about him and M." She squeezed my shoulder in earnest. "Russell is not going to blame them for your involvement – they will just say you offered a freebie."

"So, we'll tell her about that – come clean, and then she'll at least know the full situation with your scummy pimp."

Daisy came back into the room, sat down, leaned back in her chair, and regarded us.

"Mandy, you will be paid for your shift, but just know that Jeff is covering for you, until we are finished this conversation. Got it?" I nodded.

"Daisy, we have something to share," Jessi began.

"Please do."

"As I had said, a situation with one of the johns got out of control." Jessi took a shaky breath and flushed.

I realized at that moment that this sweet girl had likely never told anyone the sordid details of her prostitution and that the last person she'd want to voice it to was Daisy.

"I had come to Jessi because I had nowhere else to go – that much you already know," I interjected. "In doing so, I placed Jessi in a position that was unfair." The hated tears welled up in my eyes, and I grabbed Jessi's hand, "but being the beautiful soul that she is, Jessi let me stay until I could arrange another place."

Daisy said nothing.

"One night, Russell brought a john to the unit unexpectedly – caught us unawares, and I had to dive under the bed to hide. Jessi would have received rough treatment from Russell if he knew about me." I continued.

"This was not the first time for this john – we call him *SD*. But this night, he had a *friend* with him. " I couldn't stop my derisive snort of disgust.

"Once things got going," I looked at Jessi apologetically, "I sneezed – couldn't hold it back, and my cover was blown. They hauled me out and insisted that I participate – either that or let Russell in the know." I sighed. "That was out of the question."

"Two nights later, they showed up again – without Russell this time." Jessi began to cry, silent tears flowing down her cheeks. I squeezed her hand.

"There were four of them now, and they had us by the short ones." I closed my eyes, willing the trauma away from the event that I was reliving in the telling.

"They bound and blindfolded us and proceeded to rape us, in every disgusting way imaginable - then left us there, helpless. For three fucking hours!" I lost my battle and fought back, gulping sobs. "We fled that night."

"That prick Russell won't find you here or at the motel." The dangerous glint in her eyes would have sent the bravest cad scurrying for cover. A shiver shimmied down my spine.

"It's time for me to share with you now." Daisy leaned forward. "I needed to be sure you were willing to come clean about this, at least. She drilled me with a warning glare.

"Normally, I'd be scooting your asses out of a dive like the Speak Eazy, but I happen to know the owner." She grinned. "Let's just say you'll be under my protection there – but only for a while until we can sort this out!"

A glance at Jessi suggested to me that both of us were likely unable to conceal our stupefied expressions. Daisy's ring of laughter confirmed it.

"I do have friends in low places, but this particular guy has a heart of gold and will make sure you come to no harm. Let's just say his tenants are loyal to him."

The bikers! I was beginning to get the picture that was unfolding here. What the hell kind of life had Daisy led? Curiosity was eating me up but now was not the time.

"Thank you," my gratitude was genuine, especially for Jessi's sake. The thought of that loathsome asshole getting anywhere near her again made me want to vomit – and filled me with an all-consuming rage that was a bit frightening, even for me.

"You, too, will be under my wing." Daisy eyed me intently. Something in her pointed gaze set alarms off in my brain. Best to remain silent now!

"Jess, I want you to go now to see Liz at the little Italian shop on Fifth, just down from the motel." Daisy scribbled something on a note and handed it to Jessi. "Tell her I sent you." Jessi had been effectively dismissed.

"Mandy and I have a few more things to discuss."

Oh, shit! With Jessi gone, my anxiety was at its peak. Crap – I felt like a bug under a microscope! She continued her regard with that expectant gleam in her eye, and I began to squirm.

"Mandy," her soft tone put me further off-kilter, "I know who you are; where you've been," she leaned toward me and took my hand, "and – who you are running from."

Well, fuck – what the hell was she talking about? Could it be she knows about it all? And how?

"It's OK, Mandy," she kept a firm grip on the hand that I was desperately trying to pull out of her grasp, "You are safe right now." She leaned back with a solemn expression. "But even I can't keep you that way without your help."

Oh God – somehow, she knew about my flight from the

foster home. Crap! She knew I was under government care – I'd be sent back for sure. Damn it! Panic welled within me – the urge to flee was overwhelming! But what about Jessi?

"Take a deep breath, girl," Daisy began to soothe, "shh, it's OK, let it out."

I hadn't realized that I was crying. Huge hiccupping sobs were wracking my whole body. Her gentle words were a catalyst, and when she came around and took me into her arms, I lost it completely. I had not allowed anyone close to me like this since Millie. It was both wonderful and terrifying. As the tremors subsided, Daisy leaned back and continued.

"Del Greenwood from Child Protection Services came to visit me."

Oh my God! So, it wasn't coincidental. How on earth did she make the connection? The confusion must have been evident on my face.

"She had a visit with Millie."

Millie betrayed me?

"Don't go getting your shit in a knot over Millie – she was a tough nut to crack, apparently." Daisy smiled. "And you know that she would never have talked about you and Jessi if she didn't feel it was the best thing for you."

"I cannot go back! He will kill me!" Along with all the other unspeakable things that he will resume! I started to cry again. What the fuck? Have I lost all my power, too? Deep inside, though, I knew it was because of Daisy – I trusted her. But she was helpless against the system. Damn it!

"You're not going back, Honey, I promise you that."

"You can't make that promise and keep it!" There was the anger that I so desperately needed – my strength!

"Not if you work with *her* – she can't do a damn thing to save me. There's no fucking way out unless I find a way to make it on my own! I was almost there, and now…"

"Now, you need to listen to me."

Daisy's calm voice drew me in.

"The Millers' time is up – Paul Miller is not his real name, and he will soon be behind bars if all goes well. At the very least, those two no longer have a foster home licence."

I hung my head – a wave of pure weakness washed over me. The relief – Oh my God! Was it true? How?

"Del Greenwood is one impressive lady – very determined!"

Yeah, I remember that about her – scared the hell out of me!

"And she's on your side – she's on our team!"

Team? My side? Ha – they were all on my side. But the darker forces were stronger and beyond their reach. I blurted that out now.

"Mandy," she lifted my chin gently, "This time is different – you need to trust me. You have both myself and Millie, to make sure of it!" She smiled gently into my eyes.

"I can't wait to meet that lady," Daisy chuckled, "You are well-loved! I know that you were ripped away from her when you finally found a home, and I am so sorry for what you've been through." Her gaze was full of compassion.

"But, think of the strength that you've gained – you are one formidable young lady! The spark of your anger, your strong will, and your tenacious drive for survival – will all serve to help you set the world on fire once you are out there on your own. I do believe, too, that you would lay down your life for a trusted friend, such as Jessi, without a second thought." She gave me a fierce hug.

"I don't know what to say right now," damn, I hated the feeling of reliance on others for my survival, "it's not that I don't trust you, believe me! But if you knew how many foster homes I've had the misfortune to land in, the abuse and cruelty…"

"Del has filled me in – has had a thorough look through your file," Daisy maintained steady eye contact, "and she's well aware that a great many of the atrocities are solidly locked away, only for your knowledge." She sat back and crossed her arms.

"How would you feel to know that we, three adults, are committed to keeping you from the trauma of any further foster homes?" Her smile was conspiring.

"Of course, that sounds like sweet freedom to me – I've never had this until the last couple of weeks," I couldn't believe my ears. "But how?"

"Del is going to make some arrangements for you to live independently, within government support still." She put up her hand as I began to spout.

"It is not foster care; rather, a home with supervision. Mandy, these places are a catalyst to moving out completely on your own." She pinned me with a serious gaze. "You are fifteen years-old, and this necessarily puts you at a disadvantage in this world."

"Do you really believe that you can properly support yourself on the meager wage that I am able to pay you now? And moving forward, what employment do you think you could secure with a grade-nine education?" She let that sink in for a minute.

Damn! She was implanting doubts, and it was fucking with my head. I had been so hopeful…

"In such a home, you will be able to keep your income, albeit part-time, because you will also be enrolled in schooling to finish your education. And, you will still have the advantage of government funding, paying for it."

But Jessi!

"And the best part?" She had well anticipated my fear. "Del will move mountains to ensure that you and Jessi will do this together – hopefully even in the same home."

Holy shit! I was beginning to see a light somewhere within this plan.

"Through all of your years of suffering, the Universe has arranged for all of these events to unwind at just the perfect moment. Fifteen is the youngest qualifying age for these types of programs, and not all kids are eligible or able to manage it." She smiled.

"Del Greenwood is advocating for you – she believes that you and Jessi are both shoo-ins for the program due to the severe trauma you've both endured, together with your strength and iron-will determination.

"It will take awhile to put this together – no sudden adjustments yet! Thankfully, Jessi's adoptive parents surrendered her guardianship back to government care, so that won't be an issue. You will be safe with Joe at the motel, in the interim." At my speculative look, she laughed softly. "Yes, Joe, who also owns this diner. That's a story for another day."

It was all too much to take in. I started to shake, and she gathered me back into her embrace.

"Honey, if you need the day off, it's with pay – I'll cover for you."

It hit me like a brick. Sudden gratitude overcame me. Here was a woman willing to risk all for two young girls that she genuinely cared about. A really, good person! For maybe the first time in my life, I set aside all my fears, anger, and doubts to honor this. I felt an overwhelming compulsion to embrace this gift.

Had the Universe arranged this, as she had eluded? Well, it has never had my back before, but I had to agree that the timing worked out perfectly. Who knew the reason for anybody's situation in life? I never before held any belief that it could be different and had only felt victimized.

It resonated somewhere inside! Today had changed me – something had shifted. It was both exhilarating and unnerving. I knew I couldn't afford to put aside all of the coping skills and strategies that I'd built so meticulously for survival. But perhaps I could have both – hope for the future while preserving this intricate part of me.

Time to buck up, girl!

"No, it's OK, I'm going to work," I smiled and gave Daisy a quick hug. It was an awkward feeling for me, but it reminded me of Millie – a lifetime ago; a warmth seeped through every cell in my body.

Chapter Twenty-Two

"We're in."

Daisy's call was a welcome diversion to Del's current predicament. The search warrant on the Miller's home had been granted almost immediately, but the place seemed deserted when the police tried to execute it just this morning. Del's gut told her that they'd fled.

"The girls just left my office, and Mandy came clean."

"Thank God, and you, for your intervention!"

"We'll have to give her some room," Daisy warned, "this is all new to her – completely out of her comfort zone. It's a lot to take in."

"No problem there, I'm just grateful that you and Millie have both earned her trust."

"She's appreciative of what you are doing, as well – she'll come around."

A sudden vision of Amanda, defiant and fiery, flittered across Del's mind, and she smiled. She was a formidable cookie to crumble, and for the life of her, Del could not imagine Amanda, compliant and grateful. No matter, this girl was destined for a positive outcome; Del was determined to make sure of it.

With a long sigh, she glanced out from her office window, hoping that the refreshing spring shower promised a rejuvenation for more than just the ground soil, awaiting nourishment for rebirth.

Jessica Saunders had been out of the system for more than a year now. A breeze through her file pretty much mirrored Amanda's parenting situation or lack thereof. The exception was a glaring lack of documentation from her foster experiences. Del would bet her right hand on the probability that Jessi, as well, had suffered abuse – the last adoptive home she had fled was likely a source.

"Thanks, Daisy," Del took a deep breath, "I have some alarming news." Del then imparted the situation regarding the Millers.

"They could have gone anywhere, and who knows what tipped them off. However, no surprise, really. He was under suspicion for Gen's beating, and with Mandy's disappearance, the writing is on the wall."

"This is not good," Daisy lamented, "Much better that we know where he's at."

"Yes, and he didn't show up for his work shift this morning." Del let out a troubled sigh. "Your contacts will have to be on extreme guard."

"No worries there! The man won't have a chance if they get

their hands on him – I guarantee you that!"

Del rang off and decided to spend the morning, now tackling paperwork from her other case files – she'd have to arrange a couple of home visits as well in the next few days.

Sherri, of course, had her back, monitoring any updates on the Millers, as well as searching for outreach home possibilities; for both Amanda and Jessi. Keeping them together was the key to their buy-in, Del knew.

Her phone buzzed – she was surprised to see the Caller ID – Amanda's school and answered immediately.

"Ms. Greenwood," Del recognized the secretary's voice.

"Yes, how can I help you?"

"I had a visit from Gen Miller this morning," her voice was intentionally low volume, "and though I can't involve myself in any way, I wanted to let you know that she is looking for Mandy." She hesitated.

"She gave me a cell number and said they had moved. The new address she claimed not to have with her but promised she'd provide it. She was adamant that I call her, if Mandy shows up at school."

This could be a major lead! Del scribbled the number on a notepad and then added it to her phone cell contacts. Intuition guided her – don't try it yet! She buzzed for Sherri, who showed up at her door and handed Del a folder with a smile.

"Possibilities, Madam!"

"Thank you – how *do* you access this so efficiently?" Del was amazed at the list of possible homes for the two girls. Now, she handed Sherri the note.

"Amanda Goodchild's school called to give me this number, provided to them by one Gen Miller." At Sherri's lifted brow, Del continued, "I would suggest not attempting to call – it may tip them off. However, perhaps you could search the cell – see if maybe it's an option for the police to trace?"

"On it," Sherrie breezed out.

Del pondered it over and then decided she'd pay a visit to Amanda today – sending Daisy a text so she'd be in the know. Daisy immediately replied that 2:00 would be the optimum time.

The crowd was relatively sparse, when she arrived at the diner – lunch rush was past. Daisy caught her eye and nodded, disappearing into the kitchen.

Then she appeared – the same vulnerable young girl that Del remembered in her office, now standing outside the kitchen door, a look of uncertainty on her features. Del smiled, and Amanda wandered over, sitting cautiously at the booth.

"Hello Amanda," Del watched her closely, trying to read her emotions for the best approach.

"It's Mandy."

Del wondered if the slight was born from defiance or acceptance. Likely a little of both. She knew that her work was cut out for her, and it would be tenuous for a bit. Trust was earned.

"Mandy," Del maintained a gentle smile, "I am so glad to meet with you, under significantly different circumstances," she paused, "and I have something to say to you." Mandy had not moved a muscle.

"The Del Greenwood sitting across from you now, is not defined by her career. I am not here as a social worker today." The wariness peeked through, in Mandy's regard of her, and Del's heart melted a little. "I am here as your friend and mentor - as a partner in keeping you safe."

"Having said that, my connections with Child Protection Services will serve us well here. Daisy told you about my plan, correct?"

"We talked," Mandy nodded, "It sounds ideal, but as you well know – that has never been a part of my life." She drew a shaky breath.

"I have nothing against you – it's not personal." Mandy

regarded her now a little more openly.

"But it is personal for me – I want you to know that."

"Why? Why me?"

She was waiting for an answer. Del reflected on that very question. It wasn't as if her heart was not involved, in all of her cases. Then, why indeed, was she willing to risk her job – hell, even her life, for one Amanda Goodchild? Del decided that honestly was the best shot she had.

"I don't know, exactly." Del sighed and looked her straight in the eye. "Every child that comes across my plate pulls on my heartstrings – and I put all that I have into it." Del regarded her thoughtfully. "Why would I risk it all?" Mandy was no dummy and nodded sagely.

"Because you deserve it. Your nightmare, through the system is one of the most horrendous, that I have ever bore witness to. I know there are others, but you," Del paused to ensure her audience was engaged, "you are sitting right in front of me – have been, from the moment you sauntered into my office - proud, brave and scared as hell!" Del smiled compassionately.

"Mandy, you are one remarkable young lady," Del noted a shimmer of tears gleaming in her eyes now. "You possess ferocious courage, commitment, and fiercely honor a stalwart moral code."

Del paused as Daisy brought them both a light lunch and coffee, squeezing Mandy's shoulder in reassurance as she drifted away. After a shake of her head, Mandy fixed Del with an open gaze.

"And, you love deeply – this I know from your relationships. Despite all you have endured, you are passionately devoted to Jessi, and I know without a doubt, that you would also place yourself in danger, to protect both Millie and Daisy." Del grinned. "Not to mention your stellar grades in school – you are one smart girl!"

"You have asked me a profound question – *why?*" Del opened her hands on the table, as an invitation to trust in her honesty and genuine caring. "I have your answer - it is simple."

"You are worth it!"

A couple of tears escaped and trickled down Mandy's cheeks, and Del was grateful for the progress today. She accepted the ups and downs, that were likely to come with it, but Mandy had granted her an audience – not defiant or mistrustful this time. Del was aware of the level of courage this took, on Mandy's part. It was a great step!

Chapter Twenty-Three

What the hell was I supposed to do with all this emotion?

Getting back to work felt like the best remedy for now. I had thanked Jeff profusely, for covering for me. He had shrugged it off as *no big deal*, but it was huge to me. I was not accustomed to generosity in my lot, and it meant everything.

The compassion in his eyes was fleeting, but I'd seen it, and I wondered. How much did he know about me? About Jessi? He was a good friend. He never asked what Daisy and I had discussed – carried on like it was none of his business. I felt safe, working along there beside him.

At shift's end, I threw Jeff and Bree a high five in the air, and mouthed a thank you to Daisy, on the way out the door. Her affectionate smile, in return, warmed my insides.

Jessi and I had plans tonight! The motel had a small green space with a few picnic tables and a couple of barbecue pits. We had seen a group of bikers cooking up a storm the night prior, and decided it was a good idea. The prospect of fresh air and a tasty meal was too inviting, and Jessi had picked up some jumbo hot dogs and buns for the occasion, complete with chips and Smore ingredients.

It didn't take long to get the coals going, and there were hot dog sticks propped up on one of the tables. We relaxed on two of the Adirondack chairs provided, and chatted about the recent developments. The constant noise of revving bikes coming and going, didn't bother us in the least. The activity was somehow comforting, now that Daisy had indicated we'd be safe here. A few of the dudes threw a friendly smile at us, as they ambled by, but none harassed us. This was particularly shocking to Jessi.

"I keep expecting one of them to try to hire me," she giggled.

"Well, you are not in that profession any longer, and they'd have no reason to think you are." I punched her arm playfully. "But don't be surprised if you get hit on, anyhow!"

"Trust me, I'm not remotely interested in men, my friend." Her expression clouded and I squeezed her hand. She looked up earnestly.

"Do you want kids someday, Mandy?"

"I haven't given it much thought," her question took me by surprise, "I suppose maybe, but never within the life that I've known, so far. Any child that I bring into this world, will have a good home – both a mother and father," I hesitated at her vulnerable look, "or two mothers!"

"You are amazing," Jessi smiled warmly, "I was just wondering." She paused. "I've only just now considered the possibility. I remember our time with Millie and Simon – you and I looked after the other kids, like they were our own." She smiled wistfully. "It was really one of the best things I loved."

I allowed my mind to replay those couple of years – even with the pain of loss, I agreed. We had both been firmly determined to keep those kids safe, and always tried to provide for their happiness – their right to a joyful childhood. Something that had been rudely denied, to both of *us*.

"Jess, if you ever want to move on," I regarded her seriously, "I don't mean from our friendship – but, to take on a male partner in your life," I was totally genuine, "it will be OK with me."

"Mandy, right now, I can't imagine it – you are just what I need in my life, and I am completely happy, being lovers with you!" She gave me a tender hug.

"But I, too, have no expectations of you. Same leeway goes for you." Jessi sighed contentedly. "I think our friendship will survive anything, really, and that is the most important thing for me."

"Always and forever," I returned; my love for Jessi was everything. We had found each other again, and *wild horses couldn't drag us away*. I smiled at the *Rolling Stones* song lyric. I'd always loved that tune, even though it was an *oldie*. We were exposed to a lot of awesome old tunes, through Millie and Simon.

"Hey, let's eat!" Jessi had two hot dogs on each stick, primed to put over the coals. Though I would have preferred woodsmoke over charcoal, the smell was awesome and I knew it would taste great.

I had brought out the condiments earlier and we had a grand feast, laughing at each other, as we licked the ketchup and mustard; then the gooey Smores, from our fingers. Of course, some had dribbled onto my t-shirt – *you can dress me up but you can't take me out*. That adage always applied to me!

We put the food away and came back out to sit by the heat of the coals, as the spring evening was bringing in a chill. We had just settled in with a hot chocolate, when I noticed two dudes coming down the sidewalk. Something about them looked a little sketchy - I caught Jessi's eye, and motioned with my own, toward their approach.

Jessi and I had been around the block a time or two with questionable dudes, so we weren't overly concerned for our safety. We'd play it cool, if they decided to stop. I had a niggling feeling that it may just come to that, as they were now regarding us with significant interest.

They walked past right in front of us, so it seemed that they were going to carry on, but at the edge of the motel lot, they swerved around and started to advance toward us on the lawn. Both of us were instantly on full alert. Show time!

They stopped in front of us.

"Looks like you could use a little company to keep you warm." He was a druggie – unmistakable. Teeth visibly rotting and exhibiting jerky movements. His jeans were disgustingly filthy.

"No, we're fine thank you," I pinned him with a fierce glare, "feel free to go on your way." He sneered his response.

"Oh, we have nowhere to be right now," the second dude was built like a brick shit house; a bit more intimidating – he was studying me closely. They were clearly bad asses.

"Hey boys," Jessie looked them over with disdain, "we are not welcoming visitors. My friend and I wish to spend this time alone."

I knew we were in for a fight, when I saw the mean glint in the big guy's eye. I stood up to face them, heart pounding wildly in my chest. There was something about him that was familiar, but I couldn't put my finger on it.

Jessi and I did possess some self-defence training, and had been honing our skills together, the past week or so. The question was – did they have the same advantage? Druggies were dangerous, as they tended to harbor intense physical power.

Suddenly, from out of nowhere it seemed, the two deadbeats

were surrounded by a group of bikers – I counted ten. There were no weapons visible, but I had no doubt that they would materialize, if necessary.

"You girls OK?" One of the guys, who had sent me a warm smile several times over the past few days, glanced over at us both. We nodded our confirmation.

"Gentlemen," another in the group addressed the two dudes, "I suggest you be on your way now," his look was deadly, "these two ladies do not want your company," he edged up until he was nose to nose with the big guy, "and if we ever find you here again, my face will be the last thing you will ever see."

Crap! The message was crystal clear, and the dudes moved off, without a word. I couldn't believe it! Never in my life, thus far, had anyone stepped in to protect me like this – especially men. I stared at them all in amazement.

"You ladies don't need to put up with any shit from anyone, as long as you are living here." They nodded respectfully as they moved off, and I shouted my thanks after them. They merely put their hands up in acknowledgement, and disappeared as fast as they'd come.

"Holy shit!" Jessi was as pumped as I was. "That was amazing! Is it awful, that my first idea for payback, is freebies?" We both laughed at that.

"No way lady, you are no longer on that path!" I took a calming breath. "But I think we've just had a taste of the safety that Daisy promised."

"All the same," Jessi responded, "We should be careful – I don't want to put anyone else in danger." We both agreed to stay inside from now on, after supper hour and move our tails quickly, if we saw any lurking danger, before there was a need for anyone else to step in.

Lounging on the bed, it suddenly hit me!

"Jess, I forgot to ask about your meeting with… Liz, was it? At the Italian shop?"

"Oh, right! How could I forget! I start next week, sorting and filling spice containers." Jessi was positively beaming. "It's awesome – they import the spices directly from Italy, and then sell them in smaller containers."

"Wow, Jess – that's great news!" I was so happy for her. She went on to share, that it would be full time for now, until Daisy and Del came up with a more permanent plan for us both.

"Free spices come with it – we are going to become culinary wizards!" We laughed at that and shut down the lights.

I was thoroughly exhausted. It had been a day, for sure! After a quick shower, Jessi and I made love, and I dropped off immediately.

My newfound sense of security was novel, and it was strange that I remained ever vigilant – reluctant to lay any trust in it, during my conscious hours. Yet somehow, my subconscious allowed me to rest peacefully. I had never slept so soundly – ever! My entire existence had required that I be on my toes at all times, and I knew it would be hard to let that guard go – if even possible.

Chapter Twenty-Four

"It's a "pay-as-you-go" disposable – and it seems that they were smart enough to turn off the location settings – so the police haven't been able to trace it." Sherri threw Del an empathetic glance.

"Plus, if they have any sense, they'll likely replace the phone every few days – not overly pricey to do so – lots available; dirt cheap, on the black market."

Damn! It had been a positive thread of hope to find out where the Millers had relocated to.

"OK, thanks, Sherri! Maybe the detective will get a break, working with the school on it. With any luck, Gen Miller will try again." Del sighed heavily. "God knows they probably have good reason to want to keep Amanda quiet." The mere act of voicing the horrible suspicion sent a shudder of apprehension down her spine.

Del wondered, for the umpteenth time, if she should have warned Amanda about the Miller's dive under the radar. She, Millie, and Daisy had pondered on it and decided that it didn't matter where the Millers were – they didn't know the girls' whereabouts anyhow, and there were no common denominators between Jessi and Amanda's worlds, at least as not as far as any one knew. Still…something niggled.

On her way over to the diner, Sherri's office line popped up.

"Hey, what's up?"

"Paul Miller does not legally exist – at least not *our* Paul Miller." Del sighed at Sherri's words – not a surprise. "Of course, we knew that, but he didn't even officially change his name."

"As you know, we do have his government ID on file, which I've learned clearly does not exist. He has obtained a false ID from somewhere."

Del knew these were easily procured – a dime a dozen! If she were to be generous with the screening process performed, she supposed there would have been no reason to question it, with Gen Miller being his alleged wife. She thanked Sherri and made a quick decision.

They had agreed to meet at Millie's right after Mandy's shift was over. It was time that the five of them had a chat together. Del figured that the two girls would be impacted positively, to witness the power of partnership between their three mentors – the ones who cared the most about them both in this wicked world.

"Hey, thanks for picking me up." Jessi was dressed casually, in a faded pair of denim Levi's and a bright yellow t-shirt. Del mused that this girl was stunningly gorgeous!

"We thought it would be good for all of us to get together – compare notes, and just generally visit!" Del threw her a friendly smile. She had already let Jessi know that Daisy was bringing Mandy.

Draped comfortably together on Millie's loveseat, Mandy and Jessi giggled while regaling some fond memories of their life with Millie and Simon.

"Oh, Lordy, girls – you were both such imps!" Millie regarded them fondly, her features softening as strong affection shone through. "I have not seen you together since that time." The break in her voice betrayed her sentiment.

"Well, let's plan to make this a regular thing," Jessi squeezed her hand.

"It warms my heart," Daisy took the lead now.

"I think it's important that we review together your current circumstances and possible plans for the future." she smiled at the girls reassuringly.

"The three of us have agreed that moving forward, any placements, choices, and opportunities for you both will be undertaken with your full input and approval." Daisy continued.

"However, we will ask for unequivocal full trust in the process. There will be some elements that are non-negotiable – such as your education."

Both girls nodded agreeably. Del was aware that Mandy

seemed to thrive at almost all of the schools she had attended. Kids develop a variety of coping skills when fed with a life of trauma and sometimes choose to immerse themselves into learning – whether it be for that sense of accomplishment and worthiness or simply a positive escape – it was often hard to tell. Others are unable to handle the social and academic pressure. Del thanked God that Amanda Goodchild was quite the scholar! Many doors would open for both girls if they earned their diplomas.

"As long as we can do it together," Mandy's first round of input incited nods from all three adults.

"We will do our very best to ensure this," Del promised. "We do have an idea to run by you both, which we'll discuss a bit later." She heaved a deep sigh and faced both girls, making deliberate eye contact.

"There are things we feel you should be made aware of." She had their full attention. "First, you need to know that from the moment I connected with both Daisy and Millie, my scope of operation has significantly compromised the terms and conditions of my position with the government." She smiled at them both affectionately.

"Suffice to say that if you breath a word of what I am about to tell you, they will fire my ass quicker than lightning. Not to mention the complex legalities I could face." Del's tone was deadly serious.

"I've asked for your trust in me, and now I want you to promise that my trust in *you* will be well-placed. Having said all of this, everything that I've just told you is secondary to your safety. Everything must remain confidential to that end. Things have an uncanny way of coming back to bite when shared with the wrong people." Del straightened up.

"So, do I have your word – all that we share stays between the five of us?" Both girls nodded solemnly and Del smiled her appreciation.

"First, we've learned that Paul Miller is not who he portrays." Del went on to explain his unspeakable child abuse and prison sentence, as well as the department's inefficiency in properly investigating their backgrounds. She noticed the hardness fall over Mandy's features.

"I am sorry this happened," Del reached out to touch her arm, "the honest truth is that I can't do a damn thing about it now. But how we manage this moving forward is critical for your safety and for that of all other at-risk children in the system." Del paused.

"There was a young girl placed with them before you, Mandy, who disappeared." Del regarded her intently, not wishing to create more trauma than the poor girl had already experienced at that home, but it was important that she knew all.

"She has never been found - assumed to be a run-away, perhaps on the streets. As you well know," Del eyed them, "often these young girls are never found once they hit there." Jessi nodded solemnly.

"The remains of a young girl were discovered a few months later, which they have not yet been able to identify." Del heaved a sigh of resignation, "My fear is that it could be the same girl."

"Geezus, I would pretty much bank on it!" The vehemence in Mandy's tone took Del unawares.

"Mandy," Del questioned gently. "Would you please let us know what happened at the Miller home?"

"The scum of the earth raped my ass at every opportunity," Mandy was shaking so hard, and tears began to fall, "I had found a hiding spot in the basement, but if I used it too many times, he'd become enraged; the abuse would then be particularly violent." She looked up at Del and sniffed back her tears. "He lays into Gen all the time."

"He is a monster – evil, and you can, one hundred percent, count on me to do whatever is within my power, to see the bastard put away for a lifetime." Jessi grabbed Mandy in a fierce hug.

"Thank you, Mandy – that is very courageous." Del smiled. "And, a game changer – if you would be willing to testify when the time comes."

"Bring on the bastard," was Mandy's passionate response. "I know without a doubt, he'll kill me first if he gets the chance."

"We need to ensure he does not!" Daisy added. "He knows nothing of your connection with Jessi, her neighborhood, or where you both are now – we need to keep it that way."

"There is one other thing you should be aware of, though it likely doesn't change much," Del stated. "As you know, Gen and Paul Miller no longer have a licence to operate the foster home. However, they appear to have abandoned the house and have moved on. The police showed up with a search warrant and found nothing left behind." Del noticed the thoughtful expression on Mandy's face, throwing her a questioning glance.

"I just thought of something – it might be nothing," Mandy quickly asserted, "but when I first moved in, I found this little heart pendant – the necklace portion was missing – in the corner of the top drawer of the dresser." Mandy smiled sadly. "I remember thinking that it must have mattered to someone at one time, but it was likely lost to them forever, so I decided that from then on, it would matter to me." She looked at each of them.

"Do you still have it?" Del found it difficult to contain her enthusiasm – this may very well be a key to the little girl's identity if her suspicions were correct.

"Yeah, it's in a little pouch at the motel." Mandy supplied easily. "Do you think it could belong to her?" Everyone in the room knew who she was referring to.

"Let's hope it brings answers," Del replied softly.

"But before we go," all eyes turned to Millie, "we need to discuss possibilities for your future." Love and affection radiated from her expression as she regarded Jessi and Mandy.

"We've all been talking and agree that it might be possible for you girls to stay with me." She laughed aloud at the look of incredulity on the girls' faces. "It's not in stone yet, and details need to be worked out, but Del can explain the process of how this will unfold."

"Oh my God!" Jessi gushed beside a speechless Mandy. "That would be beyond fantastic!" Tears threatened to spill, and Millie got up to give both girls an emotional hug.

"It's important that Del explain it to you," Millie was clearly having her own struggle containing her emotions, "things have to fall into place, in order for us to ensure safety and success."

"I was wracking my brains, trying to find a group home that would take you both and be willing to tackle the education and work balance." Del smiled mischievously.

"Out of the blue, one brilliant lady named Millie put forth an idea that took root – why could she not serve as your guardian?"

"Of course, initially, it seemed simple enough," Millie chimed in, "but Del, in her infinite experience and wisdom, pointed out some of the hurdles we'd have to scale."

"As you are both officially wards of the government," Del addressed them intently, "it could take up to a year for Millie to attain legal guardianship – assuming she was even successful."

"We don't have a year!" Mandy found her voice, "Why can't we just move in and start paying rent to Millie?"

"We need to do this upfront in order to protect Millie. She no longer has a foster licence, and if you were found here…"

"We agreed we'd be careful with that!"

"I know, Mandy, but *I* found Millie, right?" Del reminded her gently, "so it's reasonable to assume others would too – in looking for you, and sooner or later, I will need to disclose this journey."

"So…we've come up with a plan." She met Millie's eyes with a smile. "We are going to process an application for Millie to operate a group home – which can be in effect, with as little as two minor residents, who are presently wards of the government – no need for guardianship changes."

"I happen to have had some experience with kids in these

situations and can make sure we tick all the boxes for Millie to be approved; fast-tracked, hopefully. Your ages are perfect – both old enough for work experience programs, and your education can be obtained through distance learning if you wish so that you can also stay employed on a part-time basis. There is an outreach campus near Millie's place to attend for help with the module work if you need it." Del smiled at the girls' expressions as she watched them process this information.

"It won't be easy - I'll guarantee you that," Del warned.

"Easy is nothing I've ever experienced," Mandy grinned at the faces surrounding her. "Could this really be possible?"

"It is, and we are going to work hard to make this happen," Del determined. "This means, though, that you'll have to stay at the motel a while longer."

"As you know now, many people are looking out for your welfare," Daisy commented, "the boys put the word out on your two unwelcome visitors last night."

Jessi and Mandy exchanged glances and related the details of this event, thanking Daisy for arranging their protection and promising to be more careful in the future. Daisy chuckled at the curiosity evident in their regard.

"Joe is a very dear friend of mine – my late husband's best

friend." It's OK," she waved off their compassion, "It's been many years now. "For the past two decades, we have worked together to try and make this world just a little better."

"When Peter died, I still owed a significant amount on the loan for the diner, and without his income, I could not keep up." She sighed wistfully.

"Joe took over the loan, and though he fought me on it, I had the ownership changed to his name until such time I could pay him back. The diner is mine again, but I always consider Joe as the boss – without him, it would be history."

"Meanwhile, we've worked together, trying to help the less than-fortunate get off the streets. His motel, not exactly the dive I alluded to, has a steady income from the bikers – he gives them a good deal and a break now and again as well. They are very loyal and have become an integral part of our partnership."

"So," Daisy concluded, "you are in good hands until these arrangements are in place and Millie is ready to rock."

"That is so cool," Jessi murmured.

"We can come over to help prepare the house, at least, right?" Del knew Mandy was on a roll now.

"Of course," she agreed.

"My fondest dream was to adopt the two of you," Millie

related softly, "but this is the quickest way to keep you both safe and secure a future for you."

Jessi got up and clutched Millie in a long embrace.

"Millie, from the moment that Mandy and I left your home, each under totally different circumstances – we've grieved and wished that someday, our paths would come back to you." Tears were flowing free from both her and an emotionally overcome Mandy. "First, we found each other, and now we found you - the only mother either one of us has ever known."

Del sniffed back her own emotion, certain that she was on the right road. Lose her job – be damned – at least she would have her integrity. Now, it was time to set the wheels in motion meticulously and timely. She sat back and sighed deeply – thinking that poor Jack would never have survived the meeting of minds in this house today. There was a reason for everything.

Chapter Twenty-Five

Holy shit! It was almost too much to take in at once! What the hell is wrong with me? Why can't I roll with good fortune? It seems that I never have any hesitation to tackle the bad shit – accept it as a given, without question.

Deep down, I knew the difference. Everything that has ever happened in my life has been about survival – no choice but to buck up and face it with a fight!

I really had no idea how to deal with this positive turn. Jessi seemed to be handling it all with grace and gratitude. Oh, it was not about a lack of that, for sure – I was overwhelmed by everyone's kindness and caring!

And more than a little shocked at Del Greenwood's commitment. She said it was personal. There had been something about her that stirred unwelcome emotions from the moment I met her. Hope? In any case, I believed her now. Hell, she was sticking her neck out for us – risking everything!

"Hey, talk to me," Jessi poked me in the ribs as she finished drying the few supper dishes that we had accumulated.

"I don't know, Jess," I responded, "I struggle to put my finger on it, but something is niggling at my senses. I hope it's just that I can't manage to wrap my head around our good luck."

"It's all-new, Mandy," she squeezed my shoulder, "and I get it. My situation has been a bit different. I've had the blessing of Daisy's love and affection, plus the reunion with Millie, for almost a year now."

Her words rang true – perhaps I just needed to calm the fuck down and focus on the gratitude – embrace all this help. But something was holding me back…

It was a foreboding – intuition. I knew it! This is the one thing that I've learned to rely on all of my life, and it's never failed me – warning me to be extra wary. I have always listened.

I concentrated hard to shake it off now and stay in the moment with Jessi. Affection for her melted my heart and I smiled – she was in exceptionally good spirits, filled with hope for the future. I had to jump on this ride with her now and put aside my misgivings.

Jessi and I spent the evening catching up on all the things that were paramount to our new plans. We both desired the education – astute enough to know that it was key to making a half-decent living in this world. As deeply as I appreciated my current job with Daisy, I was under no illusion - it would not be enough to fulfill my dreams for the future.

"Pretty cool – Daisy's story, huh?" Jessi marvelled.

Impressive was more the word. I wondered what her life had been like over the past two decades. She had clearly been widowed young. I voiced all this now.

"Did you know about all this? And why, I wonder, did she not have you living in that motel a year ago?" Admittedly, I was curious about Daisy and Jessi's relationship.

"No, I wasn't aware of any of it." Jessi shrugged, "I thought Joe was the owner, and she's never talked about her husband."

"And, believe me, she did try to rescue my butt several times," Jessi chuckled, "I had no idea just how resourceful the woman could be, with kick-ass connections of her own."

"And to be honest, no matter how much of a scuzzball Russell is, he was really good to me – I wanted for nothing, and he offered protection from all sources of danger."

"Until recently, of course." Jessi sighed deeply.

"Well, that was my fucking fault," I admitted, feeling the dead weight of responsibility pulling me under.

"Bullshit! I was aware that someday I would fall from his list of favorites – through aging, at least. I've seen his bad side and always knew that I was on borrowed time."

"Besides," Jessi grabbed my arm passionately, "how can you not see that your presence in this picture is what has catapulted us into this awesome future?" She shook me a little. "There is no question – you are my good luck charm!"

"Hell of a way to skid into your life, though!" We both giggled. "We'll be OK as long as we are together." I grabbed her in a fierce bear hug, throwing in all the emotion that had my senses in a muddle. And I felt safe – for now.

"What do you think about school and work – do you believe it's manageable?" Jessi regarded me thoughtfully.

"Hell, yes!" Anything was better than the life we had been fated for up to this point. "Del told me that our employment would be part-time, and we wouldn't have to pay living expenses, so we can easily save money for the future." I threw her a bright smile.

"There was a girl about your age that lived in the home I was in before the Millers. She was managing distance learning and told me that it only required half the hours in comparison to public school."

I often wondered what had happened to her. Jolene – that was her name! The foster home had been abruptly shut down when Child Protection Services had sprung a surprise visit and found drugs on the premises. Other than being high most of the time, they had been decent caregivers, I supposed.

"I might be a tad freakish, but I actually enjoy school." I

grinned sheepishly.

"No, I totally get it," Jessi replied, "I do too!" She smiled, "We can help each other too!"

It was true - Jessi had lost one more year of school than I had, so we'd, for sure, be studying at the same grade level.

"Do you really think they murdered that girl?" Jessi's introspection mirrored my own thoughts.

"I would not put it past that piece of shit!" Vehemence overtook me. "If so, my guess is that Gen was an accomplice. As much as I hate her weakness, she is under the ruthless control of that man and has reason to fear for her life if she defies him. Hell, he almost killed her the night before I ran." Jessi gave me a warm hug.

"Well, I am ever grateful that you did! It is beyond cool that we both already have jobs in place," she mused cheerfully.

"For sure – I know I could get to work early enough to manage the lunch dishes and then work through the supper hour." I already had the plan worked out.

"Honestly, it was only the dishwasher that they missed anyhow." I smiled wistfully, shaking my head in wonder. "Bree and Jeff manage the prep and cooking like pros, so Daisy has given me far more hours than she needed to."

"That's Daisy," Jessi agreed. "And Millie – shit! Is she truly up for this, do you think?" Worry etched Jessi's brow.

"I thought about that, but we are not little kids anymore – she won't need to do a thing for us." I was adamant, "In fact, we can make her life easier in this process – all the housework, laundry etc."

"Of course, you are right," Jessi and I exchanged a high-five.

We went to bed and lay there, continuing to share our hopes and dreams and make plans for our future. We held hands as we drifted off into pre-slumber, lost in our own worlds - totally content together.

I contemplated the little heart pendant that I had handed over to Del when she dropped us off. Its absence felt odd. On one hand, there was a measure of letting go – I suppose it was an important piece to escaping Gen and Paul Miller. But on the other hand, I was also struck with a sense of loneliness and vulnerability without it. I realized now that it had been the only beacon of hope I'd had – a link to someone else like me, who maybe had escaped to a better life.

I wished with all my heart now that it did not belong to the little girl who used to live and breathe in that abandoned pile of bones that they had found almost a year ago.

Del Greenwood came to mind – she was one tough lady! My admiration for her had grown considerably. We seemed two peas in a pod in a very strange and resilient kind of way. She had effectively stood up to all of my tricks to push her away and broken through the thick barrier that was comprised of my carefully well-constructed walls. No one else had ever managed that – not even Millie.

I was duly impressed!

Suddenly, I saw myself in her shoes – fiercely determined to help others. One thing I had going for me – I had lived their stories; I could relate on an even playing ground.

But that was a distant dream – there was a long road to travel before I could even think of what might come after my secondary school education. I could feel it burning, though, that spark of ignition, fueling a passion for something greater than I – a fated purpose.

Chapter Twenty-Six

Del pondered significantly on the issue of what to divulge to Sherri. It wasn't a question of trust – hell, she had no reservations there. Her main concern was protection. Every little detail, outside of agency protocol, that she revealed to Sherri placed her assistant in a compromised position. As she continued to mull it over, the very source of her worry knocked on the door.

"Here you go – ready for Millie's signature," Sherri smiled fondly, "I love that woman – was so sad when she shut down her home. She used to bring in bribe material of the food variety – to enlist our cooperation" she giggled.

"Millie is, hands down, a great asset to our cause," Del agreed fervently, "and I'm more than ecstatic that she's agreed to run this transitional home for these two girls, whom she lost due to circumstances totally beyond her control."

"Brilliant idea, Miss Smarty Pants!" Sherri winked astutely.

"Well, it was a strategic meeting of minds." Del knew that Sherri was no fool and had come to some conclusions of her own. It was time.

"I have known where Amanda Goodchild has been for a couple of weeks now," She noted the lack of surprise in Sherri's expression. "She ran to Jessi, straight from the Millers, the morning of Gen's beating. I'm sorry to have kept you in the dark…"

"Please – no need to go there! I totally get it, and I trust implicitly that you have your reasons. Besides, the less I know, the better!"

"Exactly," Del heaved a sigh of relief, "I contacted Millie, who happened to know Jessi's whereabouts, and it went from there." Del pinned her with serious regard.

"That is pretty much the sum of what I can share and is exactly what I will update the files with once we have Millie's home operational and things are in place to protect the girls." She had left out Daisy's involvement and the details of the relevant physical locations. It would remain off-record – the element of danger, even for the unforeseeable future, was far too great.

The beauty of this arrangement was that the funding included around-the-clock house supervision. Daisy had already enlisted four of the biker gentlemen for the jobs. It was perfect – steady income and two of them were permanent residents at the motel – no longer transient. All would split their shifts to ensure one of them would be present, always.

Del had laughed at Daisy's description of the recruitment. There had been at least a dozen of them lined up and vying for the position, having devoted themselves unequivocally to the girls' protection. Most of these guys usually held security jobs – many as bouncers in the bars, and this was by far a step up in their eyes. There would be opportunities for the others as well, down the road. She had already put a bug in the ear of the program manager for some of their other transition homes. Daisy assured her that Joe was thoroughly selective with his tenants.

She decided to head over to Millie's – get this application submitted; ASAP, and with any luck, the red tape merry-go-round would release the permit within the next three weeks.

Reflecting on the protocol adherence required to be in place, as she negotiated the short drive, Del was satisfied that all was in good order. Millie was a perfect shoo-in for the program. Hell, the department jumped at the opportunity for stable homes and, in this case, had the benefit of a stellar foster care history in play. She'd be approved, Del was certain.

Millie ushered her in swiftly, clearly bothered, with something on her mind.

"I'll get us some tea – we need to talk," Millie shuffled off to the kitchen and quickly returned.

"Are the girls OK?" Del was a bit alarmed at her agitation.

"Yes, they are fine." She quickly nodded her reassurance, took a deep breath, and dove in.

"Daisy's boys have gotten to Jessi's pimp – apparently

worked him over pretty good." Worry was etched on Millie's features.

"How did this come about?" Del's mind was a whirling mass of confusion. Had he found Jessi and Mandy?

"Apparently, he's been checking out all the local, cheap motels, figuring Jessi may have found a way to hide out." Millie's teacup clattered against the saucer with a slight shake of her hand as she took a sip.

"We knew it was a likelihood that the johns had told her pimp about the second girl at Jessi's apartment – thank God they had never asked for her name," Millie sighed. "but they could well have figured that Mandy had money, and may be helping Jessi to hide – hence the motel search."

"Makes sense, go on!" Del was impatient for the outcome.

"For some reason, the slimy pimp, Russell, did not show up at the Sleep Eazy himself – sent another guy in his place, who talked to Joe." Millie took a breath. "He spun some story about how this girl, named Destiny, owed his boss a significant amount of money – had stolen it and run."

"Joe suggested to him that she likely would have picked a much nicer place if she did have all that cash, but the guy insisted that it would be less obvious to hide out in a dive like Joe's."

"Joe sent him packing, but not before he got a number to call *in case she showed up at the motel.* Meanwhile, the man had been stupid enough to hit on one of the biker's ladies in the parking lot, offering money for her services. She declined, of course, but the boys were understandably on board for a good thrashing."

This morning, Joe had one of them call that number, advising the fool that he may have a lead on her whereabouts. It was arranged to meet *the boss*, whom they correctly assumed was Russell, under the guise of leading him to Destiny's alleged location."

"Instead of Joe, Russell came face to face with about a half dozen bikers, who quickly herded him into a back alley and strategically coerced him to call in the motel visitor from the previous night. Once the man arrived, they beat the snot out of them both. Russell is apparently in bad shape. They told him they would kill him if he came near the place again."

"Holy shit!" Del's brain swirled with possible ramifications.

"My young neighbor confirmed it all – they are both in the hospital."

"So, Russell is not aware that the girls are at the motel, correct?"

"Apparently, he was given a clear message that the beating was on behalf of his cohort's harassment of one of their women. Of course, unbeknownst to the recipients, it was also in honor of Jessi and Mandy." Millie smiled sagely. "Daisy claims that the boys avoid violence whenever possible, but they know how to take care of business when necessary – clearly!"

"Joe also had a talk with the local police, who have plans to raid the building this evening." Millie took a deep breath. "It seems that Russell's convenient operation will be shut down permanently. Don't worry, at this point, the police have no knowledge of Mandy in this picture or of Jessi's whereabouts."

"The other girls…" Del began.

"Will be taken to shelters – no arrests or consequences."

"OK," Del sighed with relief, "Given that Jessi actually had nothing of Russell's, it might be safe to assume that he'll be willing to let it go now, even from the far reaches of a prison cell."

A swift knock and Daisy bustled through the door.

"I assume Millie filled you in?"

"Yes, I'm just trying to wrap my head around the girls' safety from here on in." Del sighed deeply.

"Russell is done," Daisy's tone was deadly, "the man will be lucky to walk straight, never mind sport an erection again, in this lifetime." She snickered. "I know - nasty! But if you knew…" her expression hardened, "suffice to say that the prick has had this coming for a long time."

"And his slimy accomplice – turns out to be one of the bastards that abused our girls the night they fled, according to a sniveling Russell, who was trying to weasel out of it all – blame it all on the other dickhead. So, a bit of justice is served."

"Jesus!" Del sank back into the loveseat and closed her eyes. "I am not sure I can maintain confidence in their safety, though I am grateful, Daisy, for the protection that you and Joe have secured."

"There's a reason Russell did not come to the motel himself," Daisy imparted with a sigh of resignation.

"Peter and I had a daughter – Julie." Daisy took a moment to collect herself, "she was beautiful – had everything going for her. When she was sixteen, she met Russell." Daisy's expression was bitter with the painful memories, "he was a very charismatic young man, wooing her with flowers and fancy words. Julie was completely smitten, and though we tried to limit the time she spent with him, it was to no avail." Daisy sniffed back tears.

"She would sneak out in the middle of the night to meet with him. We tried talking to them both – he was five years older and clearly more experienced in this world."

"We started noticing Julie's behavioral changes – moody, distant, agitated, failing grades and were terrified that she was doing drugs. As time went on, things escalated for the worse, and we caught her shooting up in the bathroom. All the treatments and interventions were fruitless – then one day, she came to us, distraught." Tears were trickling down her cheeks as she spoke softly, "Julie was pregnant, and the dirtbag had turned her away. Russell was making her turn tricks for the drugs and claimed he would not be responsible for any bastard of hers." She took a deep breath.

"We went to the police with no results. Unless Julie testified that she had been forced and confined, there could be no charges laid, and even if she did – it would come down to hearsay."

"Julie was despondent, and though we managed to get her into rehabilitation and off the drugs, she sank into a deep depression. We were helpless to change any of it – living a nightmare. We just wanted to give our baby the life she deserved, but our Julie was gone.

"One day, Peter forced the lock on her bedroom door and found her – she'd slit her wrists and took her own life. We lost both her and our grandchild that day. Then, six months later, Peter lost his will to carry on and chose to leave this life as well." Daisy was shaking with wracking sobs.

Del and Millie enwrapped her in their arms, knowing that this comfort only went so far in alleviating the awful painful memories. Daisy finally pulled away and smiled, patting their arms.

"It was twenty years ago now – seems like forever, yet it still has the power to totally gut me."

"Anyhow, Russell will stay away for good now – times are different; the pimps often pay the piper - if there's proof, and with our two brilliant girls willing to testify, along with a host of others, he's powerless. Russell is but a small-time parasite – operates pretty much solo."

Del collected Millie's signature and headed to the office to submit an electronic copy, along with the standard screening forms to accompany it. She had never felt more exhausted from working a case.

Heading home, she reflected on her current state. While Jack had been in the picture, there was no question of keeping things bottled up; they had shared it all – ranted and vented properly. Tonight was a night for a confidential. But damn it to hell – there was no one with whom she could confide in.

Settling in front of her crackling fireplace with a cup of hot tea and a blanket, she sighed and laid her head back on the cushion. Did she want another love relationship in her life? It would surely assuage her loneliness, but that was a poor reason to seek it out. No, her life was far too complicated right now.

A tearjerker movie was what the doctor would order! She settled on an old favorite – *Terms of Endearment*. Deeply immersed in her choice of escape, she laughed along with the humorous antics and reflected on how life's tough pills went down a little smoother, with a good dose of hilarity. But when the tragic climax hit – and Emma died, Del sobbed like a baby, knowing that the source of her tears ran far deeper than this story.

It was a while before she crawled under the covers, thoroughly drained from her emotional outpour but feeling somewhat lighter from the release.

Tomorrow was another day.

Chapter Twenty-Seven

"Hit me!"

Jeff groaned – an ace. I had a queen face-up and took his last nickel with the win! I chortled with glee at his mock move to strangle me.

The diner was slow, so we managed an entire hour to chill on our break. It was Victoria Day weekend, and many of the regular patrons were away or with family.

"Next time..." Bree smiled as she shoveled her meager coinage over to me – I had fronted her so she could join in. The three of us often managed a game or two but rarely had a chance to finish when the diner was in full swing. Daisy breezed over and sat with us.

"Hey, can I ask a favor on your way home – I'll let you go thirty minutes earlier?" She addressed me.

"Sure!"

Truth be told, I would do anything for the woman. Without her, my life would be the same nightmare that I had always known. Millie had shared Daisy's story with us, insisting that we promise to never bring it up. Hell, I would never want to cause her pain. I couldn't help thinking about Jessi – her fate may have mirrored Julie's if not for the street smarts that Jessi had necessarily accumulated and the intervention of Daisy. I shook it off.

"I need to drop off some documents to my lawyer – it's a few blocks out of your way." She regarded me apologetically. "There are some urgent calls that I need to attend to that just can't wait."

After assuring her it was no big deal, I returned to the kitchen and worked on automatic, grating cheese and zucchini for Jeff's awesome fritters – normally a brunch fare, he'd incorporated it as an appetizer, into the dinner menu.

Daisy and I had chatted about my future hours at the diner, and she was totally on board with the suggestions I had laid out, adding that any extra hours I might want on the weekend were totally available. I had been jumping at those and had already stuffed a fair amount of cash under our mattress. I was always up for a shift. Hell, the work was enjoyable! How many people could say that in this life?

Prep work done, I set out to the lawyer's office. It was on a busy street, where old, sturdier brick buildings, in recent years, had undergone a facelift, creating a modern, convenient professional district. A friendly receptionist took the envelope, and I carried on.

My route included back-tracking a bit, and rather than take the main streets, I decided on a few shortcuts through the buildings. It would shave ten minutes off my trek. Soon, I emerged from the last alley to the opposite end of the street to the motel, from where I usually walked.

Without warning, I was roughly grabbed from behind, my arms ruthlessly and immediately immobilized with a strong rope. A meaty, filthy hand covered my mouth, rendering my screams of outrage totally ineffective.

What the fuck? My heart was blasting through my chest, and terror filled every fiber of my being. Why the hell had I let my guard down? Protection, my ass! If I could only scream loud enough – it would probably be a far different outcome.

There were two of them, now dragging me back into the dismal, shadowy alley. The beefy guy cursed as my teeth dug into his hand while he was securing a gag. A ringing blow to my head shook my senses, and I fought to stay conscious. Who the fuck were they? A sack was thrown over my head, and though I kicked with all my might, I was blind; they managed to shepherd me into some sort of vehicle.

"She's a feisty one for sure!"

My heart dropped into my stomach – I knew that voice from our altercation at the motel. He was *some kind of stupid* to risk another run-in with the bikers. Was he one of Russel's associates?

"Yeah, it's a shame that her days are numbered," the other

sneered, "but we'll get our share first, I promise you that."

Paralyzing panic flooded me – Paul Miller!

It all came back to me now – the beefy guy had stopped by the house one night; I had only gotten a fleeting glimpse. But he must have recognized me at the motel! Fuck! I couldn't stop the trembling, which quickly escalated into violent shudders.

As the van – I figured out by the floor space, started to move, I tried to memorize the route they were taking and, somehow, burn it firmly into my memory. Dread flooded every cell in my body – what the hell good would that do? I would be dead before I could ever chance to escape. I knew now how dangerous the man was. Fuck!

I wasn't sure yet who was driving, but it was fast and jerky. My body slammed back and forth against opposite ends of the van, shooting shards of pain throughout. I inhaled as deeply as possible – slow breaths…I needed to think. No way in hell was I going to go down like this! Especially now – with all the good things I had going on. More than ever, I had a reason to fight!

The van stopped, and my stomach lurched. They moved away, and I couldn't hear their words, but a certain stench permeated the stuffy air. I should recognize it! The silence was almost deafening. The only sounds were of chirping birds and buzzing insects. I pushed back a hysterical giggle at the irony of such a peaceful setting for this horrific nightmare!

They were moving closer again – I held my breath.

"What about the other one? She probably knows about you."

"Yeah, but she doesn't know where we are – we'll get her later on." The cruel guffaw made me ill.

No, not Jessi too! Think, think…my mind whirled.

The doors jerked open – a cargo van – and I was dragged painfully across the ground. I made a note that it was earthy – long field grass? My breath was knocked out as they flung me ruthlessly a few yards away. I heard them rummaging through something.

"Here! Use this one – not quite as scummy."

Suddenly, I was picked up by the burly one and thrown back into the van, now on top of some stench-filled pad – I suspected it to be on an old mattress. He quickly hopped in and further secured my hands to the wall of the van, binding my feet with more rope. I could not stop the whimpers of fear, and he laughed mercilessly, fondling me savagely.

They closed the doors and left me there. My sense of hearing was on overdrive, taking note of every little move they made. Another vehicle engine started – I tried to determine what make and model it could be. There were more undecipherable words – some vehement – in apparent disagreement, and then doors slammed. As the vehicle took off, I knew that I should welcome the abandonment, but I was frozen in terror.

Hell, it was not as if I could move anyhow, but the feeling of helplessness was amplified by the terrifying claustrophobia taking over my sanity. What if they left me to die here like this? My inner screams threatened to completely obliterate all of my senses.

Get a grip! Get a grip! I dragged air through my nostrils, forcing myself to calm down, but I still couldn't seem to get enough. I needed to keep my mind busy!

OK, first off – it was likely that they would return. Bile churned in my stomach at their words – *they would get their share first*. And Jessi – oh my God! What if they brought her here, too? It was all on me! I couldn't bear to think of them killing us both. No…don't go there!

Where the hell was I? It was clearly in a wooded, remote location. And now, I knew – amidst rotting garbage all around. The burning smell indicated to me that it was likely a dump site. Nausea once again threatened at the thought of the filthy mattress under me.

But this was good, right? How many refuse sites would be within fifteen or so minutes of the city? Not hard to trace! A little voice niggled - *assuming that you had the chance to alert anyone.* Fuck that! Couldn't afford the negativity. Think!

By now, Jessi would be wondering where I was and hopefully check in with Daisy. If I could just lose this gag, at least I'd be able to breath. Of course, I had to somehow get this sack off my head first. I realized that the stupid buffoon had secured my hands but not my positioning, and my legs, though bound, were free to move – at least together.

Though it robbed me of precious air, I shuffled my body while pulling with my arms and managed to get into a sitting position with my arms behind me. The pain was excruciating due to the angle that was necessary. Now – how to get at the sack? I couldn't bend over very far, but if I shifted a bit sideways, I might be able to walk my feet onto the wall of the van. The body twist would be brutal, but with knees bent, I could maybe reach with my head.

Oh God – breathe through the pain…there! I needed to break for a minute, but I was now able to shuffle myself closer to my feet and thereby bend my knees. It felt like every bone in my body would surely snap, but finally, my head made contact. I knew I couldn't stay in this position for long, though. Frantically, I rubbed my face against my knees, over and over, until it was raw.

There! I had it – the sack slipped away, and I blinked, even in the darkness of the van. Holy crap! I'd managed it! Oh, I knew it wasn't freedom yet, but it sure lent a measure of confidence to what

I might accomplish! I looked around now, with my eyes adjusting to the dim light. What a fucking pigsty! There must be something useful in this mess!

My wrists were screaming for relief, but I needed to stay this way while I surveyed my surroundings. There! In the corner, just within my reach, was a rusty nail protruding from a rotting two-by-four. I could shift so that my feet were close enough, but what then? Discouragement was a poison that I desperately needed to fight against.

I would find a way. Exhaustion set in, and I surrendered. For a time, I drifted in and out of awareness, honoring my mind and body's need for respite from the trauma, the impossible situation that I was facing.

Images of Jessi swam before me, rousing my consciousness. Were they after her now? I embraced the silence, terrified of the implications should they return.

But Jessi was smart! At this point, my absence would have all of her cautionary measures in full tune. A tiny thread of hope slipped through, knowing that Daisy's boys would also be searching.

Chapter Twenty-Eight

"We got him!"

Del was shaking with the implication. Paul Miller - rather, Everett Richards, was going down!

"What's happening?" Sherri burst into the tiny office space.

"Sherri, the little locket is our key to putting that asshole away for good!"

"Were you able to find the owner, then?"

"Better than that!" Del took a deep breath. "On a whim, I managed to contact the Miller's foster child's mother, whom they had taken her from due to a drug overdose. Though she remains an addict, living on the streets, the mother is understandably a mess, with her daughter's whereabouts currently unknown." Del's expression clouded.

"Bittersweet justice – the poor woman is about to find out that her daughter has been identified as the remains of the young murdered girl." She released a deep, troubled sigh.

"I know, I know – back up, Del," she verbally chided herself, "I took the little locket to the mother, hoping that it belonged to her daughter. Indeed, she had given it to the little girl on her last birthday before her disappearance." Del paused.

"I then contacted the lead homicide detective in the deceased girl's case, and we compared notes. Apparently, there was a chain found on the girl's remains that matches the link on the locket – it had been ripped away at some point, and the trauma on the links match." Another deep breath.

"I dropped it off to be included as possible evidence." Del leaned forward and pinned her assistant with a burning stare.

"Sherri, there were fingerprints on both the locket and the chain, matching Everett Richards! All of this unequivocally ties the Miller's foster child to the girl's remains." Del was excited now.

"Furthermore, the detective confirmed that the cause of death was a homicide. Of course, we had already tipped them off to the fact that Paul Miller and Everett Richards are one and the same. Granted, that alone does not constitute solid proof of the murder…" She sighed her frustration.

"Another problem is that we have no idea where the man is," Sherri contributed.

Del's cell buzzed – it was Daisy. She nodded at Sherri apologetically.

"Hey, how are things?"

"Mandy is missing. She should have been home more than an hour ago, and Jessi is beside herself!" Daisy paused. "Del, it is my fault – I sent her off course on the way home on an errand."

"Don't go there, Daisy – we have no idea what happened yet." Del's mind was whirling, thoughts flying into her head in a frenzied jumble. "I'll be right over - I have things to share."

Del filled Sherri in and headed straight to the diner. How on earth had this happened? The security was solid. But she had to acknowledge that it couldn't be everywhere. OK – no getting ahead of yourself here! Mandy could be anywhere. Maybe she just stopped off to shop, on her way. Del headed straight for the little office to find a sobbing Jessi with Daisy.

"Hey, we will find her," Del took the teen in a comforting embrace, but the look she exchanged with Daisy spoke of fear and trepidation.

"I contacted the lawyer's office, who said she left there at approximately 3:45 – it's past 5:00 now. Mandy should have reached the motel just before 4:00," Daisy reasoned. "The boys are scouting the area for any clues, with a couple watching for her return."

"You said that Russell operated alone? But what if…"

"I know, I've wracked my brains on that one," Daisy looked miserable, "but we've kept a vigil on that man, especially when he had this sweet girl in his clutches," Daisy squeezed Jessi, "and I'm pretty certain that there is no one acting on his behalf. The only connection that the other beating victim had with Russell is his status as a john." Daisy took a breath.

"The man has come clean – out of necessity, and for now, has pleaded that the police keep it under wraps for the sake of his wife and family." Daisy threw Del a derisive grin.

"His story mirrors that of the girls'," she confirmed, "and he has admitted his weakness toward illicit sexual diversions. He was furious over the girls' disappearance because he had a pretty good set-up for a good price." Daisy sneered.

"However, it will all soon come out because he'll be charged, not only with unlawful solicitation – in addition, rape, assault and battery, which will most likely earn him a healthy prison term."

"In any case," Daisy huffed out her frustration, "I'm pretty confident that Russel is not behind this."

Del felt a chill permeate her spine as she related all the developments on Everett Richards and the findings of the police investigation into the murdered girl. They somehow needed solid evidence!

"My gut is telling me that Everett Richards is behind this, though I can't imagine how." Daisy emitted a troubled sigh.

"Well, let's review this." Del eyed both of them, "Other than Russell's attempt to find you, Jessi, and the two deadbeats who approached you at the motel that night, is there anything else you can think of that might ring a bell?"

"No…" Jessi trembled and forcibly reigned in her tears, "I mean…we are young chicks, so we get ogled all the time. And both of us are tuned in, you know? We are always aware of what's going on around us."

"What about in the diner?" Daisy suggested, "Anything at all that might give you pause to wonder? Had Mandy mentioned anything?"

"No, but your clientele is pretty tame – predictable and stable." Jessi shook her head. "Of course, I'm not there when Mandy is working – but she's in the kitchen, right?" It was rhetorical, and the women fell silent.

"There was maybe something…" Jessi mused, "Those two dudes who harassed us that night," she looked at them both now with a shred of hope in her gaze.

"Mandy said something that I think we both shrugged off," she continued, "the burly guy gave her the creeps, almost like she'd had a run-in with him before." Jessi drew in a shaky breath, "but Mandy laughed it off, saying that he probably just reminded her of some badass from the past."

Daisy immediately picked up the phone and waited, a determined gleam in her eyes.

"Yes, Buck, I need you here at the diner." She rang off and took a deep breath. "My boys are nothing if not thorough, so let's take a breather for a moment – get a coffee."

It was impossible to put aside their worry, and all three women sighed audibly as Buck sat down at the booth. Daisy wasted no time.

"The two guys you confronted at the motel that night – do you have any leads on their identities?"

"Unfortunately, I have no idea who they are, but we did tail them separately after they parted ways on the street."

Oh my God! This was incredible! Del wanted to throw herself at him in a monster hug as he continued.

"The obvious addict was tracked to a known drug house on Hastings, and the brick-shit-house dude, to a run-down home about ten blocks further down the road. We have a screenshot of the plate number on an old blue Ford pickup that was parked in the drive – 90s vintage," he hesitated, eyeing them all with a good measure of empathy.

Del noted there was something else in his demeanor…tenacity – that was it – he had every intention of following through, like a dog with a bone. She was duly impressed and ever appreciative of his intervention. Jessi sat erect beside her, melting into silent sobs, unable to speak at that moment, but gratitude shone through as she regarded Buck.

"You are welcome, little lady," her hand was lost within his as he reached out, in a comforting grip of reassurance, "Whatever it takes, we will find Mandy." He exchanged a long look with Daisy and was gone.

Chapter Twenty-Nine

Oh, Sweet Jesus! My bladder finally let go at the sound of the approaching vehicle. It was an old truck, I knew – recognizing the pistons and carburetor noise. My newfound confidence bled into the waves of panic that were currently assaulting me – and I froze in place.

Fuck! He'll be royally pissed at my current state – especially without the sack. God, did they have Jessi? I prayed not and listened intently for any indication as the doors slammed in the distance. I could hear their mumbles, escalating to some form of argument. There was no sound of a struggle, so perhaps they hadn't picked her up yet?

My mind raced. I knew that they didn't dare go near the motel – the burly guy had received the message, loud and clear, from our protectors. Would they be brazened enough to watch the place, though – track Jessi's movements to the spice shop or the diner?

Through the panic, I reasoned that it didn't matter who had taken me. Daisy would ensure that Jessi was well-protected now. Please let that be so…

Suddenly, the truck door slammed, and the vehicle peeled out. Relief flooded me, though I knew it was a momentary reprieve – I relaxed against my bonds, not caring about the biting pain.

Creak…the van doors suddenly opened, and I screamed in terror, though no one could hear me through the sickening gag. But I could see him – and wished to hell that I hadn't removed the damn sack. I whimpered like a baby as he slowly climbed in, and for the life of me, I could not tear my frightened gaze away from the cruel sneer on his face. I knew my fear was palpable and would fuel his violent lust.

He tore off my clothing with ruthless yanks – for once, not seeming to care about my shameful incontinence. His eyes seared my flesh as they roamed over me – with devil's intent. I gagged. He smiled – he had me just where he wanted me.

"Girlie, you and I are going to have some fun today," he fondled me roughly, "and this time, we are in no rush," he wheedled, pinching ruthlessly, "no fucking Gen to whine and spy on us," he moved further down, "no Goddamn time limits at all," he unzipped his filthy jeans and sat back, chortling.

"Oh, I promised my buddy that I'd wait, but what's a little secret, between you and me, going to hurt," he murmured, "and I've been waiting for this moment – yearning for it ever since you fled the house. I've thought of nothing else – you are such a tempting little whore. I could not help myself around you – your steamy little body, begging for me – aching for me! Hell, I'll bet you're even ready right now! You get the benefit of a man who's been deprived of female delights for a long while now – with that whore, Gen, out of commission."

His evil snicker sent shivers of revulsion down my spine. He ceased his self-fondling and eyed me speculatively.

"You sure are a damn sight more delectable than the last scrawny little foster whore bitch – didn't even have any tits yet," he licked his lips, and his eyes glazed over, "but, oh, Nikki was delicious – virgin too! I gave it to her good – and she'll never be able to tell on me anymore, not from where she ended up – no longer of this earth. But with you, I plan to extend the delights before you get to greet her."

His cruel guffaw sent my stomach into heaving spasms! He had killed her, then! I wanted to rip his eyes out and castrate him right there, with my teeth, if necessary. My impotence was a poison, choking my soul! Now, he regarded me with ruthless purpose.

"Have to go slow – extend this pleasure. You are one lucky bitch – I have kept you around for much longer than intended – longer than I should have. Not overly wise, perhaps, but you are like a drug! So feisty and clever. Look at you, managing to unmask yourself." He looked into my eyes with admiration.

"But that, unfortunately, was a stupid move on your part." His gaze held deadly intent. "Sealed your fate now." The sickening grin was back. "However, you'll first get the benefit of my carnal administrations – trust me, my friends will pale in comparison," he shrugged in mock apology, "I would remove the gag to allow your moans and groans of ecstasy, their due freedom," he sniggered, "however, your teeth are a formidable weapon – I'm in no mood for pain today."

I wriggled against my restraints in a desperate and useless ploy for escape. He smiled slowly.

"Oh, I know you want it desperately. But the anticipation will increase the pleasure – tenfold!"

He resumed the disgusting stroking, and his eyes roved hungrily over my naked body. I closed my own as his breathing became heavier, and his disgusting moans filled my ears – seeming to bounce off the walls of the van to molest every part of me.

OK – I had been through worse with him before. This was not new. My inner pep talk did little to assuage the horror as he moved over me now, straddling me. Though the violence was somehow less than usual, it did nothing to lessen the dread and disgust as he began the onslaught.

I willed myself gone, detached from the entire experience. Intuition guided me toward caution – I made all the moves of awareness, including the pleas for mercy and whimpering that he so craved. That, too, was not forced – God knows how fucking horrible his rape and torture were to endure, but I had another world now, apart from him. One he could never fucking touch!

With the absence of his buddy, Paul's excitement grew to alarming proportions, and as darkness loomed, with a sickening dread, I resigned myself to the reality that he would continue the merciless molestation; three more times that night before he finally passed out beside me. At some point, I had managed my escape – manifesting Jessi's essence into my arms.

I lay there in the dark, softly weeping and trying to ignore the grotesque snoring that was aggravated by his increased imbibement of alcohol. He was a dangerous man, and I knew that my every move would determine my outcome if there was to be any hope at all for survival.

Where the hell was Burly Dude?

Miraculously, I managed to drift off and woke to shreds of morning light, peeking in through the filthy back window and rusted-out holes in the side of the van. My arms were completely numb, and I desperately needed water.

Moving my head to check on him, I found the asshole wide awake and regarding me curiously. I fought back a wave of nausea at the sight of him and moved against my restraints.

"Well, now. Sleeping Beauty has roused."

The putrid smell of alcohol nearly made me vomit as he

came closer. I knew he had been shocked, as I had mentally escaped with Jessi during the abhorrent assault, abandoning my resistance to his filthy acts upon me. Watching the speculative gleam in his eyes now, it was apparent that he was thoroughly unsure of what to do with it.

"Well, too bad for you that I'm all out of steam for now, but later, we can resume our delightful activity. Right now, I gotta piss and get you some water." He jumped out of the van and returned with the promised hydration, holding it in front of me mercilessly. At my whimper, he relented.

"All right, I'll lift the gag, but if you bite me – you'll regret it." His tone was menacing as he allowed me to drink liberally from the water bottle. It was pure heaven! He sat back on his haunches and studied me.

"You know, we might be able to give you a little leeway if you promise to behave. There are other, more beguiling reasons to leave the gag off," his eyes took on a lustful gleam, "and with your obvious lack of struggle last night," he licked his lips, "I find myself craving the sounds of your lewd little moans and groans." He smiled wickedly.

"Hell, I may even lengthen the rope a little – let you get the blood flow back into your arms, so you can squirm and pretend to fight properly then," he nodded, "but first, we need to move to a new location. Something's up; the useless prick is not answering his cell."

With that, he hopped out and started the van. I estimated only five minutes on the move as he parked again. This time, I took careful note of the tree line as we went. He got out, and though he was out of my sight, I heard him shuffling around a bit. I had no idea what he was up to but entirely welcomed the break from his nauseating presence. I closed my eyes and miraculously managed to drift off.

Chapter Thirty

Del was frantic, waiting to hear. Had they gone back to the house, where the truck was parked? Did they see the son-of-a-bitch? Intuition screamed that it was their sole hope of finding Mandy!

Daisy had warned the boys to use extreme caution – they couldn't afford to tip the man off. And if they were lucky – he would take them straight to her. They also needed to ensure that they didn't beat the crap out of the dicks, in order to avoid jeopardizing any criminal charges and proceedings. She had chuckled as she talked with Del about it.

"My boys know exactly how to scare the living shit out of the toughest dudes without harming a hair on their bodies."

Del nearly jumped out of her skin at the chime of her cell and picked up immediately.

"We meet at Millie's. Can you be there in ten?"

"Absolutely!" Del's hands were shaking with anticipation as she rushed out the door. She had not even managed to snag one wink of sleep through the night, terrified at the possible outcomes, but exhaustion could come later. She willfully pushed the images from her brain – Mandy lying in a ditch, brutally assaulted and murdered. She knew with certainty now that Everett Richards would likely do just that if he got his hands on her.

The four women settled in around Millie's kitchen table, coffee in hand, as they waited for Buck. Jessi had stayed the night and would do so until they found Mandy.

Millie ushered the gentle giant of a man – Del's astute assessment of Buck - into her home with a quick hug of gratitude. He pulled up an extra chair and joined them.

"I know you are all anxious for information," he regarded Jessi with tenderness in his gaze, "but we haven't found Mandy yet." He put his hand up to continue.

"We do have a constant tail on the truck now," he sighed, "it wasn't there until later in the day, and we've since followed the man three times to a parking lot close to the motel." He pinned them with a purposeful gaze.

"As we speak, the man has a vigil down the road from there – we assume he's watching for you, Jessi." He looked imploringly into her eyes. "It's imperative that you stay here." Jessi nodded her agreement and Buck heaved a sigh of relief.

"We've searched the plate number on the truck and traced the owner – one Harry Watts, and discovered that he is employed at the same company as Paul Miller." At the ladies' reactive gasps of fear, he forged ahead.

"Turns out, both men served time in prison together, though

Harry's sentence was much lighter, and he's been out for several years now – likely managed to get Everett Richards this job under the alias of Paul Miller."

"Thank you, Buck," Daisy found her voice, "this is good progress – at least we know for sure who we are dealing with now."

"OK, we will not let that truck out of our sight – our hope is to follow it straight to Mandy." He smiled at them gently. "Don't lose faith, ladies – we will find her. There are three of us on the watch today – I need to get back to my post."

Buck gave Jessi's shoulder a gentle squeeze as he made his way to the door, and she suddenly jumped up and ran over to him, immediately melting into his warm, comforting embrace. He kissed her gently on the forehead and was gone.

Del regarded the strain on the faces around the table and wondered how in hell they were going to endure the waiting. But it was all they could do now. They had decided not to contact the police just yet to avoid impeding complications and the possibility that if Richards got wind of it, the danger would escalate to a fatal outcome for Mandy. Truth be told, Del held infinitely more trust in Daisy's boys than the police.

So, what did she know about Everett Richards? His previous behaviors? Certainly, he was a deadly threat. This was amplified by his apparent instability – taking significant risks with his criminal activities. Del speculated on his penchant for drawing out the precarious behavior. How many times had he abused Gen, knowing that one day, she may full well decide to turn his ass in. Was he really that gullible to believe she'd remain loyal? And at least two of the young women that he'd raped and tortured – he'd kept around for his evil sexual exploitation; for an extended period of time – even risking the consequences from their possible escapes.

Del knew in her gut – Everett Richards was not gullible or stupid. He was quite simply and unpredictably volatile – unable to control his compulsions toward violence and sexual deviancy. This played in their favor. After all, he was convicted once, right?

"Let's assume that Mandy is alive," Del regarded them all solemnly, "We know that he is sadistic and cruel, and while that is horrific, to say the least, history tells us that he gets morbid delight in torturing and playing with his victims." At Jessi and Millie's renewed tears, Del continued.

"Mandy is tough – we know that," Del heaved a sigh, "She's dealt with his abuse already and knows what to expect – how he ticks and how to handle him." She motioned for them to put their hands together on the table.

"Mandy deserves our faith in her!" They all nodded emphatically and squeezed each other's hands in affirmation.

"Besides," Del continued, "we have a distinct advantage – Everett Richards has no idea yet that the police have evidence enough to tie the murdered child to him and perhaps lock him away for the rest of his life."

Chapter Thirty-One

"What the fuck are you telling me here?"

I was jerked awake by Paul Miller – Everett Richards' – raging rant to someone on the other end of his cell.

"What do you mean, she's not fucking there? You must have missed her, you idiot!"

Jessi! They must be talking about her! Good girl, Jess – you are smarter than these stupid assholes! I gained a measure of satisfaction from this development, even through the fear of my own precarious predicament.

"Well, get your ass back here! We need to deal with this one – can't wait any longer," he spewed, "and remember - we are on the next road in, to the south, now. Make damn sure you aren't followed!" He cussed liberally as he cut the call.

I braced myself – knowing how his anger would fuel the violence. My next strategy had my gut rolling in disgust. He was about to be seduced. It was a risk, I knew – he had an insatiable lust for the power he gained through my fear. However, it was a delicate balance. His attraction to my strength and resistance – my furious fight – was equally alluring for him, and I needed to find that sweet spot.

First and foremost, it required that I disarm the anger.

The doors flew open. My heart dropped to my toes – the glaze of unbridled violent lust in his eyes had me gulping in the air – calming breaths! I never broke eye contact as I began to whimper a little. A crazed grin marked his face, and he climbed in, inching closer. I let the natural tremors of fear induce his excitement.

"I have to wait for that asshole partner of mine, but," his eyes moved down my body, "we are going to have a little fun along the way." I pushed down the vomit as he licked his lips and groaned. He dropped his pants to reveal the evidence of his readiness and straddled me.

He paused, staring intently down into my face and whipped a pocket knife out of the jeans that were now down around his knees. He severed the gag with one swift motion. I gulped in blessed air, and his eyes gleamed.

Next, he reached up and worked to loosen the rope that held my bound hands flush to the van's wall. I cried out with intense pain from the sudden blood rush and was sickened by the feel of his further excitement.

"Oh, sweet little whore, I wonder if I dare release your wrists - yes, you are a hellcat, but I find that I'm quite in for the fight."

This, I wasn't expecting, and my mind raced, trying to incorporate it into my plan of action. I needed to factor in that soon, there'd be two of them, and the burly guy was particularly intimidating.

"Fight you will, and then you'll surrender," he began to fondle my body, and his breathing increased, "just as you did last night!"

Suddenly, my hands were mobile, but he immediately locked them in an iron grip above my head, continuing his brutal exploration with the other hand, leaving no part of me untouched. Just as I thought that he would lose control, he moved back, panting and groaning deeply, but stopped abruptly when the rumble of an engine signalled the truck's return.

"Fuck, damn it! Fuck the bastard!" He scrambled back into his pants, cursing a blue streak. "Only fucking time I can count on that piece of shit to be punctual." He gazed down at me - the crazed gleam of lust still burning in his eyes.

I didn't dare move! Directly behind him, within my vision, was the board, armed with a protruding nail, rusty and sharp. While Richards gathered his wits and gained some control, I considered the uses for this possible weapon.

Unfortunately, its length was compromised by the thickness of the two-by-four, so any penetration, even if I should be so lucky as to push one of the men onto the board, would likely do minimal damage and only serve to escalate the peril from their ensuing rage.

The ominous slam of the truck door sent panic flooding through my bones. Fuck! They were about to thoroughly ravage me and then kill me – leave me there to rot like the trash! What was I thinking? That I would be successful in single-handedly taking them down? I knew from other murder cases I'd read about – the killing frenzy would incite them to commit unspeakable atrocities upon my body before the mercy of death.

I whimpered in my terror as the burly dude showed up and climbed in. I gagged as he immediately began to undress; both men were now fully ready to take the next step. I lost my fight to hold back the tears and screeches as they reached for my body, touching me everywhere.

"Unbind her legs," the burly dude suggested, "so much more we can enjoy that way," he grinned suggestively, "judging by the state of my friend here," he eyed Richards with a lewd grin, "you haven't recently satiated his appetite."

What the fuck did I have to lose? I kicked with both legs as hard as I could, one of them sending Richards flying backwards and the other landing square in the crotch of the big guy. I screamed in terror as Richards came off the board with a look of raging incredulity, glancing at the blood on the nail.

I scrambled into a ball in the corner of the van as Richards slowly advanced toward me. The burly dude was still retching and curled in a ball on the floor but was eyeing me with deadly intent while screaming obscenities. I blubbered pleas for mercy as Richards grabbed me and roughly threw me down on the mattress, rattling every bone in my body.

His lust was all-consuming now – the rage palpable. The first blow to my face rendered me senseless as he immediately took savage possession of me. I screamed as the burly dude swam into my vision just behind him, hell-bent on the same.

Jessi, Jessi – please come. I called out in my mind – and she appeared, as always. My saving grace, holding me close and safe, in her arms – trying to protect me. I was aware of intense pain, but there wasn't a damn thing they could do to me now that could drag me away from here. At that moment, I prayed for the mercy of death – because I knew I would no longer be able to meet Jessi on this level in our earthly existence. They had already broken me. But damn it - I'd given it everything that I had.

I'm so sorry, Jessi!

Chapter Thirty-Two

Del hung on to Jessi as tightly as she could. Daisy was talking on the phone with Buck.

"OK, we will wait here." She rang off and came to help. Jessi was thrashing wildly against Del – intent on going with Buck and the boys to find Mandy.

"Stop!" Daisy thundered, and Jessi collapsed against them, sobbing uncontrollably. "There's not a damn thing you could hope to accomplish, save for get in their way – it's too critical to risk it." Millie opened her arms and drew Jessi over to the loveseat, cradling her in a loving embrace.

"So, Buck had the boys plant a tracking device under the truck," it was a recap – they had all heard Buck on speaker, "and followed safely behind. About a half-hour ago, the truck stopped at a remote location near the Vancouver Transfer Station." She took a deep, calming breath.

"Our boys are parked about a half-mile from there. Buck and five others are trekking in through a deeply wooded area as we speak." Daisy eyed the worried faces around her.

"This is good, everyone!" Del hung firmly onto her conviction that Everett Richards was not yet finished with Mandy. "The fact that they are still out there speaks to her survival thus far."

As soon as the boys managed the rescue and had the situation under control, Del would call the detective at the police station. He would likely be thoroughly miffed that she hadn't called him in sooner, but she'd found him to be a reasonable guy and was pretty certain that she'd gain his collaboration.

All they could do for now was wait. The guys were equipped with blankets and extra clothing for Mandy – no one had any idea what to expect.

The four of them yearned to be allowed closer to the site – to be there for Mandy when she was finally freed. Del knew that each of them battled their own level of fear for her. Her heart went out, specifically to Jessi. The two girls had survived so much trauma together – creating a bond like none other. If the unspeakable should happen, it would be a long road to recovery for Jessi.

No matter what the outcome – how sad or successful it was, Del needed to focus on the global perspective. It looked like a wrap! They were about to apprehend one evil man – Everett Richards, a.k.a. Paul Miller. This would literally save the lives of who knows how many other children? And secure justice for the parents of lost babies.

Del wondered about Gen Miller. True – she had reaped what she'd sown, but it wasn't that simple. No person would choose that life if they had faith in a better, alternate pathway. There are so many inner demons and insecurities driving one's choices. An old adage – *we are one decision away from the gutter* – came to mind. In her profession, Del had witnessed that reality firsthand. She made a mental note to connect with Gen once they found her.

They all jumped at Daisy's cell chime. She put it immediately on speaker.

"We are at the perimeter of the site now – we are about to move in," Buck's voice was low volume, "Jessi, we've got her – she's alive." The line went dead.

"OK," Daisy heaved an emotional sigh, "we won't hear from him again until it's secure." Jessi broke down in renewed sobbing.

Del was thankful he'd taken the time and risk to affirm her survival. She knew they would all hold their breaths until the next call. Then Del would be busy with the police. It could take some time – caution was key. Every step the boys took could mean the difference between life and death for Mandy. If Richards and his cohort were alerted – if the boys moved in just a shade too quickly – one swift movement with a knife could make for a tragic outcome. But Del had faith in them!

Chapter Thirty-Three

What the fuck? Reality slammed into me, intense pain and terror, as a grand commotion ensued around me. Confusion rendered me senseless, and I was unable to figure out what was happening. I could hear pathetic whimpers and wailing from somewhere. I was stunned to realize that it was coming from me.

I was cognizant of the fact that I'd been momentarily freed from the horrific assault and began shuddering uncontrollably. So damn cold! Grunts and groans assailed my auditory perception, and it finally hit me! My attackers were under siege, themselves. I recognized Buck's voice and a few of the other bikers and slowly slid into myself – into a place of refuge. I figured I was safe, physically. My mental state was an entirely different story.

I was vaguely aware of being covered – a warm blanket? Someone picked me up, cradled me into their arms and carried me to…somewhere…I was gone again – in a cocoon.

It was a long-forgotten but familiar haven - still under construction, and I immersed in the memory of having begun the build when I was still a toddler. It was a place that I'd had a critical need for at that time – to escape and rest, to die. Now, it required sturdier walls – I was much older and bigger, with a horrific history of prophecy-fulfilled realities.

Pain stabbed me unmercifully, launching me rudely out of the warm refuge. I was pissed about that and fought against it, but its intensity held me captive.

"It's OK," a gentle assurance from Brad, one of the younger biker dudes that I remembered. "You are going to be OK – you are alive, and we got these fuckers – they are going down!"

I focused on his face – he was still holding me, and the compassion and comfort in his eyes were my undoing. I began to bawl like a baby, and he murmured affectionate words of consolation – over and over until I cried it out through a ruthless veil of intense pain.

All around me was an activity – guys on their phones, barking orders – I heard them talking with 911, and Buck came over to relate, as best he could, my condition to the operator.

I was stunned at his description – facial lacerations and serious wounds to various parts of my body, some of which he related from memory, refusing to expose me to the indignity of removing the warm blanket, which would have been necessary, to inspect my naked body.

"I think she has at least one separated joint – shoulder, and possibly pelvic – definitely trauma there." He paused with a catch in his voice. "Her pulse is good, though a tad fast, and her breathing is unrestricted, but she displays signs of intense pain when we move her, so perhaps some broken ribs? And, of course, she's in shock – we are keeping her warm."

Buck met Brad's eyes as he walked out of earshot, keeping the line with 911 open as per protocol. I began to survey my surroundings and winced heavily as Brad gently settled us both down into a bed of spruce branches that someone had ingeniously prepared. He smiled gently, keeping me on his lap.

Suddenly, I spotted them – off to the side, by one of the biker's vehicles – some kind of SUV. They were both fully confined, bound by ropes and chains around their wrists and ankles, perched none-too-comfortably on the ground.

But it was too good for them. A seething rage consumed me, and I began to scream at them. My voice was hoarse and raspy - barely audible, but I railed at them, with my breath coming in short gasps. My throat and ribs were on fire, and I suddenly remembered them choking me.

"Fuckers! Scum suckers!" I spewed all the hatred and outrage that they had planted into me, along with their disgustingly sick bodily fluids. I continued the tirade, using every fowl description that I could come up with.

"You go, girl!" Brad chuckled into my ear. "Give it all you got – it's good to see the life come back into your soul!"

"You think you've beaten me? You pathetic worms – sorry excuses for human beings?" I forged on, "Well, you are nothing but a couple of sick-ass losers!" I sneered at them, "I am the winner here! Me! And you will have to live with that for the rest of your worthless lives!" I was finally spent.

The two fuckers had no power left – looking thoroughly miserable and more than a little frightened at their predicament while eyeing the bikers warily.

I took note of the lack of trauma evident. The guys had been merciful, so it seemed. While this both enraged and confused me a little, my gratitude for being alive and safe overrode it all! I collapsed back into Brad's arms, drinking in my freedom.

Sirens wailed in the distance, and I knew they were coming our way – for sure, an ambulance. My former foster provider and his deadbeat buddy were about to lose their game for good. I understood this, but so many questions rolled around in my head. How on earth did they find me? No one had a clue where Everett Richards had disappeared to, nor his connection to the burly dude, which I knew had been my demise.

The very act of thinking was just too much right now. I watched the first responders fly into view, with police cars trailing right behind them, feeling as though I was in surveillance from above, floating on a cloud.

Shit! This was all so surreal.

Brad pressed a lingering, gentle kiss upon my cheek as he surrendered me to the paramedics, who carefully loaded me onto a stretcher – the pain was so fucking intense. But I looked over at the source of it all – the two low lives, still sprawled in the dirt, and I refused to vocalize it. My screams remained silent.

I would not give those fuckers the satisfaction! Instead, I willed every ounce of strength I could muster and laughed in their faces, producing my middle finger for a farewell gesture as I was carried past.

Once loaded in the vehicle, I couldn't suppress agonized whimpers from the pain, but by the time we arrived at Vancouver General Emergency, whatever drugs they'd loaded me with had taken a considerable edge off my discomfort.

I was blessedly safe.

Chapter Thirty-Four

"They've got her!" Daisy's scream reverberated off the walls of the room that had served as the women's prison for the past day – it seemed like forever! Tears of joy were streaming down her face, and the others joined in.

"She's alive and presently being transported to Vancouver General by ambulance." Daisy let out a shaky breath. "We can wait at the hospital, but it will be some time before they'll let us see her." She regarded them solemnly.

"Buck warned that she's in pretty rough shape. She will need some surgery and stitches. There's a shoulder separation, and possible pelvic as well – he wasn't sure, but said that the abuse in that area was horrific." Daisy paused to gain control of her emotions.

"There are extensive bite marks – they will need to re-attach one of her nipples, a piece of her lip, and a partially severed finger. In addition, several ribs are broken, and she may have internal organ damage; he felt it best we were prepared."

Jessi cried out and folded over in emotional agony. The others held her while she wailed out her sorrow. Daisy cleared her throat.

"Buck reported that her feistiness won out in the end, as she bolstered her courage to face them with her outrage." Tears flooded

Daisy's eyes. "He was choking up, the whole time he was telling me all of this. I've never seen that big buffoon so broken up over anything." She straightened up.

"Suffice to say, we'll need to toughen up before we go see her."

Del stood up, putting her phone away. "I have to go see a detective about a crime," she smiled through her own tears. "I explained everything, and he's pretty sure that with the rape kit, and the evidence already in place, we'll have a clear conviction. He also requested that I relay his admiration to us all for the diligence and care that we took with the situation."

"That's awesome, Del. Go get 'im!" Millie smiled warmly.

"Oh, he will still take me to task!" Del hurried out the door after a round of warm hugs.

~~~

On the drive to the precinct, Del considered her first impression of Detective Devon McMullen. His smile was warm and genuine and reached his eyes the few times he had bestowed one upon her. That, she decided, was a major plus in her current precarious position.

An added bonus, she conceded, was his roguish good looks – dark and thoroughly masculine – handed down, likely from Irish
~~~

or Scottish heritage. The absence of an accent suggested that he was born, or at least raised, somewhere on North American soil. She estimated him to be close to her own age, perhaps a year or two older, with a hint of graying beginning at the sideburns.

Reigning in her curiosity, she deduced that the man was likely happily married, and that suited her fine - not in the market for a man, no matter how attractive the eye candy.

The direction that her thoughts had taken took Del by surprise, with the horror that Mandy had and was still enduring. But, she supposed, the news of Mandy's survival had afforded a much-needed reprieve from the emotional turmoil that had wreaked complete inner havoc and imprisoned them all over the past few days.

In any case, there were far more pressing matters at hand - she snapped her focus in line with the purpose of this appointment as she parked the car in the visitor section.

Wandering into the main reception area, she was struck by the intense hustle and bustle – frenzied energy. This was a central precinct dealing with a large variety of policing matters and within an area that was rife with homelessness, prostitution, drugs and petty crime – a colorful mix, to say the least.

As directed by the desk Sargent, she took the stairs to the second floor and followed the signs – there it was – *Homicide*. She and Devon McMullen had met in person only once, at a café down the road, in honor of their colliding, crazy schedules. It was then that she had passed on the locket to him.

Suddenly, he was before her, having been alerted to her arrival, and she was ushered down a hallway to a space with several desks. Carrying on through to a back office, he motioned for her to take a seat and closed the door.

"Thanks for coming my way," his gentle smile revealed compassion as he took a chair directly across from her rather than behind his desk.

Another good sign.

"Can I get you a coffee or snack?"

Damn, that smile was a killer!

"No, it's fine – I've had too many already!" Del held up the water bottle she retrieved from her bag with a returning grin.

"I know this has been an impossibly stressful situation, and though the outcome is the best you could hope for," he reached out to touch her arm, "the strain from all the stress and worry must be taking its toll. We can just sit for a minute for you to catch your breath if you'd like."

Del felt an immediate, comforting wave wash over her and closed her eyes for a minute. It meant everything to her – she'd been holding it together by an invisible thread, it seemed. All of the ladies were struggling with their own nightmarish guilt for Mandy's predicament. She sighed deeply and faced him.

"First off, I want to offer my sincere apologies for the delay in contacting you. The situation was somewhat volatile," she gave him an assessing glance, "and to be honest, there were those whose identities and situations I needed to protect."

"Fair enough," he returned the scrutinizing appraisal, "I think, however, you and I need to clear the air and establish a circle of trust between us." He reached over for his notebook.

"Agreed," Del sighed and fixed him with a firm stare, "on the condition that some of what I have to say will need to remain off the record." She sat back.

"Sounds reasonable," he grinned affably, "how about we start with reviewing the facts that we both are aware of, and go from there."

Del nodded and they got to work, comparing notes – known facts, timelines, key players, etc. Along the way, she weaved in additional information – some admissible, clearly defining that which had to remain between them.

Throughout the entire session, Devon afforded his full attention – obviously, a well-trained and active listener, nodding and stepping in to paraphrase when appropriate. Most of the information Devon offered was already known to both of them.

"Sorry, I guess I'm the only one with secrets," Del grinned sheepishly.

"That does make you a woman of mystery." Devon searched her eyes. "I am both grateful and somewhat surprised that you trusted me with all of this."

"I trust my intuition – and I, in turn, appreciate your understanding and willingness to hear me out." Del was sure that she blushed like a teenager when she met his thoroughly alluring gaze.

"May I suggest that we review the game plan from here?" Devon cleared his throat. Del nodded.

"We now have the asshole in custody," he smiled, "and have substantial evidence to initiate murder charges against him for the death of their former foster child – Nikki Leeds." He took a deep breath and sat back in the chair. "Apparently, Mandy informed the attending officer that Richards verbally admitted to murdering the child during her recent ordeal."

Oh my God – while this was horrific, Del was elated at this news – there was no question now!

"The tricky part is always weighing out the probability of

which charge will stick. In this case, as you are aware, the jury would have the option of first-degree murder, second-degree murder, or manslaughter. Of course, there is always the possibility of a non-guilty verdict." Devon leaned toward her once again.

"We have a lot leaning in our favor," he smiled, "his fingerprints on the locket and the perfect match on the remains; his prior rape, assault and battery convictions with minors; an extensive previous criminal record for violence and assault, and a secondary charge."

"Yes, Mandy…" Del nodded her understanding.

"Due to the serious threat the man poses, it is imperative that we keep him behind bars until the outcome of the trial, which, as you know, can take a considerable amount of time."

"So, the question is – do we first slap the rape and assault charge – possibly escalating that to an attempted murder of Mandy? This is almost a given success, with evidence and witnesses. You are confident they will come forward?"

"Even through the mess of pain that he left her in, Mandy is chomping at the bit for that very opportunity. I've no doubt!"

"Good." He nodded.

"Normally, we would likely opt for this; the downside being that bail could be set for much lower than the murder charge, and there's a possibility he'll disappear or worse." He gave her a serious, knowing look.

Yep! Mandy may never have a life without terror – always looking behind her – wondering where he was.

"So, you'll put forth the murder charge first, then?"

"I've spoken with the D.A., and yes, that's our plan of action. The charges for Mandy's horrific assault will be laid as secondary." The intensity of his gaze sent a shiver up Del's spine.

"Mandy will likely have to testify in both cases," he sighed apologetically, "I wish we could avoid that. In addition, you may be put on the stand for the assault and battery of Gen Miller – but that assumes she'll cooperate."

"I have no issue with that, and I'll do my best to convince her. That would be charge number three?"

"Indeed, it would," he chuckled, "We've got this bastard. However, Gen may be up for an accessory to murder charge – which could serve as a negotiating tool for her testimony."

"Thank you, Detective – a lot to think about!" Del sighed. "You will call me, with any next steps? And I'll let you know, if I catch up to Gen first." He nodded.

"*Devon,* please! We can't have you calling me *Detective* all through dinner, now, can we?"

His warm smile immediately snuffed out any objections Del may have considered to a dinner invitation. She felt her face flush furiously.

"So, would you consider having dinner with me? I promise not to regale you with boring courtroom jargon!"

"That would be nice," Del returned his smile, with warmth radiating from somewhere deep inside. They shook hands, his holding hers just a second longer than customary, and she breezed out of the building with a sudden lightness to her step.

Ok, what the fuck did you just do, lady? She berated herself. What about his assumed happy marriage? Did you bother to find that out before agreeing to a date? A little voice egged her on – *there is no one else…* She didn't think it was too far off the mark, with that hint of smoldering delight in his eyes.

Truth? Somehow, she knew – or a least trusted, that this man would never have asked her out if there was a wife in the mix. That feeling of rightness accompanied her all the way to the hospital.

Chapter Thirty-Five

Fuck, that hurt! Even through the masking haze of painkillers, this was a nightmare. I had to admit that the relief was immediate – wrapping up the arm in a sling and securing my torso in a belt-like bandage provided instant ease for breathing and movement. The X-ray had shown no indication of free-floating bones or lung punctures, so apparently, in six weeks, I might be able to do a jig or two! The bastards had broken eleven of my twenty-four ribs!

I tried in vain to push away a vague memory of the two assholes, one inflicting cruel bites while the other pulled brutally on my arms to keep me from fighting against it. I retched violently, only producing dry heaves – so far, having only ingested water - and that was long gone!

They had stitched up some of the wounds – I wept like a baby when they'd worked on the nipple so painstakingly. These guys are fucking amazing! A plastic surgeon had rushed here, straight from his family dinner table – wow - to spend two hours on the nipple, a finger, facial contusions, and my lip, which Richards tore into after I clamped down on his disgusting member.

Meanwhile, they handled the tests for the rape kit – that was another scream fest – geezus – the fucktards messed me up good, down there! Again, it is all blessedly foggy, but I know that there were more objects, beyond their two pathetic dicks, in play.

Finally! The medical team left me to rest for a bit – to give me a breather, and I drifted in and out of consciousness, trapped somewhere between a nightmare and the mirroring pain of reality.

"Hey, young lady, how are you feeling?" a pleasant face peered down at me. "I'm Doctor Vance." He laid his hand on my forehead for just a second or two and smiled sheepishly as I fought my way out of a drugged stupor and tried to focus.

"I know that was a pretty foolish question – you feel like poop, right?"

Oh God, it hurt to laugh! Instead, I smiled through the mass of bruises and swelling that was currently on my face.

"I think we've pretty much completed torturing you for the moment," compassion shone from his eyes, "I am very sorry for what you have endured, Mandy."

Sweet – he may be the only professional in the world who chose to throw formality out the door. Through my haze of tears, I decided that I liked him.

"So, what's *your* form of torment?" I couldn't resist the jab, pleased that I could almost articulate my words…cool!

"Oh, I'll think of something," he chuckled. "Actually, I am the surgeon who will be repairing your pelvic displacement." His tone was serious now.

"We want to give you a day or two to let some of the trauma from your injuries settle down to a dull roar and ensure that you are at optimal strength for the surgery." He raised a brow.

"To be honest, I think you are one of the strongest ladies I have ever had the blessing to meet, so I have no qualms about this – you'll come through with flying colors."

Fuck – surgery?

"Will I walk?"

"Absolutely, but not so well for the first few weeks. You will need some time. But with physio, you'll be like new!" He patted her hand.

"One thing I cannot address is the internal damage. Dr. Knowles will be taking care of that, but I have good news!" he grinned widely.

"Hell, I could use some of that," I mumbled awkwardly.

"Dr. K., as we call her around here, will come in just before me to clean you up and do her repairs, which means you will *not* have to endure two separate surgeries and will be completely knocked out for it all! It works better for us to complete the necessary procedures all in one shot." I nodded my gratitude.

"Another bonus – your facial bone breaks – cheek and eye

socket, along with a small skull fracture, did not crush; so, will heal on their own – apparently your brain is indestructible, too!"

"Further, all X-rays and internal scans indicate no need for further surgeries. You certainly have some formidable organ bruising – kidneys, liver, spleen, lungs and almost every muscle you own! It's going to be a little while before you feel close to normal again, but each day, you'll find improvements." He squeezed my hand for a long moment before heading out and abruptly turned at the door.

"Hey, no dramatic escapes, young lady!"

Damn, I wish he'd quit making me laugh! Truthfully, this wasn't my first adventure with pain. Especially if you include sexual assault. Actually, it *is* pretty damn amazing that there's anything left of me down yonder!

As I began to drift off once again, I reflected on my good fortune – I was learning to embrace gratitude as opposed to mistrusting everything that came my way.

Oh my God, Oh my God! A horrific flash of awareness struck me. The bastards were in the process of trying to mutilate me *- not an ounce of pleasure will ever be yours again, you fucking little whore!* The excruciating pain that they'd been inflicting in that area had paused when the boys got there! Did they? Was I? I remembered a shitload of blood. Panic set in, and I screamed in terror – pushing the call button frantically.

A nurse flew into the room, followed by another and an ER doctor.

"Mandy, tell us what's wrong. Calm down, honey! Where does it hurt?"

With my free hand, I frantically gestured between my legs, gulping sobs, rendering me voiceless.

"Honey, are you hurt? Is it the catheter?"

"No, no…circumcision!" I finally managed to blurt it out. One of the nurses rubbed my arm, dawning realization flooding her features. I wept silently.

"Sweetie, everything is fine there," she smiled gently, "your angels must have arrived in time – the cuts were not deep enough to do any damage, and the Emergency doctor stitched that up shortly after you arrived. You were pretty much out of it!'

Hell, yeah! Relief washed over me. Out of all the things I could have lost my shit over – why that? My sexual organs had caused me nothing but grief throughout my entire life. Targeted me for repeated abuse. As a little girl, I used to pray that I would turn into a boy. But then, I grew up to find out that boys, sadly, were not spared either.

Still, my female genitalia are an integral part of my essence – my feminine power and strength – and my bond with Jessi! I surrendered gratefully to my body's need for rest.

Chapter Thirty-Six

Del joined the others, who were clearly physically and emotionally drained from the worry over Mandy. They huddled together in the ER waiting room, among the moans of pain, constant intercom communication, and busy medical professionals, frantically zooming, at warp speed, to wherever they were needed. The four women shared encouragement for strength and a sunny, positive demeanor, critical for when they were finally allowed to see her.

A doctor approached.

"Are you here for Amanda Goodchild?" At their affirming nods, he smiled and continued.

"Richard Bell here," he gestured toward himself. "One of the emergency physicians on call today. There are several things in play here for Amanda's treatment, and I think it's best that we chat a bit before you go in to see her."

"Of course," Del and Daisy replied in unison. They all followed him down the hallway to what appeared to be a small meeting room.

"Mandy – that is what she prefers, correct?" He grinned, "She took me to task for that a couple of times when I was trying to assess her condition – great spirit!"

"As you know," he cleared his throat and took a deep breath, looking each one of them in the eye, "Mandy has been through hell and back during the last twenty-four hours. She would likely insist that she is still there; her pain from the extensive injuries is intense," he sighed deeply, "however, she is finally resting in relative comfort, at the moment."

"Thank you for talking with us," Millie voiced all of their feelings, tears rolling down her cheeks. The doctor smiled compassionately.

"Mandy should achieve a full recovery from her physical injuries – but it will take some time." He went on to explain the details of her afflictions and the upcoming and ongoing treatment that will be necessary.

The four women wept silently as they listened, in shocked dismay, to the details of the horrific atrocities that were committed upon Mandy's body – and her psyche. It was unthinkable that anyone could treat another human in this way.

"I am so sorry," the doctor hung his head and paused, "no one should have to endure what has happened to Mandy."

"My greatest concern, at this point, is that of her state of mind – her mental well-being." He took a deep breath and regarded them solemnly. "Mandy is still suffering some shock from her trauma. That is why we have not yet given her a solid food diet. For now, she will be nourished intravenously – maybe for another day or two, at the most; along with some pretty powerful antibiotics.

"It is critical that we put support in place for her mental well-being. I have a list here." Del reached out to accept a page from him, with several resource contact numbers and a website at the bottom, where all could be accessed online.

"Thank you," Del smiled, "I am her child protection worker, and so I will make sure that this is put into place for her.

"It seems that she has a great support team sitting here before me – she's fortunate on that score." He got up to leave. "I'll have someone let you know when she's awake."

"She's tough as nails!" Jessi spouted passionately, through a haze of tears, "The strongest person I've ever known, and I can promise you that I'll be right there beside her!"

"Awesome," Dr. Bell replied softly as he disappeared into the emergency fray.

The four women made their way back to their seats and collapsed in utter exhaustion. They fell silent, each lost in a private reverie, and Del pondered the future.

Hell – tough, only went so far! Mandy had a formidable road ahead with recovery and the testimony she would be providing - not only for Everett Richards' multiple convictions but possibly Gen

Miller's and the slimy pimp, Russell.

Del was no stranger to the complexities of criminal proceedings, and the mountain of red tape that necessarily accompanied it. Not to mention the miscarriage of justice. She prayed the latter would not play into these cases.

Her key concern was the testimony, knowing all too well that the defense team would, with ruthless skill, eat her alive and mercilessly spit her out before it was all over. She heaved a troubled sigh, vowing to assist in bolstering Mandy's confidence and conviction - that *she* not be the one on trial here.

She had almost drifted off when a nurse came to advise them that Mandy was awake and could handle a short visit. She further relayed that they were in the process of finding a room in one of the wards to admit her; visiting would be easier there.

Del had prepared herself, knowing it would not be pretty. Still, she felt as if she had been sucker-punched when she gazed upon Mandy's mangled face, which appeared to have been pulverized. She mustered a smile and squeezed her hand.

Del monitored the others closely. Especially Jessi, who, quite simply, was unable to hold back her tears. Both she and Mandy sobbed it out together, and Del was aware that their unique and incredible bond provided that special space for them. She, Millie and Daisy held back to give the two girls privacy while fighting their own battles with emotion.

Jessi plunked firmly down, claiming the only available visitor chair in the small emergency cubicle, and glued herself to Mandy's side. They had moved her recently from the ICU when it was determined that her condition, though horrific, was not critical.

After the initial emotional exchanges were shared, each one contributed an effort to lighten the mood with little quips and jokes. Daisy swore that *never again would she send a teenager on an old lady's errand*, rolling her eyes dramatically. Del knew that this was a necessary piece of their support for Mandy, and it warmed her heart to share it with these beautiful souls. She marveled at the close, life-long bonds that they had forged together.

A nurse popped her head through the curtain to advise that they were moving Mandy to a ward and requested that everyone come back later in the day to visit her there.

Del decided that this was an opportune time to do a little investigation on Gen Miller and beelined her way to the school. She returned Lou Harris' welcoming smile as she approached the office counter.

"Hello there, it's so nice to see a friendly face – so far today, I've mostly encountered animosity – ranging from grunts, growls and middle fingers to shrugs of indifference," the secretary whined in mock outrage.

"What can I do for you?"

"I am just wondering if you have heard from our friend," Del threw her a knowing glance.

"As a matter of fact, she did indeed call a couple of days ago to see if her daughter had made it to school on time and reported that nothing had changed." Del knew that Lou Harris had just made a specific reference to the phone number.

"Thank you so much, Mrs. Harris. I hope you have a lovely day – and be assured that *my* girl is also in good hands!" Del noted the woman's instant relief and smiled her own gratitude before exiting the building. It was a gift to the sweet woman, who obviously cared for Mandy – at least she could rest easier knowing Mandy was safe and under someone's watchful eye.

Once in her car, she considered the options. It was unbelievable that Gen Miller had not been astute enough to change phones. But hey, Del would take her wins where she could.

First off, Gen may not even be aware that her husband had been arrested – unless he'd called her from jail, perhaps. It could be a viable gamble to contact her. The risk to that, of course, was that she might flee. Del decided to run it by Devon McMullen first and called him now through Blue Tooth.

"Hey, I didn't expect to hear from you so soon," his voice

was throaty and downright sexy – geesh!

"I wanted to run something by you – it really can't wait."

"No problem – any chance we could grab a bite together tonight?"

Del's heart raced at the prospect of meeting him under more casual circumstances. But this issue was anything but, and she paused.

"No worries – if you'd rather just chat now, it's all good," he hesitated, "however, it's 4:00, and I really don't want to eat alone; I promise to be on my best behavior!"

"I would love to, really," Del caved, "it's just that I have this pressing issue that needs to be dealt with."

"Absolutely – I think we are made of similar stuff, and will always put our work collaboration on high priority. Let's meet and start with that. Then, if you still feel like hanging with me, I'm in!"

"OK – deal!" she laughed.

Chapter Thirty-Seven

They had firmed plans to meet – 5:30 at Kozak's; she was always in for an authentic Ukrainian feed! Flutters dominated her stomach as she made her way to the office to catch up on a few calls before heading home to change into something more appropriate for the occasion.

She spotted him right away, tucked into a cozy booth in a private corner. Del was grateful now that she had opted for a quick shower to rinse the hospital odors from her being. She had donned a pair of black stretch jeans and a loose sweater with a fuchsia floral pattern that fell slightly off her shoulders. He appeared equally comfortable in jeans and a casual shirt.

"I think you clean up much better than I." He stood now and greeted her with an appreciative glance.

"Looks can be deceiving," she quipped in return. They laughed easily, and she settled in across from him.

"Del, let's order our drinks and deal with your issue," his tone was serious.

"Thank you, I'd appreciate that." The waitress appeared before them with two glasses of iced water and took their drink order. They had both immediately opted for non-alcoholic. This pleased her – it wasn't that his consumption of alcohol would have been an issue, but it meant something to her that they had partnered in avoiding alcohol on a weeknight.

Devon sat back now and gave her his full attention.

"As you know, we have Gen Miller's cell number, and though we were unsuccessful in having it traced to a location, I checked in with my school contact for Mandy, who reported that Gen called from that number two days ago." Del took a deep breath.

"I have a strong compulsion to call her – I am thinking that she may not even know that Richards is in custody."

"But you are worried she'll run," he observed keenly.

"Exactly! Although I have no idea where she'd go without him…"

"I *can* tell you this – there has been no communication between him and Gen for the past several days. At least, not on his cell, which we confiscated during his arrest." He regarded her thoughtfully. "Do you know if she has any work pals?"

Del knew exactly where he was going with that train of thought. Gen had not returned to work since the beating, as she still struggled to walk and was facing further corrective surgeries. But that wasn't to say that she didn't keep in touch with them.

Mandy! She would perhaps remember if Gen had mentioned anyone who she worked with, that may be of particular interest. She voiced this to Devon now.

"I think that's a great idea! Maybe *you* should be the detective," Devon teased.

"Not in this life!" Del returned with a smile. She visibly relaxed now, with a plan to chat with Mandy in the morning. She'd take it from there and maybe even get a little more insight into Gen. She regarded her dinner date, who was studying her intently now from across the table.

"You are an amazing woman, Del Greenwood." His glance was a warm caress, and she flushed. "I know your profession requires heart, and I've always admired that, but I have never before known anyone quite like you, not only staunchly devoted to the outcome but determined to blaze new pathways to get there – and God help anyone who errs to get in your way!"

"Oh, I think you've elevated me a few notches too high."

"You could have lost your job over this."

"Why do you think I accepted your dinner invite?" she teased, "I had to make damn sure that you would not go running to my boss!" He had astutely pinned it quite accurately. She needed to lighten this up a little.

Devon laughed out loud, and she was struck by the hearty, rich depth of tone. Was it possible to fall in love with a voice –

regardless of the person? Del met his gaze, and their eyes locked, each searching within.

"Hey, have you had a chance to decide on food yet?"

Del wanted to both hug and punch the cheery waitress in the face simultaneously with the intrusion. They both grinned up at her sheepishly, eyeing the still-closed menus.

"Give us five, please." Devon requested with a polite smile.

Del grabbed the menu and scrutinized the choices without taking in a single thing on the page. She snuck a peek to find him watching her intently and promptly gave up.

"Devon, I don't know what this is…" she gestured helplessly.

"Del, please let me explain my motives," he relaxed a little as she sat back and waited. "I won't deny it, from the moment I met you, something captivated me – even before I saw you. It was something in your voice – your manner." He shook his head.

"Tonight, I have no agenda. I am not here to seduce you into some casual fling – nor am I some needy single male who requires a relationship with a beautiful woman on my arm to feed his ego. If all you and I have is friendship – or a professional relationship, I am OK with that."

"But I'll be damned if I don't - at least, follow my gut right now. No matter what my head tells me, my heart is driving me toward you. So, I'm going to say it! Get it on the table. You can send me packing or come with me to explore it – your choice."

Del's mouth hung open. She was stunned, speechless. Yes, normally, she would consider this to be far too brazen – egotistical and entitled male behavior. But there was something about him! Now let's be honest, girl – you are totally drawn to this man!

The waitress came back, and Del looked at her in a stupor.

"I'll just have the borscht, please!" *There, now go away and leave us alone*, her nasty inner voice screamed.

"Same," Devon's eyes never left hers, and the waitress toddled off.

"OK, I admit it – there's something there for me too," Del confided, "but Devon, my life is so filled with work and complications – I just don't know if I have enough to give."

"Is there another man?"

"No, that ship sailed," she smiled, "and I swore off relationships afterward because my work is just too damn important to me and may always come first."

"Your life pretty much mirrors mine in terms of priorities. My marriage fell victim to that - I can't blame her. She remarried a few years back and had the kids that I had always dreamed we would make together," he smiled sadly.

Del looked at him with all the compassion in her soul.

"We are definitely two peas in a pod," she smiled, "my marriage also fell victim. However, not before I caught him in our bedroom with another woman after a late night at work." She shook off his condolences.

"It's been a lot of years now, and the cheating confirmed for me that he wasn't *the one*." Del sighed. "My last relationship failure bit a little – we had both lost our spouses for the same reasons and worked together. He had finally had enough – late nights, impossible odds; and moved on from the position. When I was not ready to do the same, we moved on from each other. Del smiled up at him.

"So, you have no one special in your life right now?" she asked gently. Her heart melted when he took her hand.

"If she'll agree to spend some time figuring it out with me, yes, I believe I do."

"Let's take it slow – it's the only way I know right now." Del pleaded.

"Agreed – I won't molest you – you'll have to be the one to jump my bones!" Del burst out laughing at the serious look on his face as the borscht showed up.

They ate their meal in complete, harmonic companionship,

and Del wondered at the little gifts from the Universe – she could have rejected the idea, yes - but why not explore? She realized that Devon was a man who had already earned her trust. Even though in mock gravity, his words had a ring of promise to them. She truly believed that he would not push her into anything she wasn't ready for.

Chapter Thirty-Eight

"Holy crap! Look at my face!"

It was horrific – I looked like a hideous monster from a horror movie! Over the past few days, the swelling had actually increased, and I imagined my tissue freaking out inside my body, attempting in vain to madly escape, not knowing what the fuck had happened to it!

"Shut up! You are gorgeous!" Jessi hugged me gingerly.

She was a horrible liar, but I loved her for it, anyhow. She had helped me with a sponge bath earlier – washed my hair as best she could, and it felt divine, as long as I didn't look in the mirror – ugh!

We both turned, hearing someone at the door – Del had somehow secured me a private room, and I was infinitely grateful. It kept the steady hospital noises at a low hum, and thankfully, they no longer had a need to come in so often to check vitals etc.

Shit! What was *he* doing here?

"Hey, how's the bravest lady I know?" His crooked smile was warm and caring, and I burst into tears – emotion flooding every cell in my body - I was mortified!

"Aww, hell – I didn't mean to upset you! Maybe I'll just drop these off and leave you in peace." He gently laid the spray of colorful spring flowers on my bedside tray.

"No way, get your butt in here," Jessi insisted, "it's not about you, *that* I can assure you." Jessi patted my arm and moved over to allow Brad to come and sit beside me.

Fuck – why couldn't I get my shit together? But seeing Brad just stirred up the boiling kettle of screwed-up emotions that were rolling around inside like a wrecking ball. Geezus - and I looked like this? My tears subsided, and I began to feel a little more in control, though still shaky.

"For sure – please stay," I managed what I supposed was a morbid looking smile – with my lip, still about twice the size it should be. The doc had solidly assured me that it would look normal in a couple of weeks.

Brad flashed me that awesome grin again, and I returned it as best I could. He would likely be one of my favorite humans of all time – the gratitude inside me was overwhelming, and I teared up again. Jessi had conveniently disappeared.

"Brad, I…shit!" The words wouldn't come – there was nothing I could say that would adequately express my thankfulness.

"Hey…" He reached and leaned in closely, drawing me into his embrace – it felt so damn good, such a safe place to be.

"You don't need to say anything – I would have moved the

moon and a couple of mountains to keep you safe." His expression clouded – something was troubling him.

"Don't be afraid to talk to me – I'm not that fragile," I pulled back and squeezed his hand, searching his eyes. Was there something wrong? Momentary panic set in, but I reigned it in, figuring Del would have been here in a heartbeat if anything serious had been amiss. Besides, it wasn't about me – this was about Brad, and being there for him now was a drop in the bucket in comparison to what he'd done for me.

"We arrived too late!" It was an agonized whisper, barely audible, "They never should have gotten to you - ever."

His expression was tortured, and my heart melted for him. Was he really, fucking blaming himself for what happened to me?

"I wanted to kill them both and would have, with my bare hands, if Buck hadn't been there," his expression was murderous, but now he looked into my eyes and the pain and regret there triggered a fresh round of tears to escape – free flow.

One lonely drop trickled down *his* cheek, and I reached out to gently wipe it away. I had never known a man, save for Simon, with such a good heart. He grabbed my hand now and planted a gentle kiss on my palm.

"Buck was pure focus, man!" Admiration shone from his

eyes. "He knew what needed to happen to ensure that we nailed those pricks! I saw it in his eyes – he wanted to kill them as much as I did." He shook his head and smiled at me, "But we got 'em!"

"Hell, yes!" I returned his smile painfully, "and if I ever hear you blaming yourself for what happened to me, again," passion drove my words now, "you'll feel the sting from this *brave* chick!" I took a deep, cleansing breath. "I get it! I lived it, so I know how horrific it must have been to see." I hung my head down, unable to meet the compassion in his eyes.

God, it was humiliating, knowing the man had seen me completely naked, vulnerable, and totally helpless. I fought to stave down the all-encompassing blanket of shame shrouding my sense of self-worth. Where the fuck was my anger now? Hell, the shame was always a part of it, but I'd never let it overshadow my outrage before – not until this moment.

Not until it mattered.

"Hey you," he lifted my chin, and I slowly met his gaze, "you need not carry *one ounce* of accountability for what happened to you – don't ever let anyone tell you otherwise!" He held my gaze intently. "The only thing that I will ever see when I look at you is a beautiful, brave and determined woman," he gave me a gentle shake, "you are *not* defined by the experiences others have forced upon you."

"Oh, hell!" I found my voice, "How did you get to be so damn smart!" I giggled through my sniffles, "I'll hold you to that!" I feigned a threatening glare.

"But," all serious now, "*thank you*, just doesn't seem to come close to how I feel," I met the gentle caress in his eyes, "what it meant to me – your comfort, caring, and protection," I paused to gather my thoughts, "you were my safety net – I survived – in mind, body, and spirit; because you held me in your arms." I looked at him imploringly - it was so important to me, at this moment, that he understood.

"You made me feel special," emotion welled within me, "and that's so new to me – I've never felt that way before," I grinned at him, "and now, here you go, doing it again!"

"You *are* special!"

It was simple and authentic – I knew it – felt his genuine words seep into my soul like a balm.

"If you ever need a reminder," he grinned, "I'm here. But, don't go thinking you had to survive trauma and danger to earn that status," he eyed me sternly, 'because you already owned it before any of this happened – from the moment I met you. You and I chatted a few times at the motel if you remember."

I remembered. Brad had stuck out for me, too, as being one

hell of a nice dude. It had lifted my spirits every time I ran into him.

"I do," I confirmed, "and now, it's a wrap," I smiled into his eyes, "you are officially the kindest, coolest dude that I have the good fortune to know."

"Mandy," his expression turned serious, "I want you to see me the way I was before this shitstorm hit you – any one of the guys would have done the same for you."

I took a deep breath – I'd have to roll that around in my psyche for a bit, but it made sense. I nodded.

"I think I really need some time to sort things out in my head – not about you, but everything!"

"Of course, is it OK if I visit again?"

"Absolutely! I'll chase you down if you don't!" We both laughed and with a gentle hug, he departed.

I laid back, mulling over my feelings. I came up with the best descriptor – full – that was it! My heart was full, and I realized that his visit was a catalyst – something I needed to move forward in my recovery. I couldn't deny my feelings surrounding the man. They ran deep, and I would need to explore it. A little niggle of guilt assailed me as Jessi breezed back into the room.

"Wow, you two had a great visit!" She seemed genuinely happy about that. "Methinks that you have an admirer, my girl!" She giggled at my shocked expression. "Hey, what's wrong with that?"

"Nothing, but I think you are misreading the situation – the guy is truly the genuine article. He's gentle, caring, and concerned for my welfare. He picked me up from the depths of hell and cradled me in a safe nest. I think it's pure concern for my welfare."

"OK, I can buy that," Jessie regarded me thoughtfully, "but I noticed his attention on you, even at the motel, "he's a really nice guy, Mandy – you could land worse."

"I thought we weren't into men," I raised my brow.

"Mandy, I think we need to honor the path our hearts lead us to," she smiled gently, "and we've discussed it already – nothing could damage our sisterhood – nothing!"

"Gotcha," I sighed deeply. She was right. She had her own admirers – a handful of bikers, for a few; one in particular – Buck. The man was clearly drawn to Jessi, and I knew that she was aware of it. I wasn't sure how she felt about him, but there were sparks – acknowledged or not.

In any case, we had both made a firm commitment to finishing our education first as a priority, so there was a lot of time to sort out the issue of relationships. Hell, I was only fifteen – though I felt at least a decade older.

It was a great comfort to know that I would be perfectly fine if Jessi decided she wanted to pursue a relationship with Buck. Oh, hell yes, I would have to fight back the little green monster if it got intimate. Jessi and I had shared physical pleasures now for a time, but I knew it wasn't about the sex.

We gifted each other with honoring our femininity – the beauty of our bodies, our innocence, and the right to pleasure. In essence, I supposed, we preserved that right – fostered the survival of our womanhood, and our sexuality, alongside surviving the atrocities of abuse from men. Without it, I doubt either one of us would be able to experience that satisfaction with anybody else – man or woman. I looked at her now, all the love shining from my eyes.

"Jessi, I love you so much!" I hugged her as tightly as my injuries would permit, "You are my rock and the reason for my survival – relatively intact, I think!" I giggled.

"Shit, girl – if you hadn't blasted into my life the way you did, all spitfire and bravado, I'd still be turning tricks! It works both ways." Jessi returned the embrace.

"I promise you that, if and when I may develop romantic feelings for Brad or anyone else, I will allow the freedom to explore it," I breathed deeply, "but for now, I need to focus on my recovery, the future, and sort out all of the jumbled feelings," I met her soft gaze, "we've been through a lot of changes – most of it awesome."

"Oh my God, Mandy!" Jessi grinned, a look of astonishment on her face. "Only *you* could emerge from a brutal rape, assault and attempted murder – near death, to talk about positivity in your life!"

We both laughed aloud at this. Yeah, it was true! Hell, we were both tough as nails! Even through all the pain, I felt that I was in a pretty good place. I guess the knowledge that the perverted asshole was headed for the clink took a considerable edge off of the trauma; it boded very well for the future! My introspection brought me to a profound epiphany…

"It just occurred to me," I met Jessi's eyes, "that all of our experiences since we've been reunited have opened new perspectives for me." I had her attention.

"My entire life has been about survival – all the crap that I was having to deal with and negotiate. I don't think that I ever really considered anyone else's predicament. I just assumed that most people who weren't in our shoes were full of shit-ass luck! They'd all been dealt a good hand in life. I was stuck with trash; bottom of the barrel!" I sighed and took a deep breath.

"Hell, I looked down upon people like Del and Daisy – figuring they had it made – what the hell did they have to complain about? But now that I've allowed myself to get closer – really gotten to know who they are and their stories; I realize that they've had their own pile of refuse to deal with. It's all relative."

"The part that I have never given any consideration to, is the fact that many of them devote their lives to those of us less fortunate. They don't *have* to do that! They are not obligated to *me* in any way! It makes me feel like an ungrateful little shit – I have made everything all about me!"

"Aww, Mandy," Jessi hugged me tenderly, "give yourself a break here. You absolutely and necessarily have been consumed with survival – that part is not on you! Your true character is shining through now that you have the opportunity to breathe and really look at it all."

"You are truly good for my soul, you know that?" I smiled affectionately.

"Well, you don't think I'd adore a little shit, do you?" We both guffawed over that one.

Her words made sense, and hell, I had a lot of years left to make something of my life. Until I had found Jessi again, there had been no one who cared about what happened to me. At least, it *seemed* that way. I picked up my phone and took a selfie – this would serve as the *before* pic. Oh Gawd!

Chapter Thirty-Nine

Del knocked softly on the door frame of Mandy's hospital room, with Devon hanging back slightly. They had decided to meet here together, as Devon wished to speak briefly with Mandy regarding the locket she had found, Richards' confession to her, and the pathway forward – figuring that it would be less intimidating for their first meeting, with Del in the room.

"Hey," Mandy smiled and motioned them in, curiosity in her expression, as she eyed the detective. "It's good to see you – I wanted to thank you again." A lone tear trickled down her cheek.

"Mandy, it is *I* who am indebted to *you*," Del hugged her warmly, "for letting me in!" She pinned her with a determined gaze, "Truly, you orchestrated your own survival through this; without your trust, none of the key players would have been in place." Del smiled.

"Nor would we have bagged Everett Richards," she gestured toward Devon, "I'd like you to meet Detective Devon McMullen – he's been working on the murder case involving their former foster child, Nikki Leeds, and would like to have a quick word with you."

Del's heart lurched at the emotional pain suddenly evident in Mandy's expression. She was well aware of the significance, knowing the inner bond that Mandy had forged with a little girl she had never met, deeply connected through a delicate, little locket.

"Hello, Mandy." Devon lifted an inquiring brow, gesturing to a seat next to the bed, and with her nod, settled in with a sigh. "Words are not near adequate," he established firm eye contact, "but I am thankful that you are still here with us, and I want to echo Del with my gratitude for your courage, fortitude and cooperation."

"I need you to nail that bastard!" Mandy growled vehemently. "So, whatever it takes – if I can help, I'll do it!"

Devon responded with a firm nod. Del knew that in this, Mandy's full focus and drive was on behalf of one little, lost soul – the innocent murder victim, who did not deserve an ounce of the treatment that she had received at the hands of Everett Richards and Gen Miller.

Del was well aware of how deeply Mandy had been messed up after learning that her identity had been confirmed - consumed with grief over the little girl, almost as if she was her own. In truth, both Mandy and Jessi had stepped into the role of mothering the younger kids, who had none other, while they were with Simon and Millie and likely at other homes. Del could only imagine how deeply the pain of this loss ran for Mandy.

"I think it will be a cut-and-dried case in terms of the murder," Devon began, "however, establishing intent is another matter." He sat back and sighed. "We will call upon your testimony for the locket – should be short and sweet – assuming there is nothing further to tell. Also, you'll be called upon to testify about his confession to murdering Nikki Leeds." He regarded her with compassion.

"But the jury will need to decide on whether or not it was premeditated – which would constitute a first-degree murder charge – or if it was accidental, etc."

"It was no accident," Mandy whispered. "Nikki Leeds…" The name rolled off her tongue, mirroring the unchecked tear sliding down her cheek.

"I believe this too," Devon responded solemnly, "and your conviction in this will be very important as testimony. The Crown will need to establish the man's character and his normal mode of operation as a foster father." He pinned her with a meaningful glance. "In this, you can offer first-hand experience."

"I'm in," she nodded firmly.

"I want to warn you, the Defense will make every attempt to tear you down – weaken your credibility." Devon and Del shared a knowing look between them.

"Bring it on," Mandy was adamant, which brought a smile of admiration from both.

"OK – we will chat more on it, when the time draws nearer

– thank you!" Devon gave her hand a warm squeeze. "I will let you and Del visit now, as duty calls for me – it was an honor to meet you, Mandy!" He and Del shared a warm smile as he touched her shoulder and then was gone.

"Hey, I'm sorry if you feel that I sprung that on you," Del offered, "but he wanted to lay out the ground that they will need to tread with you."

"It's all good," Mandy assured, "We need to make sure that scumbag pays for what he did to that little girl!"

The fire in Mandy's eyes provided a measure of confidence to Del in her ability to weather the fierce storm that would brew and peak during the upcoming trial. It was likely going to get ugly.

"Agreed," Del responded, with warmth in her gaze, as she regarded Mandy. "Detective McMullen is the right guy to head this up," she assured, "He's just as stubborn and dedicated as I am!" she laughed a little.

"Oh, you mean *Devon*," Mandy gave Del a knowing smile.

"Yes, of course," Del felt a betraying blush wash over her face.

"Oh, c'mon – I saw the way he touched you on the way out. And the tender looks between you." Mandy giggled.

"OK, I won't deny that we've forged a…friendship of late."

At Mandy's raised brow, she felt determined to relay the correct message.

"Mandy, the work is the first priority for both of us!" She was adamant, but her features softened as she continued, "Devon is a man of heart and deep principle, and I am so grateful that he is the lead investigator in bringing down Everett Richards." Del sighed deeply.

"I have run across a few in my day, and most of these homicide cops – I say this without judgement - become hardened and somewhat dc-sensitized. Hell – they deal with nightmarish shit on a regular basis, and more often than we'd all care to admit, justice is compromised if achieved at all. It is thoroughly discouraging. I know because it is the same in my profession."

"And here the two of you are," Mandy smiled, "teamed up, with a fierce determination – against all odds – to bring this bastard down." Del nodded with a grin of acknowledgement.

"I'm impressed!" Mandy stated firmly.

"Well, it is a quality in him that seriously appeals to me."

"Not to mention his kick-ass hottie bod!" Mandy managed a mischievous wink with her good eye.

"Yeah, that too!" Both women guffawed.

"Tell me that you are going to give the man some of your

time – off work!"

The gleam in Mandy's eyes added to the warm spark in Del's belly that reigned whenever she thought of Devon McMullen.

"We are going to take it slow."

"Seriously? You need a good lay – admit it!"

"Oh my God, Mandy!" Del regarded her in mock outrage, but they both laughed out loud. "Seriously? You are bang on!" Del sighed, "But business comes first!"

"Yeah, yeah," Mandy teased, but her expression sobered a little, "thank you, Del – for everything!"

"Mandy, at the risk of getting all mushy on you," she took her hand, "I couldn't love you more if you were my own daughter," a tear escaped, and both women shared a long embrace.

Mandy, Del knew, was speechless, unable to verbalize the strange and new feelings that were emerging – simply from having someone care for her. Devotion and love were not the norm, and it was vital that she process those emotions to allow this into her life on an ongoing basis; she needed to believe it was sustainable.

Del knew that trust was key – and that Mandy held it, with at least four women in her life – who would each lay down their lives to save hers. Yeah, that would be an incredibly overwhelming feeling, for sure.

Del reflected that she, herself, was unable to lay claim to owning this in her own life. Her parents had died when she was quite young, in an accident. Truth be told, their marriage had been rocky – infidelity on both their parts had been an issue, and her dad had smacked her mom around the few times that the woman had dared to speak out about it. Her mom had turned to alcohol and followed the same unfaithful road, albeit with only one other man that Del was aware of.

Del had left home, relieved of all the stress, at the age of seventeen after graduating from high school. She had immediately taken employment at a local bank and within two years, had earned an income sufficient to save enough funds to attend University.

Four years later, she attained her Bachelor's degree in Social Work and secured employment with Child and Family Services. She continued night school, even after her marriage, to obtain her Master's, which accredited her for the senior Child Protection Worker position that she still held today.

She supposed that her crappy family situation had inspired her passion, but it ran far deeper now. In truth, she rarely gave much thought to her deceased parents any longer and had never been close to them after she had moved out. They had tried a couple of family Christmas dinners, but it was awkward and always ended up with her mother drunk and father slamming out the door to his most recent paramour. Ironically, they had been killed together in a car crash on their way to a counselling appointment shortly after Del's marriage.

Grief was more about sadness and regret, as she had spent more time with her husband's family, though they had never accepted her as *good enough* for their incredible son, who eventually took a CEO position with his father's property investment firm. His family heaved a sigh of relief, she was certain, when the marriage ended.

Del was grateful for the monetary advantage – her home was pretty much paid for, and she had a little nest egg for emergencies. She had wanted nothing more from him.

For a time, she was quite comfortable with her own company and had never been one to seek out friendships; the proverbial introvert, she supposed. Oh, she had positive acquaintances, and was well-liked at work – always invited to various social functions. Some she attended, but mostly as an onlooker. Work was her main muse.

Frank had become her close confidante, and things had progressed from there. Presently, she admitted to harboring an aching loneliness until recent events had exploded into her life. She smiled, thinking of the powerful women whom she now counted as dear – their friendships deep and meaningful. The thing about a great female friend, she contemplated, is that they meet you on your own terms without trying to change who you are to suit their own agenda.

Men, on the other hand…her thoughts flew to Devon McMullen. While her track record was less than stellar in that department, she was drawn to giving it a chance to see where it went. And…she really enjoyed the passionate, physical element of a romantic relationship – she was not dead yet! In fact, the abstinence was driving her insane. Of course, she had her tricks and resources, but nothing compared to a sumptuous meeting of flesh.

In short, she was incredibly horny, and Devon McMullen was striking all the right sparks to create a raging inferno that sorely needed tending. So…she just might take up his challenge sooner than later!

Chapter Forty

Sweet! Del had a romantic prospect in the making! My heart was happy for her. I stuck by my original impression of the lady – she was in serious need of a good romp in the hay.

It was more than that, though, I knew. The woman was adamantly devoted to her job and truly cared about the kids, who she was trying, mostly in vain, to help. It was awe-inspiring and spoke resolutely to her character.

I teared up a little – still hated this weakness! But I was becoming accustomed to it, where it concerned people and things I cared most about. Del Greenwood had been key to my survival. It was a testament to her courage and commitment, and this humbled me completely.

Hell, she had risked her entire career for me. Who does that? And yes, I damn well struggle with it – the feeling of worthiness is so fucking foreign to me. The fact that anyone would put themselves secondary to *me*? Oh, sure, it feels great! But I'm freaking terrified to trust in it! I have only ever been able to count on one person to survive – myself!

A sudden image of Jessi floated before my mind's eye, and my heart melted. I had to concede that she was the exception. But even Jessi, along with Millie and Simon, had not been able to make the difference. It was so confusing!

Maybe *adulting* was key…it wasn't that Millie and Simon were not trustworthy. Risking a deep look inward, I had to admit that I'd had complete faith in them when both Jessi and I lived there. It was rotten life circumstances, that had crushed that bed of comfort for me. After I was ripped from there, I never let my guard down again.

Point – it's not as simple as being able to count on someone in my life. Hell, I knew Millie and Simon would have moved mountains to keep me; Millie was just not able to. I felt like shit, acknowledging the part of me that resented - even *her*, for all the trauma in my life since. It was all mixed up with my love for her, and at this moment, clarity hit.

On the surface, I knew very well that it was all about the system – I had been screwed by *the system*. But somehow, I had internalized it, within a jumble of emotions and shitty beliefs – I was unworthy. Otherwise, Millie would have found a way to keep me, right? I was born inadequate; it was meant to be; my life was fated to be garbage.

Fuck, I hated this turmoil, and every part of me wanted to stuff it back down and just carry on with my day, the business of staying alive. But I couldn't seem to stop the flood of epiphanies coming though.

I remember feeling like a worthless piece of nothing every time I fled a home, leaving the other kids behind to their horrible fate. Shame washed over me now; then, it was seeking safety, but it still had the power to rip out my heart when I dared let it surface. I had not allowed that introspection – probably ever! All those feelings were squashed firmly down in my determination to survive.

Now, the four women who are my key to feeling worthy of saving – their caring and love – are absolutely the catalyst for these seemingly rogue emotions, playing havoc with my sense of control, critical to my survival.

OK, so I know why it is coming up now, but what the hell am I supposed to do with it all? I picked up the card that Del had left on the bedside table, the counselling service, that she insisted would help me to figure out my jumbled emotions. I made a firm decision to call them after lunch.

Del's visit was interesting, to say the least. I really liked the detective, and my gut feeling about him mirrored hers. He was authentic and really cared. Shit – I was seriously willing to lay my trust in him – on this huge issue in my life! Maybe there's hope for me, yet!

Del had asked me about any possible names that I had for work friends of Gen's. She was determined to find her and perhaps convince Gen to testify against that slime. My feelings were not so optimistic, but hey – I am willing to put a bit of faith forward here, too!

I told Del there was a guy named Gary Evans who used to drive her home sometimes from work. I was pretty sure that he was a produce manager at a local grocery mart, where she regularly worked the evening shift. And just from the way Gen talked, I figured that the guy was sweet on her. A few times after one of her and Paul's epic fights surrounding the issue, Gen would gush about Gary after Paul had left the house. Gen insisted that he was a perfect gentleman and that nothing untoward had occurred between them. Gen's eyes would glaze over, though, as she promised aloud - one day, she would leave Paul for Gary; she was certain that the man would wait forever for her.

Del seemed to think this might be important information, and I was hopeful that this was the case. If Gen could be assured that Paul could not get near her, she might just come on board – who knows? But then again, she is one fucked-up woman! Still, I had the suspicion that if she truly believed it was possible to escape her deadbeat husband, she might just make the move.

In a sad and strange way, I could identify with Gen Miller. She had survived her own shitload of mistreatment throughout her miserable existence. However, her part in *my* abuse hardened my heart, and if she owned any role in the death of that little girl – then

Gen Miller had not one ounce of my sympathy.

Del believes that even if Gen is found guilty as an accessory to murder, her sentence would likely be lighter, with her testimony against Everett Richards. Another travesty of justice in the fucked-up system, but hey – if it put that scumbag away forever, then so be it.

A knock on the door brought me out of my reverie, and I smiled at Brad as he entered the room, with a huge grin on his face and something concealed behind his back.

I laughed out loud when he pulled out a mammoth, stuffed biker teddy bear, all decked out in metal and leather – a heart stitched into the vest alongside a skull. It was the absolute sweetest thing that anyone had ever given to me, and I fought back a tear. Damn, I was an emotional basket case today!

Brad held it out, and I grabbed it, hauling it in for a fervent monster hug. It felt so foreign, having gifts bestowed upon me. But as I looked up at Brad's soft, kind smile, I melted.

"Thank you!" What else could I say? "That was incredibly sweet of you." I watched him easily shrug that off as he took the seat beside me.

"How are you feeling today?" The request was in earnest, and I warmed up to his company.

"A little emotional, but otherwise, I think I might just live through this." I threw him an amicable grin. "You must be a busy guy - I do appreciate you coming by to see me."

"No place I'd rather be," he sobered, "your surgery is tomorrow." I nodded, and he continued, "Are you scared?"

I delayed my response, thinking about it.

"Not really," I mused, "I think I'm just looking forward to the recovery -and putting this all behind me. Apparently, I will be *as good as new* in every way." I sighed.

"I lucked out, Brad," I regarded him thoughtfully, "and I have *you* to thank."

"A lot of people came together, but mostly it was you," his tender look was like a warm caress, "getting away from that asshole toward a better future – brave and determined! Mandy, you may not be alive, sitting with me here, if you had not run from that home."

I shuddered – it was true. Looking into Brad's eyes now, I realized that no matter where it all went, I could count him as a friend – a lifer. It felt both strange and wonderful. On impulse, I reached to squeeze his hand in acknowledgement and gratitude.

"Don't worry, it will take more than you saving my ass to stay in my good books, "I teased him, "You're stuck with me, now!"

"Oh, that is not a problem."

The heated look in his eyes melted my bones just a little. Damned if he wasn't the sexiest man that I'd ever had the fortune to gaze upon! It was futile - supressing the warm flush that I knew was painfully obvious. This was entirely new to me.

Despite the abuse that Jessi and I had endured by the male populace, we had still dreamed…gazing upon the hottest celebs, fantasizing torrid affairs, brief though they may be, with an adoring hottie, fawning over our every desire. This of course, we knew would never be our reality.

For me, attraction wasn't about the body – it was all in the eyes. So much to read there – and crap – I could easily get lost in Brad's. OK, so his rock-solid frame is a sweet bonus – can't lie.

"Mandy," his gaze caressed my face, "I am your friend," he took my hand in a light caress, studying each finger, then pinned me with another burning gaze.

"I'd like nothing better than to kiss you right now."

His eyes roamed over my mouth, and an instant warmth spread through every cell in my body. Geezus! What appeal could he find in my grossly swollen lips?

"But," he continued, "you have a lot going on, with an education as top priority." He smiled gently, "By the time you get that under wraps, a lot of doors will be open for you." He sat back and regarded me affectionately.

"Once that comes to pass, I will check in with you," he grinned devilishly, "and if you are of the same mind – we can ignite the fireworks together."

OK, I was lost in those dark eyes – there was so much more than the promise of tantalizing, sexual adventures – ones that I couldn't even fathom the reason for pondering after what I had just been through. It was infinitely deeper, and I could not pull myself away from this man if I tried. Damn – I did not *want* to.

"It's important to me," he gently lifted my chin with his fingers, "that you come to me on equal ground – right now, you are vulnerable and haven't had the opportunity to explore this world as your own."

"Brad, I…"

"Shh…just know that I'll be here always, as your friend first," he grinned, "and we can take it from there later – we will both know when it is time," he paused, "and if it is not meant to progress, I'm not going anywhere – friends forever!"

"Deal." I met his gentle fist punch. His words oozed common sense, and I appreciated it immensely. Because at this moment, if he so much as crooked his finger in a come-on gesture, I would eagerly haul him into this hospital bed and have my way with him.

It struck me – touched me to the core, that he hadn't spouted my age as being the issue. I was pretty sure that he understood that my experiences made up for it. Deep in my soul was the knowledge that he was bestowing a gift that could very well save us both from destroying a beautiful union – one that had the potential to last forever. I was simply not ready.

I insisted on sharing my mediocre hospital lunch fare with him, and he feigned a gag at the spoonful of bland cream of mushroom soup that I held to his lips. We both giggled. When we had polished off everything remotely edible, I sat back with a sigh and thanked him for interrupting my boredom.

We spent another hour chatting easily – me excited about my release – if all went well, two days after the surgery! Of course, that included crutches, a walker, and daily physio. He was equally pumped about the work that they were accomplishing in Millie's house and relayed that Daisy figured it would be ready in a week's time to move in, provided the licence was in place. Del apparently had the power to pull strings!

How could Brad know? What words were adequate in explanation to impress that this was the absolute best lunch - despite the sketchy food – that I had ever experienced?

I felt happy and full!

Chapter Forty-One

Del left Devon's office with what she hoped was a solid plan of action. They had discussed approaching Gen's co-worker together but decided it would be best to keep it as low-key as possible, and Devon was fine with Del's lead on this one.

Her mind floated to Mandy and the surgery she would undergo the following morning. As she negotiated parking options at the little corner store, Del felt optimistic about Mandy's future. This morning, she had received the approval on Millie's transition home licence, and was beyond pumped!

Great! She managed to snag the last available spot in the little lot and headed in through the sliding glass door. Gus's Grocery was neat and tidy, with shelves well-stocked and gleaming floors. Del glanced around to locate the produce department and casually headed in that direction, where a young girl was busy stocking apples in bins.

"Hello, I'm wondering if you can help me," she approached the girl pleasantly, who smiled in response.

"Sure, I hope so – what can I do for you?"

"I'm wondering if I can have a word with your Product Manager, Gary Evans? I was told he is the person I need to speak to."

"No problem, he's just in the back, bringing out a fresh load of potatoes – you can wait for him there if you like," she nodded her head toward the appropriate section.

"I will do that – thank you so much." Del wandered off and dallied, inspecting the different types and brands of potatoes that were available for sale. She glanced up at the loud bang of a cart being pushed through the produce double doors at the back. The man headed straight in her direction with a smile of greeting. His name tag confirmed her mission.

"Hello, Gary Evans?" she greeted him warmly.

"Yes. Is there something I can help you with?"

"Del Greenwood," she held up her ID tag, "I would like to speak with you about one of your fellow employees."

"Oh, you will need to approach management if it concerns our staff."

"It's not related to her work here – it's about Gen Miller," at his wary regard, Del opted for transparency. "Gen may be in trouble, and I need to speak with her."

"I'm not sure how you think I could help you," he eyed her with growing uneasiness.

"I only want to talk, and I am aware that you and she are friends, as well as co-workers." It was a longshot, but she knew it paid off, with the softening worry etched on his face. "Can we go somewhere just for a coffee?"

"The Starbucks is two doors down. I'll meet you there in five," he carried on with unloading the potatoes, and she smiled her gratitude, hoping he wouldn't ditch her.

True to his word, he showed up and slid onto a chair across from her with a troubled expression. Del pushed a Café Mocha in his direction, and with a grateful grin, he accepted, nodding his thanks – then looked at her, waiting.

"You are aware of the volatile situation in Gen's household – in her marriage," Del took a deep breath, "her husband, Paul Miller, has been arrested and remains in custody." Shock registered on his face, but still, he said nothing.

"You may not be aware that Paul Miller is not his real name," another apparent shocker, "though I am unable to divulge anything further at this point."

"Why? What has he done?"

"I cannot speak to the details, but would it please you to hear that, at the very least, he will face an assault charge for the severe beating to Gen?" His body slumped in visible relief. "But it will not be possible without Gen's testimony."

"I can't tell you where Gen is," he began.

"Mr. Evans," Del pinned him with a pleading glance, "Gen could be in very serious trouble with the law, possibly embroiled in her husband's illegal activities," she sat back, knowing she had his full attention, "and I may not be able to help her, if I can't speak with her, very soon." Del paused, trying to assuage her positioning with him.

"It is not necessary for me to go to her location, but I'm hoping that I can count on you to bring Gen to me," she gambled, knowing he would likely not give up her whereabouts, "or at least have her contact me," she handed him a card. "I'm sure I don't need to tell you that it would be in your best interest to provide me with any information you may have regarding either Gen or Paul Miller."

"I only know that she is married to an asshole," he sighed heavily and met her eyes, "She tried to hide it, but I saw through the make-up and in some of her behaviors. I didn't know what to do for her other than provide a friendly shoulder to lean on. The one time I suggested that she talk to someone about his treatment of her, she seemed so afraid - I just let it go."

"You are a good friend, Mr. Evans," Del smiled warmly, her gut confirming that this man was open and truthful, "and you are not responsible for what has happened to her. Gen made her choices, and I am certain of the possibility that there could be healthier ones ahead for her." Del acknowledged his silent gratitude with a gentle nod.

"I know you are curious, as to how I learned of your friendship," Del grinned, "and again, I cannot speak to that just yet. But my sources tell me that she very much appreciates your presence in her life." His eyes teared, betraying deep emotion, and Del thought how very sad it was that good people are often denied their just rewards.

"I will try," he promised as they parted ways.

On her way back to the office, Del picked up Daisy, and they headed over to Millie's to chat about progress. Millie greeted them with a secretive smile as she ushered them in.

Del was certain that her jaw must have visibly dropped as she surveyed the home – the living space almost unrecognizable, with added furnishings, two new love seats and a chaise lounge added to the seating space. Wandering into the kitchen, she gawked at the addition of some quirky wall shelving and a portable island with three stools.

"How on earth?" she stammered, taking immediate notice of the new log table in the dining area – stunning!

"The boys wanted to add their touch," pride shone in Daisy's smile, "when I tried to gush my gratitude over it, Buck insisted that if they had to spend ten hours shifts in this place too, then they needed comfort." Daisy chuckled, "but I know better," she teared up a little, "Buck worked for hours, sanding and staining that impossibly heavy table."

The women ventured into the bedrooms to find that Millie's, also, was redone – floors and a walk-in shower. The smallest bedroom was rearranged into an office space. A comfortable sleeping area, with two new beds and furnishings, adorned the medium-size room.

At Del's inquiring glance, Millie led them down into the basement, and she gasped in astonishment. The entire level was completely finished – two large bedrooms, a stunning bathroom, and an enormous living/recreation space – again, fully furnished and move-in ready.

"I don't know what to say," Del found her voice, "this is amazing!" She shook her head and addressed both women, "I can tell you that I do have a budget for necessary upgrades – but it won't cover all of this cost."

"Hey," Daisy gave her a hug, "this is a gift from the boys – they all pitched in," she smiled, "and wouldn't dream of taking taxpayer dollars." She drilled Del with a stern look, "But they do insist that your budget be spent on another project for kids at risk." Del eagerly nodded her agreement.

"Thank you so much – please pass on my utmost

appreciation," Del rummaged in her tote bag and grinned widely as she pulled out a large envelope, "may I present - the official approval for your transition home licence!"

"This is such good news," Millie reached out and gushed her excitement, "it's ready! The girls can move in!"

"It seems so," Del laughed, "but it will take a couple of days to have the safety inspectors give their approval that everything is to code," she smiled and continued, "I have no doubt that the improvements are stellar, and I noticed that all smoke and CO_2 detectors are in place. It will also give you a chance to stock up the pantry!"

On her way out the door, Del reminded her that any reimbursable expenditures could be submitted through the online portal, for which Millie had already been provided some training.

Wow – shit was real now, Del mused.

It turned out to be the understatement of her day – immediately upon her return to the office, Sherri handed her a telephone message to call Gen Miller.

Seated at her desk, she punched in the number, immediately recognizing it to be different from the one on file – and waited. Finally, Gen picked up.

"Hello," the voice was faint and tentative.

"Is this Gen?" Del ventured, "thank you for reaching out."

"Against my better judgement," she whispered - Del could clearly decipher the fear in her voice.

"Tell me where I can meet you – I'll pick you up, and we'll go somewhere safe to chat." Del held her breath during a lengthy pause, "you need to trust me, Gen."

"I can't today - can we meet tomorrow at Pigeon Park? I'll be there at 2:00."

Del affirmed the arrangement and ended the connection. Her first instinct was to rush the tracing of the cell phone – she knew Devon would do his best – and she'd then swoop down on the pinned location. But she was no fool - a very cautious and light tread was key to ensuring Gen did not disappear.

How on earth was she going to sleep tonight?

Chapter Forty-Two

My eyes opened with some difficulty at a nurse's prompt. Wow – was it done, then? It seemed like I was just in the OR with a team of medical professionals, pleasantly assuring me that I was going to be fine.

Amazing that I did not feel so groggy this time – I had been adamant that they give me something other than Gravol for nausea – guess they listened. It is a whole other level of pain, puking with broken ribs!

Glancing around me, I noticed a few other patients in recovery, some awake and some still out. One was weeping and moaning – I assumed from the effects of the anesthetic.

I felt pretty damn good, actually – under no illusions, though, well aware that awesome drugs were masking pain at this point. But hey, I'll take the win! Suddenly, an orderly showed up to wheel me back to my room. He waited patiently, with a pleasant smile, while the nurses took my vitals. The trip through the hospital corridor maze was not my favorite feeling – a wee bit woozy with all the jostling. But it didn't last long, and soon, I was backed up into my original space – almost like coming home!

The feeling was intensified as my favorite four ladies strolled into the room to greet me. After a round of very gentle hugs, they settled in for a visit.

"Doctor told us it went very well – internal trauma should heal well, and the pelvic fix was smooth," Millie's blue eyes crinkled in a grin, "you won't be popping out babies anytime soon, but all should be good for the future."

It occurred to me that they must have given me an epidural to freeze, as I was unable to move or even feel my legs. Made sense and I relaxed, deciding to go with the flow.

"You are one tough cookie." Daisy pinned me with an admiring glance.

"She *is* amazing," Jessi grinned widely.

I knew she was immensely relieved for this part of my recovery to be over. Now, it was just the healing. Damn! I was one lucky chick, having so many friends on my team.

Hell, I'd never even had a team before, with the exception of my brief time with Jessi at Millie and Simon's. Even then, I didn't trust that it would last – correctly so! In brutal honesty, I still harbored a deep fear that this newfound stability would also explode in my face. I had to stop thinking like that, though.

I had set up an appointment for two weeks down the road with a counselor. During our brief conversation, she'd assured me that it would take some time to rationalize the fears from the trauma.

Post Traumatic Stress Disorder – PTSD, she called it.

"OK, I need to head out," Del's warm smile reached her striking gray eyes, "duty calls."

Soon after, Millie and Daisy bid their adieu, with the latter teasing me about missing my shifts for dish duty, and wow - how they'd piled up. Jessi was hanging back – she had taken the day off to be with me.

"I got some really cool news," she gushed, clearly excited to share.

"Hey, I can always use some of that!"

"If all goes well, you will be out of here in two days' time," her dark eyes sported a delicious secretive gleam, "and…we are moving you straight into Millie's!"

"Sweet!" This development was significant. Now, maybe I could move on with letting go of all the shit from the past and begin planning for the future! I stared at her, dumbfounded.

"Yeah, Millie got her licence," Jessi giggled, "wait until you see her – all proud, like a mama-bear. It's displayed in her little office area – I can't wait for you to see the house. You won't recognize it," Jessi's features softened, "Mandy, we are going to have such a good life there!"

All I could do was nod past the huge lump in my throat. It

was touching – watching Jessi embrace our new future with such passion and optimism. God, she was just what I needed! I reached out, and we hugged for a long time.

"We have separate bedrooms," her feigned look of horror spurred a guffaw, and we both split a gut.

"Well, we will know where to find each other," I winked, and we giggled more.

"Apparently, Buck worked around the clock, and all the boys kicked in for Millie's home makeover," Jessi sighed her appreciation and fell silent.

"I know Buck would do anything for you, Jess," I smiled gently at the tenderness in her expression, "and it feels good knowing that you have such a great friend in him."

Jessi fluffed the pillow behind me – obviously aware that I was losing my battle to stay conscious. I needed to sleep off the anesthetic and knew she would be content to lounge in the chair, scrolling on her phone and maybe reading a book that she had brought with her.

The next time I opened my eyes, Brad's face swam before my vision. As I gained focus, I noticed that Jessi was also in the room.

"Hey, Gorgeous," Brad smiled and squeezed my hand, "Jessi

and I were just discussing – busting you out of here." We all chortled.

"If my legs weren't still a bit frozen, I'd go now," I replied.

Actually, I was getting the pins and needles sensation – just as if I'd slept in a bad position and they'd fallen asleep. I commented on the absence of pain.

"OK, to be fair, the doc said that you have a nerve block as well, in your pelvis, that will help out for a day or two," Jessi reached out to touch my IV line, "not to mention the really good drugs they are pumping into you!"

The three of us spent the next couple of hours chatting about the move and the routine at Millie's. The thought of taking on home-schooling was appealing to me – something purposeful. I realized that it would be the first time – ever – that I wouldn't have to leave the school behind me every day only to face volatility and fear at home.

Home! Ha! Save for Millie and Simon's, I'd never termed my accommodations in that way. Food, shelter, clothing – maybe. But never did I have a safe haven. Until now…it hit me – home was my tribe, not a place. I pushed away the niggling fear of loss and set my focus on my awesome companions.

Chapter Forty-Three

The park was teeming with activity, and Del was not surprised that Gen had picked this location – easy to get swallowed up and indiscernible within the crowds traversing the blend of eclectic and business venues in the Gastown district.

She had texted Gen to provide landmarks for a bench she had chosen in a grassy area across from a truly incredibly tall and stunning totem pole. Del always marveled at the vibrant, colorful murals and graphic artwork that graced many of the structures. Over the years, Gastown had evolved; the 60s and 70s brought hippie culture with many independently owned, thriving shops, along with conglomerates such as Woodwards; 80s, a downturn with drugs, homelessness and poverty prevailed; and in recent decades, there came another revitalization, with a growing, thriving business community. However, homelessness and drug addiction persisted in the harbor area – as per an ongoing struggle since its early inception days.

Suddenly, there she was, walking toward Del; well – limping, to be exact, with a cane for assistance. Del stood up and greeted her warmly. Gen remained aloof and motioned to a vacant picnic table deeper into the field, and Del followed.

"I've been wondering how you are," Del plunged in as they settled onto the seats, "are you safe?" Gen looked rough, clearly still in pain, and at least a few pounds had fallen off her already thin frame.

"Safe enough," Gen sniffed, eyeing Del warily, "if there is any such thing."

"Gen, I am here to help you," Del looked directly into her eyes, "There are things you need to be aware of."

"I had no idea that Paul was arrested," Gen ventured, "but I wondered, as I haven't heard from him in almost two weeks." Fear was evident in her returning gaze, "He *is* in jail still, correct?" At Del's firm nod, she continued.

"I have no idea why, but if it has anything to do with my assault, and he gets out…" she left the sentence hanging.

"It is not about that, Gen," Del confirmed, "it's more serious, and with your help, he may never get out again."

Gen appeared truly frightened now, and Del knew she was going to have to sum this up quickly to avoid losing her. The body language spoke clearly of fight or flight.

"He's been arrested on charges of murder," Del stated, "of your former foster daughter." Del put up her hand as Gen stood up, obviously ready to flee. But Del knew that Gen was well aware of her own vulnerable position and that the woman truly had nowhere to go other than to her co-worker.

"Gary Evans is a good friend to you," Del kept her voice soft and calm, "and I know you don't want to involve him in *any* of this."

Gen tentatively sat once more, in obvious distress, as her good leg vibrated violently against the table. She surveyed her surroundings wildly, with the appearance of a caged animal.

"Please hear me out, Gen." Del pleaded, "Your safety depends on it." Gen looked directly at her now. "The authorities have recently connected the remains of a little girl, found a year ago, to the foster child, Nikki Leeds, who fled your home three months prior."

"I had nothing to do with any of it," Gen started to cry, "Paul has his weaknesses, I am aware - but murder, I know nothing about."

"They have his DNA evidence."

"Oh God!" Gen's eyes flew open wide, "So he *did* murder Nikki, then?"

At that moment, Del realized that Gen likely had not been with him at the time of the murder, which would bode well for plea bargaining on her behalf. She relaxed a little.

"Yes, Gen – the evidence is there, and he *will* be convicted," Del pinned her with a solid stare," but we need to establish motive and character in order to obtain proper justice and keep him behind bars."

"I didn't know, I didn't know," Gen was beyond upset.

"I believe you," Del reached out to provide a calming touch to her arm, "I am here to help you."

"Oh my God," Gen's tortured look pulled at Del's heart, "What will happen now?"

"First, we need to get you somewhere safe," Del insisted, "but to do so, it will require that you fully cooperate with the authorities," at Gen's panicked expression, Del forged on.

"Gen, as long as you cooperate, I assure you that he will not be able to come anywhere near you," she ascertained, "and you will be housed somewhere safely, under witness protection."

Del could see the wheels spinning in her head - and was immensely relieved at the ray of hope that was evident in Gen's expression as she regarded her.

"How about this? I'll drive you to your current living space, we'll pick up your things, and I'll take you to see the detective," Del smiled warmly, "he is very caring – knows of your tough situation and is extremely good at what he does." The emotions warring on Gen's features spurred Del to close.

"We know about Everett Richards."

Gen slumped forward, agony written all over her features, and Del gently urged her up. Guiding the struggling woman to the car, Del tried to put herself into Gen's shoes. What a fucking, rotten hand the lady had been dealt! Sure, by some of her own choices – but it was never as simple as that.

On the way to the station, Del phoned ahead – she had given Devon the heads up; if at all possible, she would bring Gen immediately in to see him. She knew he was chomping at the bit, waiting for her call.

Devon greeted them warmly and assured Gen that everything was voluntary – she was under no obligation whatsoever and reiterated Del's message of providing safety.

Once settled in the small office space, Devon regarded her kindly, and asked after her welfare – was there anything he could bring her? Gen quickly shook her head and eyed him with wary expectancy.

"I will give you a run-down of what we would like to see happen," he addressed her compassionately, "first and foremost, we will move you into protective custody immediately," he paused, "and you will remain there until after the trial, provided we have your statement and full cooperation." At Gen's nervous reaction, he continued.

"This is not conditional. We are not expecting anything from you other than the full truth. No one will try to coerce you to say anything against your husband, that is not true." he paused, "In fact, it is critical that you speak to the facts. If you try to embellish them in any way, in a possible effort to ensure his conviction, you will jeopardize the outcome."

"What about *my* position?" Gen eyed him fearfully, "Will I be in danger of conviction as well?"

"If you had no first-hand knowledge of the murder, you would not be charged," he eyed her seriously, "but if you were aware of the crime," he sighed, "you would likely face a charge of accessory to murder."

"I knew nothing about it," she whispered and looked up with a pained expression, "but I did wonder. I heard about the little girl's remains that were found, and I wondered," she sniffed back tears, "I was afraid to ask him about Nikki; if he knew it was her, and I guess I really didn't want to find out, that he may have done it – I mean, how could I love a man like that?" She regarded Devon thoughtfully.

"Why did it take so long to make the connection? As time went by, I put it out of my mind because I knew you guys were aware of Nikki missing and of the murdered child. No one had come to us, so I figured that possibility had been likely explored already."

"That is a very good question," Devon responded grimly, "one that has been haunting my dreams of late," he admitted.

"However, we are here now, and thanks to your recent foster

daughter, Amanda Goodchild, we have the physical, connecting evidence." At her questioning gaze, he continued, "Amanda had found something at your home, which, thankfully, contained Everett Richards' fingerprint."

"So, Amanda came to you?" Confusion was evident.

"I had been looking for her, as you know," Del contributed, "and managed to find her. Once I learned of Paul Miller's false identity and Everett Richards' prior conviction, I decided it was important to explore his recent activity." Del sighed deeply, knowing that she was on a thin line with what she could divulge. But Gen's cooperation was key – it was a tightrope walk. For sure, she could not disclose the confession to Mandy at this point.

"Amanda revealed the extent of the abuse she had suffered at Paul Miller's hands – and had expressed her concern about any prior foster children - the outcome of their fate. She had found something in the bureau drawer and was hopeful that another little girl had escaped," Del continued with caution, "she passed it on to me in case we ever found her."

"Wow," Gen sighed deeply, "I hope Amanda is OK."

"She's doing very well," Del assured, "and has also expressed concern about you. That was a brutal beating you withstood."

"Yes," Gen nodded, "but my police statement…"

"Is false – we know that," Devon intervened, "however, it is not relevant to the murder conviction," he smiled gently, "and is commonplace in situations such as yours. We are completely aware of the fallibility of our justice system. You have every right to protect yourself." Devon sat back and regarded her thoughtfully.

"We will still pursue the charges of rape, assault, and battery against Everett Richards for your physical abuse with your new collaborating statement. But it is the best strategy to hold him on the murder charge – thankfully, the evidence allows for this."

"Your testimony will by key for us," he pinned her with a serious gaze, "for his violent and dangerous behavior, with both you and the foster children in your care, as well as the nature of his character. Your assault charge will be separate but simultaneous to the murder trial, and hopefully, this statement, should you choose to give it now, will be admissible as evidence."

"The abuse of Amanda and the others…" Gen began to cry.

"As long as you were not a perpetrator," Devon offered, "your position is encouraging for negotiating a plea bargain for any lesser charges; likely none will be in place. Even if you were a co-conspirator, your testimony will work toward shortening your sentence."

Gen began to gasp for air as the full realization of the

situation bore down upon her.

"I do not have to give you a statement, correct?"

"As I said, you are under no obligation today to do so," Devon affirmed, "however, as the murder trial progresses, it is highly likely that you will be subpoenaed as a witness, which will mandate your presence in court. If you choose not to show, the judge can, and likely will, opt to charge you with *contempt of court* and issue a warrant for your arrest."

"You have the option," Devon continued, "to provide your statement to us today and come into the Witness Protection Program. We will provide a safe place for you, even if you take a few days to make your decision," he assured, "but know this – if you opt out of our protection, we will find you when the time comes."

"Jesus," Gen sighed shakily, "I loved him once. There was good in him - I knew it," she reminisced wistfully, "He was so loving and giving – always looking after me," her expression clouded, "but in recent years, it all changed. He drank heavily - became meaner, and more unpredictable," tears rolled down her cheeks, "and our foster children – there were only four since he was released from prison – often took the brunt of his alcoholic rages." She breathed in deeply, sniffed and wiped her eyes.

"I believed in him – he wanted to rescue children who needed love, parenting and care. It was his way of making up for some of his prior deeds. He was a changed man – I trusted him." Gen looked up, took a deep, shaky breath and met their eyes, dead on.

"I'm ready."

Chapter Forty-Four

Holy freaking hell! This was incredible! I wandered around on my crutches, surveying the kitchen and living space with Jessi as my guide. It was pure luxury compared to what Millie had lived in before, and I was completely stoked that she had managed to attain this upgrade as a bonus for taking us on.

When we reached the basement stairway, Jessi was beside herself as she pushed a button for an automatic lift. Suddenly, like magic, a chair appeared that I could sit upon, and it breezed me down to the bottom level.

"Sweet!" I couldn't believe how slick that was! I was even able to take the crutches. This would help Millie in future years, too!

"Del managed to cover that expense through some sort of upgrade budget," Jessi was beaming at me, "in a *sicko* way, I guess it's the perk to being horribly traumatized!" We both rolled our eyes at that reality.

OK – this was seriously cool! Both our bedrooms came with insanely comfortable queen-sized beds, a writing/studying desk with drawers and storage, a walk-in closet, a set of bureau drawers, and a cozy reading chair. I didn't need or deserve this luxury, but I sure did appreciate it; it made me feel so grateful that they'd given Millie a truly sick, master retreat too!

But most of it was all paid for by the guys, and it was overwhelming, to say the least. This was not in my comfort zone – that level of caring! I knew I'd have to find a way to thank them.

We ended the tour with the freaking amazing bathroom – both a shower and soaking tub, and our comfy living area; we could hang out there and chill whenever we wanted. But the absolute best thing about it all? Millie, love, and safety. The rest was just icing!

I collapsed onto the huge chaise, closed my eyes, and breathed deeply. Tomorrow morning, we were meeting with the homeschool administrators to set us up for study. I was pumped for that, bored stiff with recovery. I smiled – could not *wait* to sleep in that bed tonight! Woohoo!

Buck was due in about an hour – first shift for the guys' regime. Jessi and I had made a pact that we'd handle the bedding laundry for them – after every shift rotation. I felt a fierce need to contribute whenever I could find a way.

Del and I had chatted at the hospital about volunteering with foster kids. At first, she had seemed a little hesitant.

"Mandy, you have faced so many life changes in a very short period of time," she voiced her concern, "I know you are grateful beyond words, and I appreciate that."

"It's a fire within me, Del," I was determined to explain,

"now that I've had the privilege of good fortune – of having wonderful people – good humans – care about me and work on my behalf," I had choked up a little, "I am deeply driven to making a difference for other kids like me – like I *was*."

Del had been quiet, studying me carefully, and I knew her well enough by now – she'd find a way if it were possible. I smiled. I trusted her – knew I had no need to prove anything. She trusted me! And it meant everything. I let it go and got on with the business of getting some exercise on my crutches – up and down the hospital corridor.

Just this morning, she had dropped in to see if I needed anything to help with the move. She'd lingered and finally sat down, motioning for me to join her.

"I have an idea," her smile had carried great intent.

"I'm all ears," I had responded.

"How would you feel about working with kids, mostly elementary age to start, in a literacy incentive – helping those who struggle with literacy development?"

"Sweet! I would love that!"

"Being that you would be a volunteer, not paid, and therefore, not regimented by any public school system, you would have full autonomy to build incentives and implement creative ideas. Of course, you would partner with their teachers for maximum impact."

"That sounds amazing!" I was already pumped – ideas bouncing around in my head. I had been lucky – reading had come easy for me, but I'd watched so many kids struggle. My heart went out to them – their feelings of inadequacy and their determination to build coping skills, helping them to mask the struggle and get through school. All subjects require the ability to read and comprehend, I reflected. Not to mention the social jungle – kids who struggled were always bullied and picked on. Kids could be so fucking mean!

I knew it was important work – a sweet opportunity to make a difference – it would impact their entire lives – not just school. And though teachers tried their best, they were hampered by a structured, packed curriculum that allowed for little flex. Some managed very well, and I had learned a lot. I had been one of the students whom they'd picked for a mentor, so this was not entirely new to me.

"I'm in – totally!"

"I figured you would be," Del had chuckled, "I can also arrange that it count towards work experience for your high school diploma, along with the diner job. I will ask that you run your initial ideas through me, and we'll collaborate with each teacher, together.

The bonus is that there will likely be foster kids in the program, and this experience will lend to your skills in future volunteer work or even a possible career."

"You're the boss," I would have agreed to anything! And so, it was! I could not believe how sweet my life was unfolding.

I had been thinking about it all day, mulling design plans for tweaking their interests – and getting the kids on board. I knew that it was critical to have their buy-in. Hell, kids who struggled with it hated reading! It was right up there with getting a monster needle jabbed in your arm. But worse, because every other kid in the classroom – in the school, knew about it.

Fun was key – I had to find a way to make it enjoyable so that every other kid in the school will wish they could have the same opportunity. Yep – I was pumped!

Chapter Forty-Five

Del settled into the steamy, warm water, the mass of aromatic bubbles threatening to swallow her up whole. With a huge sigh, she embraced the tiny muscle spasms that signalled a slow relaxation was underway.

The last two days had been transforming on so many levels!

First and foremost, Mandy had been released yesterday morning from the hospital – vibrant and remarkably mobile. She would need physio for a few weeks while everything healed up, and Del had the budget to cover home visits for this purpose, along with the necessary equipment. She had incorporated a few pieces already, for a home gym – it was perfect.

Del chose, at this moment, to push away the depressing reality of the system and the dysfunctional irony – the more horrific the trauma, the greater the financial compensation through a reactive budget allowance. Instead, she fervently hung onto the positive in this situation.

It was one of those rare wins – the catalyst to continuing a soul-sucking career. Mandy's case represented the epitome of overcoming the system, dredging through unspeakable horror to emerge victorious against all odds. Del's heart was full.

Oh, there was a formidable road ahead for Mandy.

Counselling would help her continue to embrace the reality – that her new life was both deserved and stable. It would be up to Mandy to avoid self-sabotage; it was a tricky slope, but the girl had already traversed much of it. The counselors were brilliant – providing that Mandy embraced it.

The look on her face – when they brought her home – Millie had captured it on her iPhone video. Del was overcome with emotion, watching her and Jessi, totally pumped and truly appreciative of their good fortune. She, Millie, and Daisy had prepared a welcoming feast for the girls and Buck, who accepted their gratitude with quiet grace.

Del was amazed at the physical progress that Mandy had achieved with her recovery – managing those crutches like a boss and on minimum pain dosage. She had insisted that she wanted to be *present* rather than comatose. Del mused that the girl was no stranger to pain. She had endured much worse, unmedicated. The fact that she had managed to avoid emotional self-medication for all these years was a wonder – and a testament to her fortitude and strength.

The same could be said for Jessi, given the circumstances she had endured. Del could not ask for a greater healthy support sister for Mandy and sent a silent prayer of gratitude that both girls had found each other. Millie was key. Sometimes, the Universe lined things up in perfect harmony.

Then there was Gen. Holy hell – Del had brooked no idea which way *that* situation was fated to play out. It had been like sitting on the edge of her seat in a horror flick, where one wrong move could tip the scales precariously.

Thankfully, Gen had come on board. Del had carried on to the office, once Gen had agreed to give her statement. Devon reported that she had left nothing out – it was all there. The woman was now safely tucked away in an entirely new neighborhood, clear across the city, under a false ID. Of course, she would still appear as Gen Miller in court. Del reflected as she blew soapy bubbles from her nose, that the woman had likely not experienced this level of relaxed security for a long time – if ever. It was inevitable, though, that she'd struggle with guilt for her part in all of it.

A piquant sip of wine warmed her belly as she continued her recap of the proverbial ducks that had fallen so neatly in a row. Sighing deeply, she sank her luxurious auburn mane into the water. Coming up for air, she smiled, remembering Mandy's adamant stance that she please refrain from coloring it – after Del had mentioned her intention to do so to the group

"Don't you dare!" Mandy spouted, "You have gorgeous hair, and you've earned those distinguished gray streaks – also, I suspect that we share ownership of some of those! So, I should have a say."

Everyone had burst out laughing at that.

Del had indulged in a thorough mirror inspection that evening and had arrived at the conclusion that Mandy was right. It was defining, in a way – akin to well-merited face wrinkles. And she knew too well that one could never truly match natural hair color through synthetic embellishment.

So be it! And Devon seemed to take no issue at all with the subtle gray touches – he had voiced his fascination with her soft locks – promising that one day, the opportunity would come his way to run his fingers slowly through her hair in a tantalizing caress – Lordy, she'd have no hope for resistance.

Del felt that same blush, heating her skin now, as it had on the day he had murmured it, altogether too closely to her ear. The conviction that she really should reign in her hormonal impulses, which had her emotions all in turmoil - where he was concerned, seemed to have zero impact. Fantasies were running rampant! Damn!

Pulling her attention back to business, Del pondered the girls' future. The home-schooling rep had come out today – it was all set up. The woman was thorough and provided everything, including the modules for them to get started. Their computer access was in place. Millie reported that Mandy had already been head-down, immersed in the first lesson, before the lady had even left.

Del suspected that tearing herself away for her four-hour afternoon shift at the diner would be a formidable undertaking.

Left on the table now was the upcoming trial. Devon shared that the murder charges were formally in place, and a trial date was set for three weeks away. The first step would be similar to a preliminary hearing, whereby Everett Richards would appear to hear the evidence presented against him and decide if he wished further review time with his appointed defense lawyer. He also could, at this time, advise that he wishes to seek alternate counsel. Devon assumed that he would draw it out and the trial would be adjourned to accommodate his requests.

However, the evidence was solid, and together with Gen's statement, there was little risk of the judge granting bail. Devon related his anticipation that the trial would commence with minimum delay. Further, two secondary charges for the rape and assault on Gen, and a possible upgrade to attempted murder on Mandy, were in the process of finalization. Mandy had agreed to provide her statement concerning all counts as soon as Devon called her in. Everett's cohort in the crime was also being charged with Mandy's assault.

Jessi had her own statement to provide concerning Russell's operation. She had initially decided to decline pressing charges on the gang rape, which she and Mandy had endured, but underwent a change of heart after a long chat with Daisy, who convinced her that; under no circumstances had she provided consent. Both Jessi and Mandy would testify there for the sake of the others, who were also willing to stick their necks out to put the man behind bars and permanently out of business.

That one was a wrap!

Del's attention drifted back to Devon as she finished her body cleanse, slowing with slippery, sensual abandon at the special spots as she surrendered to her fantasies.

Her cell chimed as she climbed out, wrapping the towel around her, and she picked up. Butterflies ran amok in her stomach as the object of her amorous infatuation murmured a throaty greeting. Oh, hell – hot need flooded her loins – how did he do that?

"Hi," she squeaked a reply, "to what do I owe this pleasure after work hours?"

"Well, for one – I have a strange longing to be there with you right now," he whispered huskily, "and secondly, I think you know the answer to that."

His voice was pure silky heat, and Del knew at that moment that she was hooped. With the bulk of their tricky work together now stabilized, her ethic alarm bells were no longer guiding her. She felt adrift in a sea of hopeless abandon, with no oars to guide her back to solid ground.

"I suppose I do," she stammered, "and damned if I know what to do with it," she whispered softly.

"Let me come over – let me in."

"Give me fifteen," she acquiesced, knowing that there was absolutely nothing more that she craved this night.

It took her all of five minutes to dry her hair, dress casual sexy, throw on a bit of mascara, and spritz just a subtle hint of scent. The remaining ten minutes consisted of her nervously pacing the floor, wondering if it was at all possible to wear a permanent pathway into the hardwood finish.

Del jumped at the sound of her doorbell chime. Oh God, it was getting real now. Opening the door slowly, she melted inside. Devon's eyes roamed over her face, neck and bosom in a heated caress, and she swallowed nervously, stepping back to allow him in.

To his credit, the man kept his distance, hung up his light jacket, and sauntered into the kitchen in search of a glass, to share the nearly full bottle of wine still sitting on the counter.

While Del stood motionless, not trusting herself to move at this point, she made note that his gaze had never left her the entire time. She supposed they needed to talk about this…whatever it was - but wanted nothing more than to wrap herself around him in reckless surrender. Oh God!

Devon wandered into the living room and gently placed two wine glasses on the table, then moved to start the fire. To this point, he hadn't uttered a word, and Del had the sudden urge to demand that he say something – anything! Instead, she stood and watched him, mesmerized by his every move.

He stood up and moved to take her hand, guiding her to sit on the loveseat beside him. The electric currents between them sizzled deliciously, and she took a gulp of wine to distract herself.

"I know I promised I'd wait," Devon began and paused briefly as his eyes bore into hers, "and damn it, Del – I will still if you can look me in the eye and tell me that is what you want – what you need."

Del met his gaze squarely and faltered. There was no masking the heated desire that swam in those dark orbs, and she suspected he saw the same mirrored in hers. Hell, she could no more resist him than run into a blazing building. With a shaky sigh, she reached up to trace the irresistible, sexy stubble along his jaw, her eyes following the movement.

Devon captured her hand in his, whispering so softly that she wondered if she had imagined it. He placed a sweet, tantalizing kiss on her palm.

"Are you sure?"

"I am robbed of choice," she responded throatily as she gently touched his lips with her own, thinking it was pure bliss.

Devon suddenly captured her mouth in a wild and thorough possession, melting every part of her insides. As their exploration deepened and breaths labored, it seemed Devon's sweet caress was everywhere.

She wanted it – needed it, and moaned her frantic desire for him. They moved as one, stumbling together into her bedroom and tumbled onto the mattress. There, it slowed once again as they intentionally took their time, peeling clothing from each other, piece by piece, and kissing the exposed flesh as they went.

It was pure sensuality, and Del was aware that he was fighting the same battle as she to fend off a frantic coupling, release of the sexual tension that had been tortuously building between them for days now – since the moment they'd met. Both were trembling with anticipation, their hearts beating wildly, breathing reduced to moaning gasps – still, they took their time in adoring reverence as they explored each other's naked bodies, building the delicious inferno that they both knew would soon consume them completely.

"It's been a long time, and I'm not sure how..." it was an agonized moan, his voice shaky.

"Shh…" Del cut in, "do you really think once will be enough tonight?" She wriggled against him, and they melded, moaning their pleasure as they engaged in the ancient ritual of physical love. And despite his apologetic prophecy, Del met him, wave after wave, as they immersed themselves in ecstasy – the sweet, sumptuous pleasure of their mutual release.

Del was astounded; she had never experienced anything so utterly, physically satisfying with any other man before him. It was physical, emotional – sweet and wickedly carnal – all wrapped up together. She sighed in total satiated euphoria and entwined herself with him, knowing that the night would be a blissfully long one.

Chapter Forty-Six

Scraping the last of the peelings into the compost bucket, I flicked on the burner to start the potato boil. Garlic mashed was on the menu tonight. No one could perfect it like Jeff! I sent a silent prayer into the Universe that there would be enough to snag some for tomorrow's dinner. Jeff always sent leftovers home with the staff, with Daisy's blessing, of course.

Woohoo! I no longer needed my crutches – it had been almost two weeks since the surgery, and I carried a cane to assist. Truthfully, though, I didn't seem to need it – pain was gone, and my stamina was returning. Only if I put too much pressure on the right leg did I notice a twinge. My physio gal related that this was normal, and she was amazed at my progress - insisted on the cane, though and for the most part, I reigned in my inner rebel and adhered to her better judgement.

I'd already washed and prepped the carrot sticks and snap sugar peas for a quick pan sear. Jeff would handle that and the maple, pecan, crusted pork schnitzels as the orders came in. A quick glance confirmed that lunch dishes were clean and put away. I had helped Bree with a deep counter bleach cleanse earlier, as well.

"Hey, Jeff, anything you need me to help with?"

"As usual, you are amazing and not just yet – take a break."

He threw me a crooked grin, "You are never allowed to leave here – just so you know that."

He had expressed interest in the textbook I'd brought in, with full intention of immersing myself in studies during my break. Now that I had the later shift, I worked through the dinner rush until around 7:00 but allowed flex, depending on the crowd. Evening meals were not generally as busy, and Bree was usually available to finish whatever was left. I grabbed my book and took a small booth near the kitchen.

I loved this stuff – especially Social Studies. Grade Ten was all about globalization, and I soon immersed in the reading. The more that I ingested the concept of personal identity and the factors that influence it, the greater my realization of how my journey through the foster system had impacted me – subjected me to an extremely narrow lens through which to view the world around me. This, in comparison to the norm, where kids are raised by their parents, dysfunctional for some, perhaps, but very different from my experience, still.

And Jessi – with the colonization of her indigenous people. But, were we affected in the same way, through globalization – exposed to much the same language, cultures and traditions? I recognized a strong thirst for a deeper knowledge – a hunger to learn more about other cultures – other countries. I was mesmerized as I continued, and I couldn't wait to share it with Jessi.

It seemed like only minutes before the supper crowd started straggling in. I packed up, having completed a full module, and headed to the kitchen. Jeff was perfecting the finishing touches, and I cleaned up the few utensils and dishes he'd already used. Bree was helping to take orders, and I began to assist Jeff as he filled them. The diners almost always chose Jeff's daily special, confident in the quality of cuisine and taste. There were a few creatures of habit, and I stepped in to grab ingredients for Jeff to accommodate one of those now.

The time flew – it was better busy, for sure, and before long, I was prepped for home. Daisy popped her head in to offer me a ride. It was only a twenty-minute walk – five minutes by bus and I enjoyed the *me* time. But I knew Daisy – she wanted to chat about something, and I followed her out to the car. She got right to the point.

"Sweetie – are you sure you are up for this work just yet?"

Daisy had protested when I begged her to let me come back, insisting that I needed the normalcy. After much discussion, she extracted my solemn promise that I would let her know if I needed time off, or lesser hours, etc. It was already understood that I'd need the break for the court obligations.

"I'm doing great, Daisy – don't worry!"

"I'm just concerned about all you have taken on, with your school, physio, etc., and now, the volunteer work with students you plan to engage in."

"It's all good, Daisy – I'm already two modules ahead in my school work for all subjects and loving it," I patted her shoulder, "and my volunteer hours will be flex. I promised you that I would back off if I needed to."

I knew she wasn't concerned about losing me at the diner. I had correctly assumed all along that the hours she allotted me were mostly for my benefit. I tried to go over and above, to at least make them count for her, and my heart melted, knowing that she had my back.

"I just want to be sure," she heaved a resigned sigh, "you have a lot on your plate, and Millie tells me that you girls are insisting on doing all of the laundry and housework."

I giggled, remembering the last conversation we'd had with Millie on the subject. She'd expressed her concern that she might become a lazy old cat lady if we didn't let her do some stuff. At that thought, we relented a little.

"We made some compromises with Millie – we aren't doing *every*thing any longer – quit worrying!"

"Coming in for dinner?" I asked as we pulled up to the curb.

"Nope, going to see Joe tonight." A soft smile lit up her features.

"OK, tomorrow then – thanks for the ride!" As I sauntered into the house, I reflected on my secret fervent hope that she and Joe would finally surrender to their obvious mutual devotion and attraction to one another. The sole time I had mentioned it to her, she'd spouted off about how she was just an old lady – not attractive to anybody; her time was past. Of course, she was dead wrong – still a beauty in my eyes, and I'm pretty sure, in Joe's too!

Jessi had just gotten in from her work shift, and we pitched in to help Millie with supper. Brad was on the evening shift, and it brought a warm fuzzy feeling to my insides. I knew we'd visit until it was time to call it a night. While he would stay the night, he'd be gone by the time I got up in the morning; his replacement already in residence.

Jessi and I had drifted away from our intimate relationship, both by choice. It seemed natural. It wasn't that we didn't still enjoy it – find pleasure in it. It occurred to me that we both realized just how special it was – how it had gotten us through some of the ugliest shit we'd ever been forced to endure.

I think we felt a strong need to preserve that beauty, the shared gift. Neither of us wanted to risk the possibility of complacency, of taking it for granted. Deep down, I knew that Jessi and I would never opt for a permanent romantic relationship together – raise a family etc. Hell, I want all that someday, but with a man like Brad. Bottom line, I conceded that we both are content in the certainty that we will always share our lives with each other, as soul sisters anyway – that will never change.

The three of us hung out together after dinner and cleanup, sharing the events of our day.

Jessi was gaining an admirable skill set for everything to do with spices. I was flabbergasted at the knowledge – the history and uses – wow! Our meals were vastly improved because of it, and I told her so.

"Oh, shush – when you work with it for hours, you get to know this stuff!" She laughed.

Brad had a small handyman business, taking on project work. Defined as a jack-of-all-trades, he handled anything from diagnosing appliance and furnace problems to finishing an entire basement. He seemed to be content with it and came with a story today.

"So, I answered an urgent call this morning. No matter what she did, the woman could not get her freezer door to close, and she had just picked up a huge meat order the week prior," he couldn't resist a chuckle, "she was beside herself, convinced that the meat would thaw and be wasted." He paused, suppressing a laugh, "I followed her into the back room, and sure enough – the door of her chest freezer was about six inches ajar. I walked over, pushed gently and quickly saw the problem – there was a mop bucket right beside the freezer, and the handle had clearly leaned into the hinged part, the last time she'd had it open," he grinned and shrugged his shoulders, "easiest call I ever made – moved the handle and closed the lid. She was so happy!"

"Easy earnings," Jessi laughed.

"No charge for that," Brad replied.

The more I've gotten to know Brad, the greater appreciation I have developed for his character. Damn – he really is a nice guy! How often do you get a hottie and nice guy combo? He is certainly highly skilled for one so young. When I'd commented on it one day, he'd shrugged it off, crediting one of his biker mentors, who owned a small appliance and motorcycle repair business. He had hung around the dude often, helping him out on a steady basis.

Jessi decided to pack it in early, but Brad and I continued to chat.

"How old were you when you left home?" I was curious about his past.

"For good, when I was fifteen," his expression clouded a little, "I was a runner – thankfully, had a friend whose mom would look out for me and let me stay for a few nights now and again." He looked up and met my gaze.

"My mom died from cancer when I was five," he murmured softly, "and I guess my pop just fell apart without her – started drinking heavily, lost one job after another, and my brother and I barely survived through the bad stretches." He smiled when I reached out with a compassionate squeeze to his arm.

"Hell, it wasn't *all* bad – he was at least not violent, like some. My brother was a few years older than I and left when I was ten – that broke my heart," he choked a little, "he ended up with a street gang and died in a drive-by shooting several years later – I only knew about it through my neighbor's son, Mikey. He's the one that pretty much took me in when I left." Brad heaved a calming sigh and took my hand.

"That must have been awful for you – and here you are – turned out to be the nicest man I know." I smiled softly.

"Now you are flattering me," he chuckled softly, "I owe most of it to Mikey, who insisted that I keep in touch with Pop from time to time. Last visit, I barely recognized him – skin and bones, dying from a failing liver. He just kept mumbling his apologies and cried like a baby," Brad smiled sadly, "I held him closely and gave him my forgiveness. A couple of hours later, he was gone – thankfully before my brother died."

Brad reached out and pulled me close. We sat there, just cuddling, and said nothing for a long while.

"Thank you for that," he pinched my nose, and I giggled, "So, tell me about your life – I know it's been rough, and I fully understand if you don't want to."

I hesitated, not wanting to incite pity or seem like I needed attention drawn to my pathetic existence before now – or worse - needed saving. But as I gazed into his dark eyes, I realized that he was truly interested. Hell, he'd *already* rescued me from one of the worst nightmares that I'd ever endured. And in my heart, I knew our growing relationship was not born out of obligation or fascination. We simply shared a deep caring for one another.

Brad truly respects who I am – it hit me – recognizes the strengths and vulnerabilities that are a part of me, and is willing to accept me rather than try to change me.

"I was born a crack addict – literally," I began, "it was meth actually, but somehow, I never made it into foster care until I was four, when my father beat my mother to near death, causing severe brain damage," I took a deep breath, "apparently I was in pretty rough shape by then, and there was evidence of possible sexual abuse," Brad squeezed my hand ever so slightly, "thank God I don't remember my toddler years."

I continued on with the entire sordid story – it poured out of me like lava from a volcano that just couldn't hold back – eruption ensued. I had never told another human being the entire story before – not even Jessi knew all of the details, but now Brad did.

He held me close through it all and never said a word – just let me go on – spewing the anger and pain. His occasional gentle squeeze assured that he was listening with all of his heart – to mine.

I took a breather for a few minutes and then related everything that I had suffered at the hands of Everett Richards. I stopped short at the details of Jessi and my shared abuse – it wasn't mine alone to tell, but I was aware that he already knew most of it from Daisy.

"And now," I raised my tear-streaked face to his – compassion and empathy reflected in his gaze, "I have entrusted you with my shitty, messy baggage," I smiled softly, "because I *do* trust you – that you won't treat me like a broken doll or a weak, vulnerable female, who needs your constant protection," I sat back and surveyed his features – now dear to my heart, "I am a survivor, and I thank you for respecting that about me – all the good and bad that comes with it." I kissed his cheek.

"Woman, you have my utmost respect," he sighed deeply, "I can't deny that I want to find every one of your abusers throughout your life story and pummel them to death," his eyes were stormy, "but not because you need me to do that - hell, you've already taken your power back from them, just in who you are today – your survival," his gaze softened, as it roamed over my face, "I just can't abide by any adult human being forcing abuse on another – and OK – I'm a man, so especially, when a male takes liberties and advantages with a child or woman, who is helpless to defend themself – it enrages and sickens me."

I got it – I knew and appreciated his feelings on that score. It fucking enrages me too! The beauty of it is that it's not specific to me – he's not choosing *me* to defend and protect. It just so happened that he was able to do so when my circumstances were dire, but I knew he wasn't alone – they were a team that day, and I was grateful to each and every one of them. I was also very aware that he would have done the same for anyone - man or woman, who found themselves at the mercy of a sadistic monster.

Damn, he is a good man! How the hell will I ever manage to wait until graduation before deepening this bond?

"Woman, we need to call it a night," he kissed me chastely on the forehead, "because if you keep looking at me like that, it's going to be a sleepless one for at least one of us." On impulse, I hugged him fiercely.

"Thank you, Brad," I smiled my gratitude, "for everything," I headed toward my room and looked back, "but mostly for saving me from myself." I knew he would stick stubbornly to his commitment, where I was concerned, and that it was the absolute best choice for any future we may have together.

As I drifted off, for the first night since my horrible rendezvous with Everett Richards, the nightmarish visions swirling around in my head - of that bastard's face above me, taunting me, were blessedly absent. Instead, Brad's sexy grin and warm gaze lulled me into instant slumber.

Chapter Forty-Seven

Instant flames suffused every cell in Del's body as her sleep-drugged eyes drifted open to meet Devon's dark, heated gaze roaming her face. Her involuntary wake-up stretch intensified the sweet fire as the friction from their bodies revealed evidence of Devon's renewed burning desire.

Surrendering to their shared passion had been inevitable – something bigger than she – Del surmised an hour later as she stood in the shower. And who was she to complain? It was delicious and steamy. She conceded that she had never felt more alive, vigorous, and happy!

And hopelessly, head over heels in love with Devon McMullen. With a contented sigh, she toweled off and quickly dressed for work. The man was wickedly insatiable in bed – just the thought brought a fresh wave of heat to her loins.

She found him in her kitchen, dressed and ready for the day. How did he look so fresh and professional? His co-workers would have absolutely no idea, she giggled inwardly, as to how the man started his day. Gratefully accepting a cup of fresh coffee, she sat down beside him at the table, where he'd placed two plates, liberally blessed with scrambled eggs and toast.

"Oh my God, I'm going to balloon in no time if you keep

this up." Del groaned - it was so delicious! "I generally skip breakfast."

"That is counterproductive to a healthy metabolism," he returned, with a lingering kiss on her neck, as he got up to clear the table.

It had been a week, from that first night of bliss with Devon, and he hadn't slept in his own bed since. Not that she was complaining. Her life had morphed into something wonderful – meaningful, aside from her career. Neither one of them, despite their good intentions to take it slowly, could manage to part ways at the end of their busy days. Devon had purchased a small condominium close to the station years ago, but it made more sense to hang together at her place, with more space and comfort.

They had an understanding – work hours would necessarily permeate their existence together – flow over into their leisure time, and create havoc with their best laid plans. The past few evenings had been filled with just that – some overlapping together with the upcoming trial.

Del's expression clouded now, as she pondered the process – she was confident that Mandy would stand her ground in the witness box, but at what cost - how deep the impact? Would it trigger the trauma? Set her back in any way?

"Penny for your thoughts," Devon swooped down for a

lingering heated kiss as they headed out the door to their respective vehicles. Del smiled her gratitude.

"Just thinking about the trial – we'll talk later." She pulled away with great reluctance, "Will you be calling Mandy today?"

"Yes, hopefully, we can wrap up her multiple statements in a few days – ample time before the evidence submission deadline."

After firming dinner plans, they parted ways, and Del decided to drop in on Mandy beforehand – prepare her for the call and check in to see how she was doing. Though her plate was already full, the girl insisted on commencing her volunteer work through it all.

Jim, one of the biker staff, let her in with a warm smile and motioned toward the living room, where Mandy was comfortably seated, working on her modules. Del smiled warmly as she approached her.

"Hey, you are one stellar student."

"Hey, yourself," Mandy returned the friendly greeting, "I am pumped – love this stuff!"

"Well, not every high school student can boast that," Del chuckled, "especially not through homeschooling method."

"To be honest," Mandy regarded Del thoughtfully, "I'm beginning to think that learning is my thing, and I may not be ready to end it after high school," she grinned sheepishly, "I am one module away from completing Social 10."

Del was thoroughly impressed, aware that Mandy had received honor marks for all of her module work, thus far. Again, worry about the upcoming trial seeped into her thoughts. How would that impact her, with less time devoted to her studies? Oh, there was no doubt that Mandy would still tackle it. Del would have to chat with Daisy about the work hours, perhaps.

"I won't keep you long – just wanted to let you know that Devon will be calling you to set up some time to obtain your statements."

"It's all good. I want that shit over and done with ASAP." Mandy's features clouded.

"I'll be right beside you, all the way." Del was compelled to provide that reassurance. She would do anything to spare Mandy the ugliness of the trial, but the best she could offer was unwavering support. Mandy met her compassionate gaze.

"I know Del – you've got my back," Mandy smiled, "and it means everything to me – I just want those assholes to pay."

Del left her with a warm hug, sought out Jessi for the same - who was in her room, deep into school work, and headed to the office. Sherri had been working on a list of possible neighborhood schools interested in Mandy's volunteer project.

Thankfully, Mandy knew the area well and, with her street smarts, could traverse even unknown territory safely. It wasn't a major concern, as her volunteer hours would be limited to school hours. In short, they weren't restricted to walking distance – Mandy had an automatic public transit pass through Social Services. But Del wanted to keep her within a reasonable perimeter.

Del traded Sherri's list for a still-warm samosa from Sitar's, which she placed - smack dab in the middle of her assistant's desk. She smiled, making her way to her office. Sherri hadn't even uttered a word as she dove into that treat immediately, rolling her eyes in delight. It was barely 10:00 a.m., and Del shook her head – it was simply inequitable – that girl could eat ten breakfasts every day and never gain an ounce!

With four possible contenders, she decided to start her search with the closest to Millie's; Elsie Roy Elementary. The secretary confirmed that the Vice-Principle would be available at 1:00 p.m. to chat. Del then contacted the largest, yet still close, Lord Strathcona Elementary, and set up another appointment for 2:00 p.m.

So much for her afternoon! She dug into her caseload – which thankfully was relatively light in view of her senior status. She would pop by one of the foster homes before lunch, grab some fast food and carry on. Beforehand, however, she needed to touch base and collaborate with another of the social workers regarding a particularly troubling case. Del suspected that they were going to have to pull the kids from their current foster home – never a pleasant experience.

Located in Yaletown, Elsie Roy Elementary School was within close proximity to many cultural sites and programs, including the Public Library, Science World, Stanley Park Ecology, the local community centre and Vancouver Art Gallery.

The VP greeted Del warmly and ushered her into an office. Del was impressed with their student-inclusive Code of Conduct – ORCAS – Ownership, Respect, Compassion, Achievement and Safety, and wondered fleetingly how long it had taken them to match it to the ocean catchphrase.

In her line of work, she paid great attention to values, theirs being – respect, truth & trust, integrity, freedom, happiness and peace. Impressive. Further, they boasted a host of social-emotional learning programs and strategies and a wonderful lunch program – always a hit. Topping that off was a stellar early literacy intervention program structured for leveled reading literacy development – fairly standard in most schools, but their protocol was impressive.

Del thanked the woman and headed off to Lord Strathcona. In contrast, the heritage building and grounds were massive - the history formidable – operating since 1873.

Located in a busier commercial area but still with a residential mix, the cultural diversity it catered to was impressive. The school shared building space with community groups and had recently undergone a multi-stage seismic update project for space allocation. Most interesting was their status as a Tier 1 Enhanced Services school, which included extra services, supports, and staff to meet the needs of vulnerable learners. The school was strongly connected to the Community Centre and had breakfast, lunch, dental, and medical support in place.

Perhaps most notable was their formidable commitment to family volunteer and support incentives – their sense of community and literacy development was their primary aim, with strong support for English Second Language learners.

The Secretary sent Del off with an informative booklet and she skimmed over the information, pondering on it, as she headed to the diner. Both schools offered great opportunities for Mandy, but Del wanted to communicate with her – the strengths and challenges, and allow her ownership in making the decision.

Daisy greeted her with a serious expression and motioned Del into her small office space immediately.

"We have a situation," Daisy related, "Russell has been released from the hospital," she heaved a troubled sigh, "apparently still in no shape to present any personal danger, and I seriously doubt if he has the balls – pardon the pun – to come near, anyhow.”

“I thought the charges were laid, and he was supposed to be released directly into police custody!” Del was immediately pissed about this!

“Yep – that's what the plan was, but somehow, the appointed defense attorney managed a bail hearing without his presence, and because there are not yet any witness statements in place, he's been granted temporary bail, conditional to the submission of further evidence.” Daisy raised her brows in frustration.

“Well, hell – we have to get the statements, pronto!”

“Yes, they led us down a flowery garden path, assuring he would be held just from his pimp status alone until all the witness statements came in. Turns out, the investigator has been *too busy* to attend to that yet.”

“Screw that shit – I'm going to see what kind of strings Devon can pull to light some formidable fires under their butts!” Damn! Del conceded that she should not have been so surprised with this news – it happened constantly in her world, but her investment in this one was mammoth.

“Yeah – good idea, and meanwhile, I have the boys tailing his ass,” Daisy chuckled, “and they are making damn sure that he knows it.”

"Awesome," Del heaved a sigh of relief, "and thanks for letting me know."

Del tracked Mandy down in the kitchen – her timing was perfect as Mandy grabbed her books for a break.

"There are two schools that I think we could work with," she handed over some reading material and grinned, "the online resource links are there too – no rush; take a look, and when you have time, we'll compare notes and chat about a plan." Mandy nodded enthusiastically and stood for a hug.

Del smiled on the way to the restaurant, where she and Devon had first engaged in googly-eyed stares with each other. Mandy would likely have that research sewed up before the morning!

For now, she was highly anticipating a great dinner and tantalizing evening with one Devon McMullen. She had every confidence that he'd get the ball rolling to ensure that Russell's bail was evoked. She was still extremely pissed that the other girls' statements had not yet been taken – hell, all that was needed was to offer them clemency in exchange for their testimony. They were all either staying in shelters or in rehab for the time being – not hard to find.

Del knew the system had waded through the mire for decades. She got it; everyone was busy – fucking overloaded, to be frank. But when it came to minors – vulnerable children, for God's sake – adherence to priority should be first and foremost. Even honoring objectivity, she reasoned that they had more than a dozen underage prostitutes - most hooking for a fix, a clear-cut rape and assault incident, directly related, and witnesses willing to testify.

Del parked the car and took a deep, calming breath. It felt so damn good to have someone special to share it with – someone who not only understood but really respected her values and passions. It was a first for her, and sauntering into the building, she felt like the luckiest woman alive.

Chapter Forty-Eight

Damn! I couldn't stop the jitters! What was wrong with me? Getting this police business over with was something I'd been looking forward to, right?

Now, as I waited on the curb outside Millie's for Devon McMullen to pick me up, an uneasy sense of dread flooded my senses. I couldn't place my finger on it, and it was driving me nuts.

Ok - fuck sake, shake it off! Let's do this. There! The car pulled up, and I climbed in.

"Hi Mandy, thanks for agreeing to come in on such short notice," Devon checked his mirrors and pulled away from the curb.

We were headed to the station, I knew. Maybe that was the source of my angst – my prior experiences at the cop shop had been less than positive – to put it mildly.

"I just want to get this done!" I smiled in his direction. I really did like this guy, and was so pumped for him and Del – they were pretty cute together!

"If you're up for it, we are going to take your statement for four separate counts – there may be some repetition; I'll apologize for that in advance."

I was trying to count the charges in my head – the murder, my multiple beatings and rapes, Gen's beating and rape…what was

I missing? I knew the character testimony would be likely necessary for all three, and I was a witness for Gen's – then there was the locket.

"OK, you got me. I only count three."

"I should have clarified," Devon offered, "We need your statement on Russell Leach's charges too, including your own unfortunate rape and assault by the johns – we have all of their names now," compassion was evident in his tone, "I'm so sorry, Mandy – if it's too much, we'll split this up."

Bile rose in my stomach, and I fought back a hysterical giggle – I hadn't even known Russell's surname – shit! Was it too much? Hell, yes – but I knew in my gut that it would be worse to split it up. It was best to suck it up now and lick my wounds later.

"Let's just do it." I started to get out as Devon parked the car, but he gently stopped me with a hand on my arm.

"Mandy, you are a remarkable girl, and I would give my right arm to save you from this messy business," he sighed heavily, "but we need your testimony – I know that you are on board. I just want to offer my sincere gratitude, for your willingness to be on the team," he smiled gently, "my job is infinitely easier, with your cooperation – rather than watching your ass dragged into it, with a court order."

I returned his smile but said nothing, as we negotiated our way to his office space. The truth was, my body was in trauma mode – fight or flight. Once we were comfortably seated across from each other, he set the recorder up on the small table between us. I practised relaxation breathing.

"There's a formal preamble once I turn on the recorder for each statement, OK?" I nodded. "We'll start with the murder charge, and I'll be asking you about finding the locket as well as Richards' confession to you," he paused, "and you will likely be called as a character witness by the prosecution at the trial."

I nodded again. Seemed straightforward.

"OK, I will turn on the recorder now," Devon moved to do so and began the process by naming the perpetrator, the charge, and my name as the individual providing the statement. Weird – hearing my full legal name.

Richards' assault, rape and attempted murder of me was not necessary at this time to address, only the confession that he had murdered Nikki Leeds. It was a breeze until repeating the evil man's vile confession that he had murdered that sweet little girl. I shuddered as Devon moved on to Gen's assault and rape charge.

My guts churned, revisiting that horror fest. The first part involved my silent witness from the neighboring bedroom – all the trauma that I had heard clamoring through the walls. Then, the morbid picture of Gen, now burned into my brain, coming into my room the next morning. I recounted everything – her rage and accusatory words.

"Fuck, I need a break," I stood up and began pacing, holding my stomach, as if, somehow, this would tamp down the threatening panic and nausea, "I'm sorry."

"No worries, take your time," Devon had flipped off the recorder. After pacing a bit, I sat down again and nodded that I was ready to continue. We resumed, and he asked me to speak to my knowledge of Richard's usual treatment of Gen. Had this happened before? Oh, hell, yes! Was he violent by nature?

Finally, Devon suggested we break for a coffee and donut; down the road. My first instinct was to just get this motherfucker done with – but I knew that the walk and fresh air would serve me well.

"You are handling this like a champ," Devon remarked as he wolfed down a warm apple fritter. I had opted out – settling for a French Vanilla cappuccino, "Are you certain you want to continue today?"

"Hell, yes – I don't think I could go through it again," I mused thoughtfully, "It's really the same shit – all of it – that comes up for every statement I'll give, so…"

"OK, we'll try to stick to the facts and keep it as brief as we can," he reached out to squeeze my hand, "it's a bitch, though; there's no easy way through it."

I nodded in acknowledgement, and we headed back to the station. The next statement was rough – dealing with my own abuse at that sadistic asshole's hands.

I took him through everything – right down to my hiding place in the basement – the fear and degradation, pain and suffering, and hideous details of the abuse. He interjected now and then with gentle clarifying questions. I was waging a tough fight with the rising hysteria, immersed in the horror as if it was still real - but we got through it.

The second part of the statement; dealing with the abduction in the van, for some reason, was easier – I think because of the seething rage that I harbored within. Somehow, I felt stronger, through revisiting that experience. Hell, I had such a wicked support system by then, and I could feel them all; standing with me, as I provided the verbal statement. Before that, I had been all alone and I know now - a lost kid; just trying to survive hell.

"One more to go."

The compassion in Devon's eyes warmed my heart – he now was part of my tribe.

"I'm ready – let's just get this done." A glance at the wall clock – holy hell – who had analog clocks on their wall anymore – showed that we'd been at it, for two grueling hours.

The last round was more about Jessi – even though it was dealing with a rape situation, that we'd both endured together. Again, I left nothing out, save for our personal time together. Bottom line – I wanted justice for Jessi.

On the way to the diner, Devon shared the reason he needed the statement on Russell's pimping charges, which included our assault. I was stoked to be able to fuel them with this ammunition; to put him back behind bars, along with the other four dickheads that were being charged. My statement would serve there too, although somewhat circumstantial, as I could only identify them in person, if it ended up in court. What a relief, to get this done – but I knew that the trial would be worse. And Devon was picking up Jessi, next. My heart would be with her, all the way!

~~~

"This is seriously so cool," I motioned furiously for Jessi to come and look at the links I had simultaneously uploaded for both schools. With an amused giggle, she came and flopped herself down beside me on the couch.

We'd cleaned up from the evening meal of roast chicken and Jeff's delectable garlic smashed potatoes. Millie had also made
~~~

oven-baked corn on the cob and parmesan asparagus. Her special Jello popsicles were now hanging from our mouths – the poignant memory of the same treat, from years ago, had caught at my heart; when she'd brought them out of the freezer earlier.

Jessi and I had first recounted our individual experiences with Devon, and we both admitted to immense relief in having that rough patch now firmly behind us.

"Holy shit," Jessi's eyes widened, "that building looks ancient, like maybe it was a residential school at one time." Her features clouded.

"It *is* a heritage building for sure, and no – it was never a residential school," I assured, with a compassionate smile, "and, Jess, the kids there need all help they can get, in any case."

"For sure, Mandy – it just gave me the willies for a sec."

I smiled at her use of one of many expressions that we'd picked up from Millie and Simon.

I knew full well, how close the issue was to Jessi's heart – hell, it was to *mine*, too! And the recent horrific discovery of unmarked graves, with forgotten little indigenous souls; buried on the school grounds, tore me apart, every time I thought about it! I knew it bothered Jess a lot – not knowing the full extent of her own family line.

Shit, some of those little lost children may even have been her ancestors! But there were no records – no way to identify them all, and so…no closure for their people.

"Look – this one has a full, two-page write-up on their literacy program," Jessi nudged me from my reverie, "it sounds impressive and extensive."

"I know – both schools have great incentives – I'll have to give it some thought," I mused pensively.

"Well, if you can't decide, maybe you could work at both," Jessi reasoned, with an easy shrug.

While I had a leaning toward one of them, I decided it was best to hold off on my choice, until I had a chance to go over it with Del – I really wanted her perspective. After all, she was neck-deep in the world of vulnerable children, and I trusted her intuition. And maybe Jessi had a point too!

Chapter Forty-Nine

With growing agitation, Del brushed back the expertly coiffured, glorious locks that gently framed her face. Despite everyone's protests, the updated hairdo, complete with a nourishing henna, brought the natural colors to vibrancy. This served to enhance her newfound, vibrant awareness of her sensual femininity. She had Devon to thank for that, she surmised, momentarily basking in the warm glow of this distraction.

The murder trial for that poor little soul was about to begin – in about two hours' time, Del confirmed as she glanced at her cell. Mandy had been well-prepped and seemed to be holding it together, though Del knew that she must be battling a shit load of anxiety.

Her heart hurt for this young woman, whom she now loved beyond measure, who had, through no choice of her own, been victimized for most of her life. Horrible, tortuous abuse, and here she was – fated to relive it once more; through enduring the testimony that she was about to impart. It was a shitty injustice.

Del took a deep breath and tried to focus on the calming exercises that she'd learned years ago as a means to manage the stress from overwhelming situations.

"Hey!"

She hadn't heard his approach but gratefully allowed Devon

to capture her hand, in a gentle reassuring squeeze. How could she have ever gotten through this without him? Far too emotionally invested – she knew. Del had tried to focus on the positivity – it was a wrap, right? But experience had taught her never to count her chickens ahead of time. Damn!

"We've got this, Del," Devon's calming voice was the balm she needed. "And Mandy will get through this – hell, she is *the* most resilient young lady that I've ever met!"

That was true. It was time to honor the faith she had in Mandy and focus solely on encouragement and support. Another cleansing breath had her feeling much more in control – within her normal realm of operation; in dealing with the never-ending, inadequate justice system.

Suddenly, there she was, flanked by Millie and Daisy on either side. She appeared the epitome of determination, her head held high. Del could have sworn the discernment of daggers, hidden just within Mandy's gaze – prepped and ready for action toward those whose fate likely rested upon her upcoming testimony.

Her casual, simple and clean demeanor lent an aura of authenticity. Del was pleased that Mandy had opted to put very little emphasis on her physical presentation, eliminating unnecessary distractions that may or may not serve well for her testimony. This would not be her first rodeo in this fucked up mess, but it was a critical one – even more than the outcome of the assault and rape charges against the man. If the murder verdict was clean – then the hope was for a maximum sentence.

Everett Richards had lost his appeal to plea bargain – the evidence was solid, and the judge had allowed his prior prison conviction to be presented. So, Everett had then, opted for trial by jury. Mandy's testimony on the stand would now serve as a critical piece to establishing intent – his character and normal mode of operation as a foster father and in general.

Gen had been shaky, and so it was not certain that she would show, in person, to testify; she was obviously terrified of the man and for good reason – poor woman. Del prayed that she would pull it together for today, but they did have her statement on file, which Del hoped would be shared with the jury. Certainly, they would understand her reluctance. However, there's no denying the delivery of such a powerful punch, should those twelve humans - integral to justice, witness her entrance, presenting as the broken and beaten woman that she is, at the hands of the accused, sitting before them all.

Del realized that she'd had her fingers crossed, and they now ached something fierce. She had assured Gen that Everett's accomplice, for whom she held equal fear, was still behind bars, awaiting the outcome of the rape, assault, and attempted murder charge of Mandy. Still, Del had learned very long ago not to invest too much energy into the decisions of others – she held zero control over them.

The bailiff opened the courtroom doors – it was time. Del had a brief moment of alarm as Mandy continued to sit, staring straight ahead while everyone else filed in. The judge had not given any order to exclude witnesses, and Del preferred to remain close to Mandy.

"Are you OK?" Del placed a gentle hand on her shoulder.

"I'm fricking awesome – just gathering all the strength that I can haul in there with me!"

Del was encouraged and relieved at the fiery determination in Mandy's gaze as she looked up.

"I'm ready." Mandy rose, and they both filed into the courtroom to take their seats.

Chapter Fifty

Damn! I needed to get a grip on the inner trembling – felt like a freaking earthquake! There was no way in hell I could let that show on the outside!

What the fuck was wrong with me? This was so important to me! I had been waiting for weeks now for the opportunity to paint a true picture of this piece of scum.

Hell, I had been in mortal danger with this man, in circumstances I had no control over! So why were my nerves getting the best of me now, in the courtroom, with him shackled and helpless?

It was all about the psyche – Devon had given me the heads up about how our brains screw around with us in these types of situations and to expect inner turmoil – it was normal.

Closing my eyes, I took a deep breath and willed my focus on the testimony. I fixed my gaze on a specific point on the hallway wall directly across from me and performed a mental review. In addition to his confession, I would be called upon as a character witness, or lack thereof – in his case. It was testimony that particularly concerned my time in the foster home. While I could speak to the rape, assault and sexual abuse there, the kidnapping incident would not be entered as testimony, as that was a separate charge that was scheduled to go to trial very quickly after this one. Devon relayed that today's testimony would likely be revisited at that trial, as well.

Time to get on with this shitshow! I was in – all the way – there was no question in my mind. I just needed to focus and get a grip here.

Del's hand on my shoulder brought me to awareness of my surroundings – the courtroom was open. I assured her that I was fine and followed her inside. God, my legs were wobbly, but I was feeling decidedly better. It felt great to know that Buck and Brad were bringing Jessi – my tribe would all be here.

As we waited, I considered the issue of power – did I hold enough to make that difference? I sure as fuck hoped so! I realized that this was the cause of my angst – a lot rested on me – establishing the asshole for the piece of violent, worthless shit that he is.

I was grateful that Devon had not dictated my choice of attire and appearance. Maybe they only actually did that on TV. There was no way in hell that I was prepared to wear some frilly, white blouse up to my neck, with my hair combed just perfect! The judge and jury would see through that in a heartbeat. No, I need to present exactly as who I am – one of the slime bucket's victims, a scarred-for-life survivor who suffers every day with the guilt of having lived through the horror; when that sweet little girl that he ruthlessly murdered had lost everything. My waking hours in the dark of night were filled with her demise – she must have been terrified and in so much pain!

Fucking bastard – he was going down if I had any power at all toward that outcome!

"All rise!" The bailiff's voiced boomed, and we did as bid. After the judge sat, we followed suit, and it quickly began. It was both fascinating and painfully boring at the same time.

I had a wild moment of panic when he was brought into the room. He made no eye contact with anyone – stared straight ahead.

"Will the accused please rise?" This from the judge, who then proceeded to read out the charges against him, asking if he understood. His reply was faint but affirmative. The sound of his voice sent shudders up and down my spine.

The prosecuting attorney rose to address the jury, in particular, regarding the circumstances and promised to provide evidence that Everett Richards did, indeed, beat, rape, and subsequently murder his former foster child, Nikki Leeds.

The evidence was laid out, and copies were given to the jury. The defense attorney appointed by the court confirmed their awareness of all evidence presented.

It was time to call witnesses, and my stomach immediately

went into a tumultuous flip-flop.

Devon was first, testifying on the evidence in play, including the locket and the accused fingerprints. It was surreal, hearing my name as the former foster child who had found and taken the locket part from the dresser before I had fled the home. I wondered now why Nikki hadn't when she'd fled. Perhaps the need for haste robbed her of the opportunity. A deep, compassionate ache flooded my senses.

There were individuals called for forensic testimony, and the defense team chose to let it rest – there were no holes there.

Suddenly, my name rang out. Shit – I felt robbed of breath! But I somehow made my way to the witness stand, grateful for the seat, and survived the formalities. I confirmed I had found the locket and passed it on to the authorities.

When asked to identify the accused, I did so quickly by pointing at his person and avoiding his gaze, which I suspected was firmly locked on me.

"Miss Goodchild, Everett Richards recently confessed to you his act of murdering young Nikki Leeds. Would you please repeat his exact words to you?"

This I did.

I was next asked how I would describe Everett Richards

(a.k.a. Paul Miller) as a foster-father. This was what I had been waiting for – now I looked directly at the murdering prick and, matter-of-factly, slowly and clearly, related my experience of the man during the time that I had been living under his and Gen's roof as their foster daughter. The prosecutor asked defining questions, which I answered with as much clarity and precision as I could.

He thanked me, and the judge invited the defense to counter.

"Miss Goodchild," the defense attorney greeted me with a deceptively friendly grin. "Could you please tell us what prompted Mr. Richards' *alleged* confession to the murder of Nikki Leeds?"

"Objection!" The prosecution attorney remained casually seated. "As the defense attorney is well aware, this information is not admissible in this murder trial, as it will serve as testimony in a separate charge and bears no relevance here."

"Sustained."

"So, Miss Goodchild," the defense attorney continued, offering no argument, "you allege that the accused has both raped and assaulted you on several occasions?"

"He absolutely has!" Alleged my ass!

"Is it not true, Miss Goodchild, that you have exhibited behaviors toward the accused, inviting sexual attention from him?"

"No, that is not true." Fuck, was this coming from him or

Gen?

"And in addition to your invitations, is it not true that because of his refusal to give you this attention, you became very jealous and vindictive? And that you tried to damage his relationship with his wife, Gen – your foster mother, by making up these lies of abuse and rape?"

"Absolutely not!" I could feel the rage boiling up within me and caught Devon's warning glance.

"Miss Goodchild, would you please tell the court the number of foster homes that you have been placed in over the years? To be more specific, how many times have you complained about being abused and/or run from your foster homes?"

Rendered speechless now, I was confused and unsure how to respond – where this was going?

"Objection!" I wanted to kiss the prosecuting attorney!

"Sustained. Miss Goodchild is not the one on trial, Counsellor," the judge warned.

"The Defense has no further questions at this time, Your Honor."

And with that, I was released. I made my way shakily back to my seat. Jessi was there and immediately wrapped her arms around me. Brad squeezed my shoulders from behind and whispered his kudos for my testimony.

Hell, Devon had gone over it with me – the fact that the Prosecution would necessarily allow certain dirt to be strewn my way as the critical opportunity arose, with the sole intent to record my rejection by claiming that it was false. They would step in to object when it was likely to be deemed irrelevant. But the defense attorney had planted his damn seed, nonetheless!

I realized that this is exactly what had happened. OK, so it's all good because I clearly denied those allegations. I regained a sense of control.

The judge called a recess, and we moved out to sit on some highly uncomfortable wooden benches that flanked the massive inner hallway of the courthouse.

"Take some deep breaths, Champ," Devon smiled his compassionate encouragement. "You did very well in there – I know how difficult that must have been!"

"How did the jury react?" I hadn't even looked their way through it all.

"Oh, they were about as outraged as you, I believe," he squeezed my shoulder, "between the evidence in play supporting his rape and murder of a minor – a child, and *your* testimony, I believe it would take a near miracle, for them to be swayed by the Defense's allegations.

"Not to mention the fact that his prior conviction and prison sentence were admissible evidence, from the onset – the jury already has been provided that information." Del's warm regard reached out in reassurance.

My spirits lifted, but still, a worry niggled at the edges of my consciousness. I was about to mention Gen's absence when I saw her walk shakily through the main doors. Oh my God!

Both Del and Devon rose and moved to meet her. They guided her over to our seating area, and I immediately rose to give her my seat. She looked in pain like she needed to get a load off her feet.

She and I hadn't been face-to-face since that horrible morning when she'd kicked me out of their home – hell, I had been primed to run anyhow…

Now she was avoiding my gaze and damned straight – she did me dirt and so deserved the pound of guilt she was struggling to swallow, I assumed. Del had shared with me that her testimony on file indicated that she'd had no knowledge or involvement in the murder. That was something – a little piece of my heart softened.

My rising elation at her presence here overshadowed all. Damn! Now, her testimony would hopefully put the last few nails in that bastard's coffin.

A sudden gush of dread rose from deep within when I realized that the Defense may very well bring up the same allegations about me to Gen for confirmation. Would she wrongly incriminate me then? Her parting words that she'd spewed at me still rang inside my brain. Did she really believe all of that shit?

"Thanks for coming." I forced a tentative smile – it was critical to be a part of her team, her support group. It suddenly dawned on me that she must be curious and even a bit terrified herself at the details of *my* testimony.

She peered at me now, fighting tears, likely unable to put into words all that was consuming her at this moment. I instinctively understood this.

"Gen, the only role you played in my testimony was of his victim; your abuse and suffering at that bastard's hands."

The prosecuting attorney came to stand beside us all.

"OK, we need to keep this under wraps – this is not the time or place to discuss it; out in the open." He had been introduced earlier – Marcus Pickering.

I studied him now – a genius in the courtroom, I'd decided – but then I acknowledged that I really had no benchmark. He was maybe fortyish, slightly younger than Del and Devon, I deduced –

held the persona of eternal youth and energy; his courtroom attire impeccable.

"One of the conference rooms just opened up. Let's take a break in there." We all filed in behind him.

Unlike with the precinct and Del's drab government-provided furnishings, the décor here was modern and sparse, and the chairs were good quality leather – the kind that you just want to sink into for the rest of the day. The solid wood table gleamed – I could see my reflection.

This was entirely out of my comfort zone – luxury had never been a part of my existence, and reflecting on it now, I realized that I had no desire nor use for it moving forward. Still…this chair was damn comfortable!

"How are you holding up, Mandy?" The smile reached his eyes.

"I'm good so far," maybe a stretch, but I thought about how much worse the reality of the actual experience with the man had been and felt a renewed surge of determination to put that bastard away.

"A little girl lost her life, horrifically, at that evil man's hands." I met his gaze steadily. Maintaining this focus would get me through it all.

"This is important business, for sure," he regarded me thoughtfully, "but still, it will get rough as we progress through his charges." Flashing a bright smile, he rose.

"The good news is that it is highly unlikely you will be called back onto the stand for this one," he glanced at his watch, "we will be summoned to return momentarily – and Mandy," he pinned me with a determined and confident gaze, "I will be here, all the way – your well-being through it all will be uppermost in my priorities."

"Thanks," I smiled my gratitude – I don't know what I would do without everyone here in this room. I knew, too, that when it got more personal, their support would get me through the nightmare.

"OK, it's time," his smartphone had beeped - an ominous echo through the cold, impersonal, and empty space.

Chapter Fifty-One

Del sat rigidly straight, her hands firmly in place upon her lap – the agitation was almost more than she could bear.

Hell, she'd been through this before – horrific trials for child molestation, porn, and yes - even murder. It was never easy – each time, tough to bear. In truth, she supposed the horror and weight of it all increased with every new case – symbolizing another possible, disastrous failure with the justice and family court system, in which she played an integral role.

Oh, she knew the drill – don't own it or take it personally. However, there was no denying collective accountability within a convoluted and flawed system. Far too often, the cards fell on the wrong side of justice or slipped through the cracks completely.

She mentally ticked off all the boxes now – was there anything she'd missed? Gen's presence was a huge bonus. Del had to admit to a niggling worry that the woman may very well have agreed to testify for the Defense – she was vulnerable and easily swayed.

Their allegations of Mandy's promiscuity toward Everett Richards had been unnerving, to say the least.

Certainly, though, Everett and Gen had, at least, not been granted the opportunity to compare notes before he had been unexpectedly apprehended.

However, Del harbored no doubt that the Defense would grill Gen on the same issue, and with Everett Richards fixed glare drilling her into the witness stand, would Gen crumble?

"All rise!"

The Prosecution wasted no time in calling Gen Miller to the stand. Marcus had ensured the opportunity for a quick meeting with her beforehand. He now masterfully guided her through the process, confirming that she'd had no official knowledge of the murder, prior to or afterward, until learning of it after Everett Richards' arrest.

"Mrs. Miller, has the accused, Everett Richards - your husband, ever threatened you or caused bodily harm to you?"

Gen visibly trembled on the stand, a lone tear sliding down her cheek, and seemed to hesitate as she gathered the courage to make eye contact with him. The silence was deafening.

"Yes, on several occasions."

"And would you describe Everett Richards as a man with a tendency toward violence?" At her affirmative reply, he continued.

"Mrs. Miller, in your opinion, with the intimate knowledge that you possess as the wife of Everett Richards, do you believe that he is capable of committing the murder of this innocent little girl, Nikki Leeds, as per the charges laid upon him?"

Gen's demeanor altered as she pinned Everett Richards with a fierce, determined glare.

"Yes, I do." Her reply was firm and spoken with conviction.

It was the Defense's opportunity now, to counter. Del held her breath. In keeping with her suspicion, their focus was on the fallibility of Mandy's character; in an attempt to eliminate her testimony as unreliable.

"Gen Miller, you yourself, accused your foster daughter, Amanda Goodchild, of taunting and teasing your husband with offers of sexual favors. Is it not true that Amanda Goodchild was jealous of your husband's attention? That she tried to put a wedge between husband and wife to win him over to her favor?"

Gen's sorrowful gaze sought Mandy's in the courtroom as she replied, softly but audible.

"No, this is not true."

"But you clearly said…"

"What I said were the words of a wild woman who'd just been beaten near to death by her own husband. Mandy – Amanda has never displayed any such behavior towards Everett Richards. If anything, she avoided him like the plague, and rightfully so, as he abused her, at his whim, whenever he got the chance."

Her eyes remained locked with Mandy, the apology shining

through her tears.

"Thank you. The Defense has no further questions."

Del's eyes immediately gravitated to the accused. The man's face was crimson with obvious rage at the betrayal by his wife on the witness stand.

God help her if he should ever be released to the public. Del made a mental note to speak with Devon about the possibility of a new life for Gen Miller – permanent identity, etc., that would ensure her safety. She wasn't overly concerned about him having dangerous connections on the outside – he was not a very well-liked man and certainly not overly bright.

But…there was still the sentencing.

The judge led the final process – both sides' summation and his strict instructions to the jury, who would now be sequestered until they reached a verdict.

Just one hour later, the judge called them back in.

"In the charge of *Murder in the First Degree*, what is your verdict?" He addressed the jury, whose spokesperson immediately replied.

"We, the jury, find the defendant guilty on the charge of *Murder in the First Degree*."

There was an audible, collective gasp in the courtroom,

followed by clapping and cheering. The judge's gavel thundered, commanding silence.

"These court proceedings are now over, and sentencing will be delivered one week from today." The courtroom was dismissed.

Spirits were high as everyone filed out. Del was alarmed as her attention focused on Gen Miller, who looked fragile – a woman defeated. Despite the positive outcome, she knew the great toll it had taken on this brave woman. Few people would, or even could, understand the crushing weight upon her as she had delivered her testimony against her own husband today.

Mandy's sudden appearance beside Gen warmed Del's heart as the young woman folded Gen into her embrace for a fierce hug of gratitude and congratulations. Damn, there was hope for that girl, yet!

Del couldn't contain her smile as she and Devon strolled out into the parking lot together.

402

Chapter Fifty-Two

"Fuck, yeah!" I was beyond ecstatic! The scum sack was going down – away for life! Though he deserved worse, I knew that his personal safety in prison would be compromised – the general inmate population had no tolerance for a child rapist – and murderer. Someone was bound to mess him up!

We reached Brad's van, and suddenly, I burst into gut-wrenching sobs. Holy hell! He immediately caught and gathered me into his arms, murmuring soft words of comfort.

What the fuck? A second ago, I was totally stoked! I leaned on Brad with all that I was – broken, for sure – and it was scaring the crap out of me! Thankfully, he had insisted on driving me back to the house, as he was on shift tonight.

But for now, we just sat, only the two of us, as I soaked in his warmth, strength and compassion. Damn – I lucked out with this man. Friends for the time being, and really? If it never went further – if he found another; after all, it *was* a long wait, then I was still gold, with our soul-deep connection, that I trusted would be forever.

Considerably calmer, by the time we walked through Millie's door, I felt an utter flood of exhaustion. Millie took one look at me, bestowed one of her motherly monster hugs, and sent me packing to lie down.

My next awareness brought disorientation. As it all came flooding back to me, I pondered the daylight that was still streaming through the windows and had a sudden suspicion that perhaps I'd slept for an entire day! But it was spring, after all – lighter later, and I went to freshen up, hearing voices in the family room down the hall.

Brad's husky laughter confirmed that I had merely had a near-dead nap. He smiled warmly as I sauntered over to drop into the loveseat beside him, immediately melting into his warmth, his arm stretched behind me. The comfort with which I had embraced the evolvement of our relationship – this routine, astounded me!

"Hey, girl – how are you doing?"'

The concern on Jessi's face was genuine, and I was quick to give her a thumbs up and grin.

"I'm good, thanks to that bastard's verdict and to Brad here for scraping me up off the pavement as I blubbered like a baby in a complete, humiliating meltdown." This brought on a reassuring squeeze to my shoulder as he dropped a chaste kiss on my head.

"Hell, girl – I can't even fathom your strength, facing that creepy filth!" Jessi pushed a plate of wings and yam fries my way - definitely a feast for all!

It felt great to get something into my stomach. I hadn't been able to keep even a grape down since yesterday morning – I was so keyed up! Truth? I was still getting used to nutritional sustenance on a regular basis! Millie was kick-ass in that department!

I felt all gooey and warm inside, with gratitude for sure, but also a deep caring and love for Millie. Even though she'd been unable to save our sorry asses back then, she'd tried her very best. Without the experience – love and caring from her and Simon, for at least a short time, I knew with certainty – I'd have morphed into a much harder pill to swallow as a human.

Let's face it! I am actually capable of feeling love for another human being. Hell of an awkward transition, but I had to concede that I treasured all the warm fuzzies from my girls and Brad.

The problem with it? The mess of emotions that came with it – was that part of the package? Was it normal? It sure as hell has the tendency to throw me for a loop! I acknowledged a potent struggle to ignore this deep well inside of me, a giant pull to return to the chick I used to be – strong, resilient – nothing could touch me or hurt me. Because I risked my trust with no one!

Intellectually, I'm fully aware that I can trust those in my circle – my tribe! My heart knows this – but my head messes with me, and the turmoil inside is overwhelming. Whenever I melt into a pile of mush, I feel completely out of my safety net – emotionally out of control and vulnerable as fuck.

I had chatted about it with my counsellor, Maggie. She assured me it's all part of growing, transitioning from complete vulnerability to relative safety, within my new support system. I bawled like a baby when she spoke those words – see? I'm a freaking mess!

She also assured me that what I am feeling is perfectly normal, and as I build a history with all the goodness I've embraced, it will be increasingly less frequent to feel so out of control. Then she pinned me with a no-nonsense eagle-eye and imparted that patience is my best friend. After all, I was revisiting all my PTSD with the trial shit.

Then that cool bitch smiled and reminded me that it would be over soon.

I can't fricking wait!

Chapter Fifty-Three

Damn! I was proud of that girl! Within the space of three weeks, she'd managed to provide rock-solid testimony in four separate court hearings – two of which had gone to trial. Del was beyond pleased!

Everett Richard's life was as good as over. The judge came through – in the murder case, a maximum life sentence of twenty-five years for first-degree murder, plus five years for the assault and rape of a minor. For the repeated rape and assault upon Mandy, the jury deemed – attempted murder a further ten years; for Gwen's rape, assault and attempted murder – add another ten years.

The man was sentenced to a total of fifty years of incarceration with no chance for parole. The judge's final words compared him to a monster with no remorse for his actions. Del knew that it would be a miracle for him to survive the sentence; even if he did live that long – someone would get to him.

Mandy's testimony fully exonerated Gen from ill intentions, insisting that her foster mother had been thoroughly controlled and victimized by her husband. Gen wept through the cross-examination of her own testimony but held her ground, gaining strength from the eye contact that she maintained with Mandy.

Richards' accomplice in the rape, beating and attempted

murder of Mandy received a fifteen-year sentence with no chance of parole. He had avoided a trial by jury in the hope of a reduced sentence, but the judge squashed that.

Russell Leach did not fare much better, as his treatment of, in particular, the underage girls that were under his control was brutal. They suffered beatings and rough treatment from the johns – all with Leach's full blessing. As a result, the judge handed him a sentence of ten years with no chance for parole. Thank God, all the girls were spared a subpoena to testify, as the judge passed the ruling based on their written statements to Devon.

The four men who brutally gang-raped Mandy and Jessi had opted for plea-bargaining to save the public exposure. They each received a five-year sentence. It seemed interminably inadequate, but it was justice, all the same. Del knew that *john* convictions were rare, with "willing" participants, as prostitutes were often deemed. In truth, the maximum sentence in Canada for rape and aggravated assault is life – twenty-five years. But it was complex, and Del was reservedly satisfied with the outcome.

It was certain that the perpetrators' familial relationships were forever damaged – two of them with young children, for fuck's sake! It was disgusting, and Del's stomach churned at the thought.

Brushing her hair back from her face, Del sighed deeply and smiled. Her girls were going to be OK. Yes, she claimed an emotional commitment and attachment to both, although Mandy commanded a piece of her heart that no other human had – ever!

She couldn't imagine loving a child of her own more deeply – with such fierce protective determination. If Del and Devon should ever decide on making babies – quite unlikely, at their seasoned ages, she knew that her bond with Mandy would still stand out as special.

A lone tear slipped down her cheek as she gazed at a photo on her phone – the five of them, with linked arms, in front of the diner – grinning from ear to ear. Brad had snapped that picture – it was directly after the last of the court proceedings – they had been on a huge high!

Del shook her head! She had spent some time earlier catching up on paperwork and calls for her other cases. She realized that Mandy had significantly impacted her perspective.

It was somewhat of a paradigm shift, really. Acknowledging the well of expected failure within her work in the system, which she had succumbed to for years - shocked her with its intensity. How on earth could a person even visualize the success that had unfolded with Mandy while stuck in that mire?

Never again! There was always hope – she had experienced that ultimate reality with Mandy and reflected on those upon whom she owed gratitude. It had been a team – Sherri, Devon, Millie,

Daisy, Joe, Jessi – but mostly, Mandy – her resilience and dogged determination for survival. The youth had hit a pivotal point through her journey – and her decision to trust in the team was an accolade for her strength and self-caring.

Damn!

With a rare tender thought of Jack, she made a mental note to give him a call – to let him know about Mandy's bright future. He had cared about the kids under his caseload. He deserved to be told.

Her cell chimed, and she picked up.

"Hey, Gorgeous, up for lunch?"

She would never get past the raw hunger and warm fuzzies that his deep voice invoked. Especially now that she was in the know - fully immersed in the pleasure of the promise!

"Give me ten. Where did you want to meet?"

~~~

"I figure a celebratory event is in order," Devon's wide grin was infectious, "We did good, Partner."

They had ordered their food, and his thumb was creating havoc with her insides as he gently rubbed the inside of her palm across the table. The warm smile was in his eyes, and as always, she was mesmerized. Lord above, how did she luck out with this man?
~~~

"Perhaps we can host a dinner this Saturday evening?"

They had given up on the notion of residing in two places, and Devon's condo had sold two days after hitting the market. He had credited this to a *very sexy realtor*, who was not a day under seventy years of age but was sharp and seasoned. He had three weeks to move in!

Normally, Del would be thoroughly uncomfortable with the speed at which their relationship was gathering, and she almost giggled at the length of time it had taken for her and Jack. Good grief – there was zero comparison to the depth of commitment, trust, and intimacy she and Devon so naturally embraced.

"Sure, and…," he paused thoughtfully, "we *could* hold it at Millie's – total potluck – the guys would come speeding up to the plate, I know – pardon the pun."

"Oh my God, they would be thrilled at the suggestion," Del laughed, "they are all besotted with Mandy and Jessi; it's so sweet – mushy bikers!"

"Ok, let's plan it!"

The waitress came with their food, and they chatted casually over lunch. When the plates were cleared, Devon resumed captivity of her hands in his own, and Del nearly swooned with the depth of his gaze.

"You must know that without *you*, the outcome of all these convictions would not have come to this," his eyes roamed over her face – a sweet caress, "I owe you, Babe."

"Hey, none of this was any one of our doings," Del's face was flushed, "Mandy was key, really!"

"Yes, there is a solid truth there," he nodded, "but Del...you have changed me."

At her look of astonishment, he quickly elaborated.

"I am loathe to admit to the depth of cynicism and staunch routine that I observed with all of my cases. You have taught me the value of risking success and trusting in a worthy partner. Not to mention the resilience of youth."

His sheepish grin melted her heart. She had known, the minute she met the man, that he was special.

"Devon, you are an incredible detective," she sighed at the look of firm resignation he bestowed upon her, "but yes, agreed – we are a fantastic team!" She squeezed his hand. The look that passed between them could have melted stone. They were brought to awareness by the waitress, clearing her throat. She regarded them with a wink and a teasing grin.

"I'm thinking the two of you are finished with food?" They laughed, and Devon snatched the bill that she had so efficiently produced. They constantly engaged in "tab wars" when dining out, but it was all in fun, and Del figured they were likely pretty even.

With reluctance, they parted and returned to their busy day.

Del reflected on their future. They had discussed the possibility of children – their own, adopted or fostered. They both acknowledged the impact that their partnership could have in a less-than-perfect world and that the priority of raising children would necessarily have an effect. It was not off the proverbial table but for now…

God, she was so hopelessly in love with this man!

Chapter Fifty-Four

Damn!

My heart was full – to near bursting, really, with all the "feels" as I gazed upon the members of my tribe – the only family I had ever really known, now sitting companionably around Millie's table. The boys had hauled in another collapsible one, along with some folding chairs, to accommodate all.

It was a total shock to Jessi and I – we'd been shooed out of the house for the afternoon, and Daisy had stated that she had some extra help this Saturday at the diner, encouraging me to take the day off. I welcomed the opportunity to spend time with Jessi.

After some window shopping – both of us were almost miserly with our money, saving almost everything we earned, we took a long walk along the ocean shore, with the salty, cool breeze stirring our senses, before heading home.

Coming in the door, we were flabbergasted! First, to see everyone waiting for us and yelling "Surprise!" at the top of their lungs. There was a huge banner in the living room that brought instant tears to us both – "To Mandy and Jessi – the winning team! The two bravest young ladies we know!" I was pretty impressed with the artwork, too – complete with cartoon "kick-ass" and "fist pump" images. And centered in the bottom was a picture of the two of us - placed, standing on top of the world, with shit-eating grins on our faces! It was epic!

We imparted our thanks, and a mountain of hugs followed. All the girls were here, along with our group of protectors, at both the motel and the house. I recognized Joe and threw Daisy a wicked grin – they were clearly a couple now!

Del introduced us to Sherri, who apparently was key to everything falling into place as it should, and I hugged her warmly. Holy shit – Gen was there – I actually hadn't expected to see her ever again. The diner staff beamed at us – unbelievable – who the heck was manning the restaurant?

As we gravitated into the dining area, I'm sure my jaw dropped to the floor. The feast that was spread out on the long tables was simply amazing.

Mouth agape, my eyes flew to Millie, and she laughed.

"No, I did not do all this work by myself! As a matter of fact, my only contribution was to cook the scalloped potatoes! Everyone brought the rest, and they all pitched in to set it up!"

I giggled at the sheepish grin plastered on Jeff's face – I knew he'd contributed a plate or five.

Relaxing a little, I began to engage in the banter. The meal was excellent, and a feeling of warm contentment flowed through every cell in my body. Brad stood up and cleared his throat.

"I have been given the privilege to bestow a toast in honor of these two amazing ladies! Buck, please join me." He pinned us with a reverent grin.

"You two ladies have not only overcome every obstacle put before you but totally kicked-ass and singlehandedly assured that proper justice was served up to the lowlifes in your story." He choked up and took a few seconds before continuing. "And I am *so* proud of you!"

Brad's eyes were keenly fixed on mine, and I couldn't hold back the emotion as I blinked back tears. I grabbed Jessi's hand as Brad motioned to Buck.

"It is true – without your courage and spitfire determination, both your fates may have taken a very different turn. Certainly, the scourge of this earth would not, today, be behind bars." Buck cleared his throat.

"Having said that, there are people in this room that maximized the positive effect of this outcome with their rock-solid commitment and belief in the two of you." Jessi and I nodded vigorously.

Buck went on to thank all in the room – especially Del, Millie, Daisy and Devon. "With you on their team, these two lovely young ladies have an awesome future ahead of them – one filled with hope and success!"

Jessi and I were reduced to tears – there wasn't any need for words beyond our whispered and fervent "thank you." We knew, without a doubt, how damn lucky we were and had already bestowed our gratitude, ongoing, toward our benefactors and now dearest friends.

They were everything in my world – the reason I jumped into the pool of risking trust that led to believing in myself – or at least discovering that it was possible.

As people departed, after warm hugs, Jessi and I immediately started cleanup, but Millie stopped us short.

"Girls, tonight is yours – this has all been in your honor, and frankly, I'll be hurt if you don't allow us to treat you."

Damn, she had us there.

"Don't worry, there's not enough room in this kitchen for everyone who wants to help! Buck and Brad are also banished!"

With that, we headed down to our happy place on the lower level and relaxed with our guys on the loveseat and couch. We chatted about the trial, leaving all the sordid details out. We'd heard them hundreds of times before – hell, we'd *lived* it.

I was freaking proud of Jessi! She had stood, regal and tall, through her Victim Impact Statement. With the lack of a trial, this was our avenue, as victims, to impact the sentencing handed down to the scums – Russell and the johns.

Jessi handled it like the boss that she is! I know that if I tried my entire life to measure up to her – I'd be miles behind. Her grace, humility, and courage – in the interest of truth and justice, were amazing. Not once did she fall into the abyss of shame and remorse for the lifestyle that so many pass judgement upon – prostitution is complex and, in most cases, a form of slavery. Jessi had definitely been indentured in her fight for survival.

She told her story – the naked truth, leaving no part of the trauma unturned. In doing so, she managed to advocate for all young girls who fall prey to vile perpetrators.

My own statement was rife with anger and hatred – I barely contained my rage, spewing it liberally, aimed directly at each of them. It was more on behalf of Jessi - for me. I had already come to terms with my own part in her ordeal, quite certain that she'd never have endured the abusive incident if I'd not been caught in her apartment that first night.

But this was about so much more – the opportunity to highlight the evil that lurks within men like these – the injustice of prostitution, the vulnerability and hopelessness of the victims. I possessed enough fuel to fire the gush of my rage to last a thousand lifetimes. Though I contained it, for Jessi's sake, my words shot out, like fiery darts, aimed directly at each of the men – there was no mistaking my message.

This one was all about Jessi…

We had made it – she and I! Our future laid before us – rife with promise and possibilities. Neither of us had ever been empowered to choose our fate up to this point.

We rocked this fucking story!

Good on us!

Epilogue

Two Years Later…

I surveyed the tiny apartment with wonder and had to give myself a pinch. Two years ago, I would not have dreamed this possible. It was bright and cheery, even with nothing in it! It was giving off great vibes and energy, and a delicious shiver ran through me.

The small galley kitchen had ample counter space, I figured, and there were just enough cupboards to house all the birthday gifts that my tribe had recently bestowed – setting Brad and I up for success.

It had been an epic party for sure – me coming of proverbial age at eighteen – hell, I didn't even think I'd live to see that day until Daisy, Millie and Del had blasted into my world.

The place was clean – at least forty years old, but with new vinyl flooring throughout. The building was well-kept – we were on the second floor. I wandered now through the spacious living room to check out the balcony. Sliding open the doors, I was struck by the pungently sweet aroma of the gardens below – petunias, roses and lilacs finishing their late spring bloom. A gentle breeze ticked my skin. This space was ginormous! Enough room for a patio table, chairs, *and* loungers!

The view was to die for – who could have imagined it in the thick of Vancouver? The unit faced a generous green space – zoned for park and recreation. It was quiet enough to hear the birds and bees, with road noise only distant in the background. Back inside, I ran my hand over the little fireplace mantle – it framed a well-contained wood stove insert. I imagined all the crackling warm fires Brad and I would enjoy – so romantic.

My thoughts flew to the man I loved – Brad was not only the most decent guy I'd ever known – he actually loved me! *Me*, with all my scars and sordid past. Our lovemaking was tender and frantically passionate – all at once. I felt like the most beautiful woman alive in his arms.

Aside from Jessi, I'd never experienced lovemaking before. It had always been sex and never for my benefit. Abuse, rape and torture. If not for Brad's patience and encouragement, I doubt I would have even risked intimacy with a man, ever!

The floor in front of that gorgeous fireplace brought forth a sudden ache in my loins – yes, we'd spend some time here! Wandering off to the bedroom, my heart warmed. The space was generous, complete with a door to the same epic balcony and a three-piece ensuite - it was sheer heaven. I imagined the bed here…

We bought our furniture and arranged delivery today. Brad had a work contract for the morning but planned to be here when the van arrived.

I was beyond excited!

The past two years had flown by! I wasn't sure that our relationship would come to this – it had seemed remotely out of my range of distance – such a long wait for Brad, who was now twenty-three. But he had stayed loyal to me in the most platonic way possible – true to his vow.

Hell, I had tested him sorely, especially that last year. I wanted nothing more than to jump his bones and, on several occasions, had shamelessly flirted, hinting at the promise of delights. I'm sure the man was part saint…but no saint could possess *that* depth of passion in bed. Lord, I was actually blushing.

Nope…he's just the most decent guy in the world!

I continued my inspection of our new home, wandering into the main bath and spare bedroom. There was also a huge storage space, with in-suite laundry, where our new sheets were washing now, and another off the balcony. It was my dream come true. My heart was nearly bursting, and I sat on the floor, bathed in the warmth of the sun's rays, continuing to reflect on the journey that brought me here.

By the time the trials had been over, I'd entered my eleventh-grade studies shortly after my sixteenth birthday. I knew that it would take me only another year to graduate. Jess and I had shared in that celebration –less than a year later, with her slightly behind me.

The party had been epic – with everyone sputtering kudos to the two of us for our success. Brad had gifted me with five hundred dollars toward my first-year tuition at the local college. I had burst into tears. With this and my savings, I had enough to enroll in the Child and Youth Care program. As it turned out, the system paid for my first year, so I had all the tuition funds for my degree! My ultimate goal was to work with Child Protection Services.

It was my calling – a certainty in my gut, and I had never been more sure of anything in my life. I knew these kids. Hell, I had lived their lives. Making a difference was a passionate focus now.

My work with the schools had been inspiring and eye-opening. Not all kids that lived in great homes had great lives. I found out that kids struggle with learning, and particularly with literacy development, for a variety of reasons.

The well-adjusted kids tend to negotiate challenges that are directly related to - diagnosed or not - disabilities, such as dyslexia, ADHD, and hard of hearing. Generally, it was easy to customize an intervention program, as the kids were usually willing and eager to participate.

But it is complex. And even some of the so-called, well-rounded kids who come from mid to high-income backgrounds are riddled with emotional issues – their busy parents often do not even realize that their kids are suffering. Bottom line – there are reasons for the deficiency.

Whatever the case, it was intense but rewarding work. Perhaps due to my age, I was able to make solid connections with these kids – in particular, the ones who were scrambling to survive with abusive, neglectful caregivers – some of them foster kids.

A whole array of obstacles face children who struggle with literacy. They are often grades behind their peers and develop deep feelings of inadequacy, leading to isolation, depression, fear and self-sabotaging behaviors – even suicide. The last thing these kids want is to be singled out for "extra help" at school.

Bullying is rampant in the school system. But I know from a gut level that it isn't simply a school problem – rather societal. Parents love to point the finger, but often, it is born out of fear for their kid – they need someone to make it stop, and it happens often on school property. But after hours, and even during, through social media - now *there* is a real fear-induced threat. Some kids spend their entire school day worried and anxious over what will happen that evening.

Truth is, teachers, administrators, community leaders…mostly have no idea how to handle it – how to make it stop! Another ugly reality is that kids are not born bullies – they learn it through role-modeling.

I hold a strong belief that adults in this world - including those who exhibit bullying behavior in homes, workplaces and socially - would benefit from the teachings and leadership of children; we need programs in place for that – I have already chatted with Del about it.

Challenging work, for sure! Though I tried my best to work one-on-one with kids to customize the intervention to their needs, there were so many in need and so little budget in place. Group work was key to reaching as many kids as I could, and my programs were all about fun – so much so that the kids who didn't struggle begged to come along. Sometimes, the teachers would allow it, as I pointed out, the benefit of connection. It wasn't all about the literacy.

I will miss this work, I know, as I plow through my college education. There would still be occasions for volunteer work, but sporadic, as my studies and job will take priority.

My heart is full – I know I have made a difference for some of the kids!

Brad…wow, that is another story.

I knew he was my guy from the moment he grabbed me, gently but firmly, from the clutches of those monsters. Naked and vulnerable, filled with shame and agony, both physically and mentally, I had felt broken – finally, I had lost my courage, fortitude and strength.

But in his arms that day, I connected with the good in the world – I knew he was gold. It was more than just gratitude, though I had a mountain of that, too. A soul connection is the most fitting description. I felt his love and calm commitment to me from a spiritual level. It was the bomb!

Six months after my seventeenth birthday, Brad lost the battle. Though we were officially dating by then, I hadn't even seduced him – trying to be fair. I was immersed in my second term of studies, and absolutely loving it. Hard work for sure, and always a few boring units to cover, but overall, I was enthralled.

Brad had taken me out to dinner – a rare treat for us – something other than eating in, fast food, pizza, etc. It was divine – the Brioche Ristorante – at their new waterfront location.

Heaven to the tastebuds – I remember it like yesterday and drifted; appetizer to start – roasted Brussels sprout chips – amazing, as I usually can't palate that vegetable, then NY steak with house-made penne in wild mushroom sauce. Of course, Italians know vino, so we shared a bottle of the best during the meal.

Feeling mellow and sated, we had strolled along the waterfront, and hit a gelato place for a dose of sweet. On the way home, Brad was pensive and quiet.

"Is everything OK?" I was suddenly concerned with the amount of cash he'd dropped – of course, not allowing me to pay for any of it.

"The best," he answered with a warm smile as he drew me to him.

"Talk to me." I wanted to peer into that mood of his – see what was driving it.

"Can we go to my place tonight?"

The fire in his eyes sent pure shots of lightning to my loins. Was he really going there? A sudden shyness, a fear, gripped me. What if he was planning to seduce me? I was pretty darn sure I couldn't resist it. But what if I couldn't measure up to his expectations? What if the actual act of sex with a man repulsed me? What if I repulsed him?

"Mandy, you are safe with me – no expectations, OK?" He must have seen the panic in my eyes.

We cuddled on the way to the motel. When we got to his door, he kissed me properly – but it was also tender and sweet. My heart melted. Once inside, we settled on the sofa bed, part of the kitchenette unit he rented from Joe. Brad drew me to him and tucked my head under his chin.

"There is absolutely no place I'd rather be right now," he murmured, "with you here or at Millie's - at the restaurant…with you." He turned my face up to meet his warm gaze, alive with feeling and fire.

"Brad…" I began – my heart was beating so loudly; I was sure he'd feel it. The sexy dimples around his mouth sent little shoots of fire to my belly. I wanted to kiss each one.

"Shh…"

With that, he bent down and captured my lips with his in a slow, sensuous, exploratory kiss. We had kissed before, but this…this was a show-stopper! Every cell in my body melted, and my loins turned to molten lava.

With obvious reluctance, he lifted his head and put a bit of distance between us. I could see him trying to get control of his breathing – on the other hand, I was a hormonal mess, needing him now more than anything in my life before. To hell with my worries – I wanted this man with every fiber of my being.

"You know how I feel about you," his eyes caressed my face, "I promised you I'd wait, and I will stick by that."

The warring agony in his gaze touched my heart. I knew he would – trusted him completely. But I was ready for this next step. I took his hand. I was well aware that I needed to respect *his* need to maintain his integrity, and his concern about my feelings for him; was it hero worship; did I have him on a pedestal? He'd spoken of this from the beginning. I knew it was neither of those things – rather, much deeper.

He closed his eyes and took a deep breath. I knew this was pivotal, and I made the wise choice to stay silent.

"Mandy, I want you with every cell in my body," the release of his exhale was jagged, "and I assure you that I will wait forever if need be," he drilled me with a determined look, "when the time is right…"

"Brad, I am seventeen – young by some standards, but I've seen so much more of the world – *the growing up too soon variety* – and consequently, I feel much more seasoned, wiser, and yes - ready for the next steps in my life – you included."

My body was on fire – is this then, how he was feeling too? I was having one hell of a time controlling this! My respect for his struggle was immense.

"I need to be sure of your well-being, Mandy – first off, your safety, both emotionally and physically…" he grasped my hand, "I promise you, when the time is right, we will take it as slow as you need," he smiled tenderly.

"But also, I have a raging fear that it's too soon, and I'll lose you."

There it was, written all over his face; the vulnerability, and I physically ached with the tenderness of loving this big bulk of a man, who was the epitome of devotion, caring and compassion.

Here he sat, shaking, with desire or fear. I wasn't certain which at this point. I wanted to wrap him in my arms and rock him, assure him of his own safety with me. Even with my body on fire for him - this overrode my physical need.

"Brad, can I hold you?"

We cuddled, embraced, and slowly - ever so slowly, with each reassuring caress, the touches morphed – our bodies began responding naturally to our needs. They were not merely physical – but enhanced by the deep, emotional soul connection that we shared.

Of course, this only served to fuel the fire, and he captured my face - his words coming out in a low groan.

"I love you, Mandy," his breathing was raspy, "please know this, but right now, I want to do things with you - wanton and downright lusty – of the X-rated variety," he paused and searched my eyes, "I don't want to scare you. Are you sure?"

We were both shaking with our need for each other. My desire for Brad was all-consuming, and I was burning up with it.

"I love you too," I rubbed against him. "Now, ravish me,

dammit!" I whispered hoarsely.

With that, this big hunk of a man lost all semblance of control – to my utter delight, and our resistance was history. We gloried in the natural unfolding of this ritual – the ancient art of lovemaking at its finest, unfettered and raw – completely open and sensual. Our bodies melted into one another as we explored and tasted.

I was completely mesmerized by the power of his tender yet virile masculinity. And hands down - ready for him. With that discovery, he groaned deeply, and the inferno escalated until neither one of us could wait any longer.

"I'm so sorry, it's been a long time for me," he gasped the apology.

"Shh...I'm pretty certain you'll have a number of opportunities to make up for it," I whispered softly, "but I don't think you'll need to worry about that, anyhow." I wriggled from beneath him to move on top – and he filled me with the glory of his maleness. At that moment, I took control, and we embraced the mind-bending, climatic ecstasy together.

Reflecting back on it now, as I switched the bedsheets to the dryer, I was elated to concede that, after six months of glorious sexual intimacy, the fire only raged hotter. We loved the exploration and new discoveries with our bodies.

Up until now, we'd limited our sensuous delights to his home at the motel, but once or twice, we had snuck in a quickie when he was on shift. We tried our best, though, to respect Millie's home and values - not that she'd likely object. She knew damn well how hotly we lusted after each other!

Now, this would be *our* home – together, and I couldn't wait!

Millie had cried when we told her, but the blow was softened with Del's sharing of her current dilemma. She was desperate to find a home for two teenage sisters – twins, who were in need. This move would reunite them, after years apart, in separate foster care homes. I was thrilled to be the catalyst in providing this opportunity.

While Brad and Buck were both moving on from the house positions, there were two eager guys well-suited to take their place.

Yes, Jessi and Buck, she - almost nineteen, had both moved out a month ago, together. Their place was only blocks from ours, and the four of us were solid friends – how could it get any better than this?

True, Buck was twenty-six, but at this point, the age difference mattered little. They were happy and crazy for each other. Jessi had overcome her own demons to embrace their intimacy and positively glowed in his presence.

She had decided to enroll in the local college as well, in

culinary studies. She was completely passionate about this journey - and so ace – it was right up her alley! I giggled, thinking that she certainly had an opportunity for practice at the diner!

~~~

It's been a journey to this – to whom I've become – where I've landed. I never dreamed it all possible. Back in the home with Gen and Paul, I was certain of only one thing – I would die in the fight for survival, if necessary. And many times, I thought I'd hit that fate.

I am still overcome with emotion every time I reflect upon my gifts – my blessings.

Brad, who has shown me love, devotion and commitment – believes in me! Novel for me! And the intimacy – I'd only ever experienced sex in the form of rape and brutal assault. A tool for men's pleasure. I had known only pain, degradation and fear. My connection with Brad is beyond fathoming – but very real. The intimacy is both exhilarating and, at the very utmost – healthy! My relationship with my own sexuality and femininity is deep in the healing stage.

I have many individuals upon which to bestow my gratitude – Jessi, who eagerly engaged in the joint preservation of our sisterhood and our womanhood – it saved us both, though she has *always* been a rock when it came to compartmentalizing her life.
~~~

I've always been a hot mess! Thank God she believed in me, too! We traded strength and support when needed. As far back as pre-teens, we had each others' backs. She will forever have my intense love, devotion and respect.

Del, who was determined to save my sorry ass, even after my ill-treatment of her! She risked so much and left no stone unturned. I smiled – remembering her and Devon's small wedding ceremony – just six months ago. He had taken her out for dinner and feigned a work purpose first – *priorities, don't you know.* He handed her an envelope and asked her to provide input – it was quite an important case he was taking on…

Del had ripped open that envelope to find a sparkling engagement ring taped to some rather intimidating-looking legal documents. Right there, in the middle of their favourite restaurant, she'd jumped into his arms and sealed the bond. They had opted to wed at City Hall and celebrate at Millie's afterward! Awesome!

Devon, for his unwavering, caring patience and calm encouragement – I never doubted his belief in me – that I had this! And he loved Del…she was getting her *happily ever after*. They both were – damn, it made my heart melt.

Millie, bless her soul for taking us back in again – it seemed a miracle, but no – it was her love for us that had never died. There was no one else like her in my world, and I would climb mountains for her.

Daisy – another wounded soul – had so much to lose but risked it all for us, including bringing Joe into our circle. Bless them both. Hell, Brad and Buck would be total strangers, unrecognizable on the street to us, if it weren't for Daisy. And she risked hiring me – such a catalyst to where I am today…

Brad and Buck – why the fuck should they risk it all on two street kids? But they did, even before they loved us. The other biker boys, too, who laid their lives on the line when the scum had kidnapped me.

Gen, for trusting us and finding the good within, to do the right thing. I was relieved that she had taken Devon's offer to build a new life – Jessica Harding was now safe from the clutches of anyone who may have been a part of Everett Richards' disgusting existence!

I owe so much to so many!

But mostly to myself, I'm realizing. For allowing trust and grace into my life, embracing compassion and letting go, daring to believe in myself – that I could become something other than a pathetic victim in this life. There had been no reason to believe otherwise. It was all I had ever known.

Until I accepted someone's hand…

I continue to work with my counselor – currently exploring forgiveness. She insists that I need to work with self-forgiveness first and assures me that it's beyond far, the hardest.

I'm not certain if I can forgive everyone who has done me wrong in this life. I can't imagine that reality with Everett Richards. A burning hatred still reigns in full-force, deep within. But I know that my counselor is right – it imprisons me still, in a place that I need to break free of, moving forward. I need to deny him that power over me!

However, I've managed some growth with forgiveness – Gen, and my former foster brother…my mother. It's a start, right?

Is it possible? Or perhaps it will take another lifetime to manage it. I don't profess to know where I will end up when I die. I do, however, have a deep, intuitive belief that should I get another chance for a human journey, I've done my time in this one. I truly believe that I'll be blessed with a better start next time around.

My story is told here – and believe me, it wasn't easy to put pen to paper, so to speak. Reliving it will always cause angst and pain. And yes, stir up my PTSD.

Author's Message

My compulsion to put this story into print has been totally gifted – a divine purpose that one day came crashing into my life with hurricane force! I harbor a burning need to share - with those of you who roam those dire streets, are suffering a horrible human fate, whose sole focus is to survive the day, are helplessly treading water in a pool of ugliness.

And to those reaching out with a helping hand. For me, this is a driving force - hence the publishing of this book.

This is for all of you; a success story – a harbinger of hope.

But it is also raw and true, chock full of appalling, horrific realities, hence the content warning preface for possible triggers.

Though the characters in this book are fictional, they are based upon and represent true-to-life, living and breathing human beings who have, in the past, will have, and are currently walking a similar pathway on this earth.

Good endings don't happen every day, but they are a tangible and real possibility for people just like you, not with ease or comfort and not without hiccups. You may have to roll several times before you'll hit the jackpot.

Remember that not everyone who fails you does so intentionally. They, too, are swimming in a sea of injustice – a system that fails us all in our humanity. Many are tired, discouraged, and simply give up on the process. They all have familial obligations, financial worries, and impossible job expectations, and most carry a host of insecurities of their own. Sleep is elusive, every time they fail someone like you. You will never know about it, just as they will never know about all that you suffer because you have never entrusted them with it.

It is true that many of these individuals – do-gooders, they are often pegged, have never lived your reality, and do not understand the depth of horror you are enduring. However, they come to you with a wealth of compassion and caring and with the sole desire to help you change your stars.

Each of us travels a unique journey with lessons to learn, armed with a soul purpose. No one who extends a branch to you is personally accountable for that which *you* are suffering – the horrific trauma that has scarred you for life; any more than you are accountable for *their lack of* your experience. Their journey and presence on your pathway are intentional and have a purpose. However, they cannot come on board without your invitation – without your permission.

I am well aware of the gaping inequity as I impart these insights in comparison with the nightmare of your own life, but believe me – these are the people to reach out to. They are your catalysts; teachers, counselors, social workers, religious leaders, friends, neighbors – anyone who extends a hand to try to help you. It doesn't matter that you may have no use for spiritual faith, have experienced only failure in school, or have been forsaken by the Social Services system countless times.

You are armed with resilience, are street smart, and necessarily geared for survival - you know how to negotiate this safely. Physically - that is. Your emotional and mental health are always at stake with every risk you take. But you are already there, completely vulnerable, in every way.

Avoid the trap of self-judgement, in your right to claim this space. Your story may not seem as horrific as Mandy's, or it may be far uglier – it's all relevant. We are all equally worthy of validation.

Please engage in a gut-level, honest conversation with yourself. What have you got to lose by taking a hand that's reaching out to help you? Perhaps it won't amount to anything.

But what if it does?

Mandy could have continued to play it safe – trust only in herself! But did she truly? She tells us now that her catalyst to success, in making a new life for herself – escaping the hell she was imprisoned within, was in mustering the courage to put trust in herself.

She could have prostituted the streets for her survival – her and Jessi may have been OK for a while. She is young – eventually, addictions may have surfaced with the need for survival and aging in that world. It was a monumental risk, taking her job with Daisy. She may have listened to those voices in her head, telling her not to trust the solution that this transition offered.

Mandy may have opted to ignore the hands that were reaching out to help her. Then, when she'd been kidnapped, her fate would have likely been sealed. Without her chosen tribe – Mandy would almost certainly no longer be with us.

I hereby implore you to reach out for that hand – as many times as necessary, to find the right road for you – and never let go!

If you are a child, youth or social worker saddled with seemingly hopeless outcomes within your caseload, please don't stop trying. Be the catalyst to empower these children, women, and men alike.

If you are a friend, family member, in a position of authority, or a concerned citizen – regarding youth at risk – please have that talk; take the risk and reach out. What is the worst that can happen? It may amount to nothing, or your offer may be rejected.

But what if it isn't? What if, on the umpteenth try, it's accepted? What if that very action you take makes a profound difference in the life of a young soul?

I urge you to take this step. Do it now…

Please be passionate about sharing this message, this book!

And never ever give up on humanity! It resides in every community – tucked into the quiet places, never afforded the same limelight as the lack thereof. Trust in that silent space – for there resides hope.

Hope for those who are vulnerable and, therefore, pushing the hardest against the hand that reaches out, not believing in a way out – not daring to. Hope for those who are reaching out and seemingly, have been granted no way in.

Never give up!

There is always a way in, and…

There is always a way out…

About The Author

Mae Strack is a devoted wife, mother, and grandmother, enjoying her life among nature in rural central Alberta. Her retirement stage of life has allowed Mae to pursue her passion for writing and editing on a full-time basis, while completely immersed in her sanctuary with the birds bees and flowers. This story marks her second published novel.

She has always embraced the gift of literature – crafting stories, songs and poetry along the way. Mae has honed her literacy skills in various career endeavors within diverse educational, professional and freelance writing and editing undertakings.

Mae is often irresistibly compelled to immerse in whimsical creation within a variety of genres; to include romance and the odd non-fiction. However, extensive work with children and young adults in various career and volunteer endeavors has sparked a burning passion within, for sharing messages of hope for these young souls, who endure significant struggles along their journey to adulthood. Mae possesses an abundant wealth of stories to share – some will evoke raw emotional responses, and others provide enlightenment and illumination through intentional light-hearted fun!

Look for further upcoming children's books and young adult novels, penned by both Mae and Lea Granwich (the latter pen name delightfully inspired by her grandchildren), that address the struggles which kids of all ages endure while negotiating their tangled web of jungle pathways through to adulthood.